JESSICA MARIN

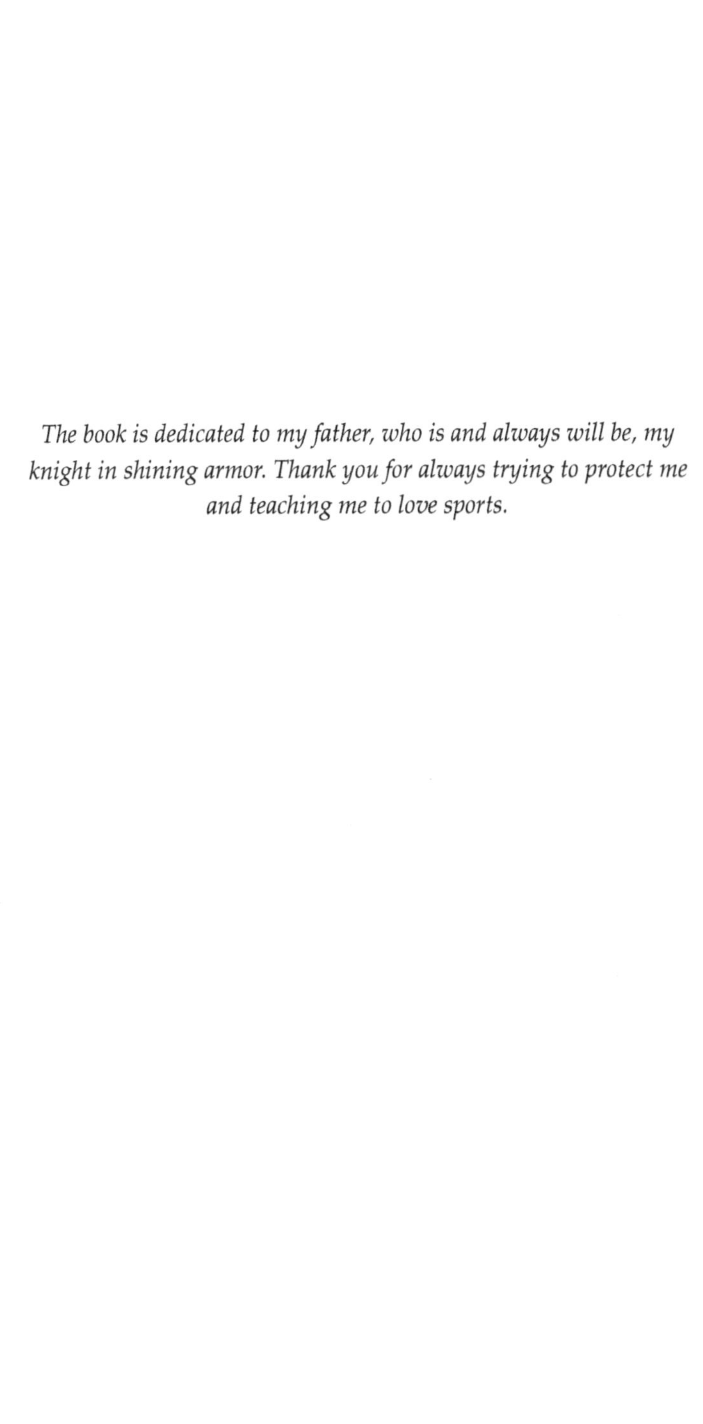

The book is dedicated to my father, who is and always will be, my knight in shining armor. Thank you for always trying to protect me and teaching me to love sports.

A NOTE FROM JESSICA MARIN

Dearest Reader,

I always say that authors sprinkle a little bit of themselves in each of their books. Some authors only do a dusting of truth, while others make it their memoir. I'm a sprinkler, but this has more of a personal connection than any of my other books. This story briefly touches upon Cassie's past trauma with her mother, which mirrors my own. I had very limited options for a release date for this book, so I think it's only fitting that The Perfect Catch is being published on my mother's birthday. Fate plays a big part in this story as well and I believe it was fate that May 6th was the last available date option for me to choose from to release this book. Like Cassie's father tells her, I think my own mother would also be proud of me if she were still alive.

If you have a loved one who struggles with addiction, I encourage you to seek help. Remember, you can't fix them. They need to want to do it on their own.

Thank you so much for your love and support. I hope you enjoy Cassie and Gunnar's love story.

All my love,

Jessica

IZZY AND CASSIE'S MOST EXCELLENT PLAYLIST

"HIGHER POWER" BY COLDPLAY

"TRUST FALL" BY PINK

"SHAKE IT OFF" BY TAYLOR SWIFT

"STRONGER" BY KELLY CLARKSON

"WALKING ON SUNSHINE" BY KATRINA AND THE WAVES

"BEAUTIFUL DAY" BY U2

"DANCING QUEEN" BY ABBA

"DON'T STOP BELIEVING" BY JOURNEY

CHAPTER 1

GUNNAR

raded.

That one-word echoes through my brain, over-taking my thoughts as my mind completely shuts off all my other senses. *That can't be what I just heard... can it?* Because no way am I being traded one week before Opening Day.

"Excuse me, but what did you just say?"

My interruption causes Craig Patterson, the general manager of the Texas Scorpions baseball team, to stop talking. He stares at me for a couple of moments before repeating his words.

"You've been traded to the Tennessee Terrors. You will be hearing from Billy Richards, their general manager, within the hour to welcome you. Their team travel coordinator will also call you to start making travel arrangements. You have seventy-two hours to report to the team. Your agent has been informed."

No. Fucking. Way.

I feel like I've just been sucker punched in the gut. My heart starts beating faster as fear and anxiety swirl through my veins. This was *NOT* what I was expecting to hear when I was called into Craig's office this morning. Sure, being traded is always a possibility since my contract doesn't have a no-trade clause, but I'm the poster child for this team. This club has been my home since I got drafted out of college. Austin is where I was born and raised. My child was born here and while being a single father has not been easy, having my parents help with childcare has made it possible for me to pursue my dreams in baseball while knowing my daughter is being raised by the best people on this planet. How the hell am I going to navigate this on my own in a new city?

Traded.

I hate that fucking word.

"Why?" I growl out, a mix of betrayal and anger making my voice harsh and menacing. I need a goddamn explanation as to why me, because right now nothing's making sense. Sure, my stats aren't the best this season, but they're not the worst either. I'm still one of the best baseball players in the league. I've given my blood, sweat, and tears to this organization and this is how I'm treated?

"Shit, Gunnar, you know this wasn't easy for me." Craig blows out a breath and rakes his hand through his hair in frustration. "You know I consider you like a son and am appreciative of all you have done for us."

"Then why the hell couldn't you give me the courtesy of having a conversation with me on what you and the scouting staff were thinking?"

"It was a last-minute conversation with Tennessee."

"Bullshit!"

"Look, Gunnar," he interrupts, bringing up his palms as a signal for me to stop talking. "You know we have an up-and-coming short-stop player in Triple A, not to mention we're looking for ways to cut salary. This trade gives us the quality closer we need and an opportunity to get a higher draft pick in the next draft. Tennessee has an exciting team this year. I know you and your family are native Texans, but I thought you would be happy to go to a contending team."

"I'm happy *here* and I believe in *this* team," I tell him, jabbing my pointer finger into his desk.

"Tennessee has positioned themselves with a great mix of seasoned veterans and talented young stars. Everyone is predicting they're going to go all the way. Let's be frank here —at thirty-five years old, you're looking at the back end of your career. You deserve a championship, Gunnar, and I just gave you a shot at getting it."

I swallow the lump that has formed in my throat. He's right and I hate it. Winning the championship is the only thing I'm missing from an otherwise picture-perfect career. We made the playoffs last year, but got beat before the finals. This team is going through a transition year, where money is tight and most of our All-Stars have left for more money else-where. It would take a miracle for us to be contenders. I know this, but it still doesn't stop the pain to my pride knowing I will not be ending my career in my home state and city.

Craig sighs and I know the end of our discussion is near-ing. "I did my job, Gunnar. I made the best decision for this team and as your friend, I made the best decision for *you*."

I nod, knowing I should be thanking him, but I'm just at a loss for words right now.

"That team needs leadership and guidance, something you excel at. You're the missing piece that can take them all the way. I know you can do it, son."

He stands up and walks around his desk. "The team has been told while you were in here, so you don't have to worry about making any announcements."

"Oh...right." My anger has started to dissipate, replaced by sadness. I stand up out of my chair and put out my hand for him to shake. "Thank you for the best thirteen years of my career, Craig. You believing in me and giving me a shot at my dreams will never be forgotten."

He looks at my hand, then looks up at me. He grabs my hand but then yanks me in for a hug. "It has been my honor to have you here. Now go kick some ass in Nashville. Get that trophy and end your career on the best high this sport can give us."

I give him a squeeze of appreciation and pat his back. I pull back to give him a small smile and notice his eyes are wet with unshed tears. Craig Patterson has been like a second father to me, so it gives me some comfort knowing this is hard for him as well.

He walks me out of his office and into the locker room, where the rest of the team is getting ready for practice. One by one, they come up to me, hug me goodbye and wish me good luck. The coaching staff is the last to say their goodbyes and when everyone is gone, the equipment manager helps me pack up my stuff.

"I will overnight your gear to the stadium. When are you heading out there?" Chris, our assistant equipment manager, asks while he throws my now old uniforms in a box.

"I have no idea. I haven't talked to anyone in their organization."

"They haven't called you yet?"

I look around for my cell phone and find it still in the top cubby of my locker. I tap the screen and see I have eight missed calls and over twenty text messages. Two of the calls are from unknown numbers and the other calls are from friends, my parents, and my brother.

Guess the news is out.

Before I can listen to my voicemails, my brother's name lights up my phone, alerting me that he's calling. If I don't pick up, I know he'll just keep calling until either I answer or shut off my phone.

"Hey, I need to call you right back," I tell him without saying hello first. I should be calling my new team to figure out logistics of where I need to report.

"Fuck yeah you better call me back! This is incredible news. You and Izzy are moving to my city, and we're going to have the best fucking time together." His excitement is contagious, and I find myself grinning at the thought of being reunited with my brother.

Gavin moved to Nashville years ago to pursue his country music career. He started out as a songwriter and once he had some hits under his belt, he then released his debut album, which skyrocketed to the top of the charts. While moving to Nashville was the best decision for him, it hurt when he left. We were thick as thieves and while it sucked watching Gavin leave, I was proud of him for chasing his dreams. Now he's married with a son, so I would have to agree that Nashville has been good to him.

I pray that it will be good for me and Izzy too.

"I promise I'll call you back and yeah, I'm excited to see you too, Gav."

We hang up and I call my parents quickly just to check in with them.

"Hey, did you hear the news?" I ask my mom when she picks up on the second ring.

"Of course I heard. I have internet alerts set up on you and your brother. Not to mention, it is all over the news. How are you holding up?"

"Mixed emotions," I answer honestly. "Shocked, angry, and now sad would sum it up."

"You're not happy?" she asks with concern lacing her voice.

"How can I be when I'm leaving you guys and the only city I've ever known. Austin has been wonderful to me. This community and their support..." My voice falters as I swallow the lump in my throat.

"Honey, it's okay to be sad and excited at the same time. This is an incredible opportunity for you to get a chance at the championship, not to mention, being in the same city as your brother."

"Yes, it's going to be great spending more time with Gavin, but he has a family of his own and is on the road a lot for his career. We'll be leaving you guys and our friends. I don't know how Izzy is going to take this news. She doesn't know yet, does she?" I panic at the thought of my parents telling her without me or worse yet, her finding it out from one of her little friends or their parents.

"No, Izzy doesn't know a thing. We figured that needs to come from you."

My shoulders sag in relief. "Thanks, Mom."

"With you and Gavin now living in the same city, this gives us an excuse to maybe buy some property there so we can come visit all the time."

"I love the sound of that."

"This is a new adventure for you and Izzy, Gunnar. Be excited. I have a good feeling about this."

"Your intuition is usually spot on, so I hope you're right. Listen, I need to go and call my new boss. I will call you back when I'm in the car heading home to pack."

"Okay. I love you, Gunnar."

"I love you, Mom."

I hang up and listen to the voicemails from the two unknown numbers. Just like Craig told me they would, Billy Richards, and Peter Kelly, the Director of Travel Operations, both called. I'm about to call one of them back when my phone rings again with the same 615 area code from the other two numbers. I take a deep breath and decide it's time to start my new life by answering the call.

"Hello?"

"Gunnar McNeer? This is Declan Wylde, Team Manager of the Tennessee Terrors."

"How are you, sir?"

"I'm great. The question is, how are *you* doing today?"

"A little surprised, sir," I answer honestly and I hear a couple of chuckles in the background.

"I have no doubt you are, but I'm here with Billy and Peter, and on behalf of the team, we want to welcome you to Nashville. We're damn excited to have you join our club."

"Thank you, sir. I'm honored that you wanted me."

"Are you kidding me? Acquiring you to our team makes us a contender to win it all. Are you ready for that, Gunnar?"

I smile and I can start to feel the bubbles of excitement building within me. "Fuck yeah I am, sir."

CHAPTER 2

"You got *traded*?"

My head snaps up at hearing that word, the crayon in my fingers skidding over the outside lines of the whale I was coloring. I narrow my gaze at Marissa, my employer and friend, and watch the emotions start playing over her face. Her cell phone is cradled between her cheek and her shoulder while she tries to juggle a squirming eighteen-month-old on her hip. As her nanny, I should get up and go help her by taking the baby off her hands, but I'm rooted in my seat, frozen with trepidation

"Are you serious?" Marissa's voice raises an octave and she turns her back to me. *Oh, no, this can't be happening again to them!* Her husband, Alec, plays professional hockey here in Nashville, and while there's always a chance for a trade if there's not a no-trade clause in your contract, I don't think they were expecting this to happen to them so soon. They were traded to Nashville four years ago and I've been their nanny for three of those years. But I guess this is just part of the business, which I don't know if I would be able to handle if I was in Marissa's shoes.

I glance at Luna, their four-year-old daughter, who is

sitting across from me coloring. She's too busy concentrating on making her elephant pink to notice something's amiss with her mother.

"Oh my God, I can't believe this!" Marissa turns around, shock registered on her face. Her eyes are watering and at first glance, I think they're tears of sadness, but then her mouth curves into a huge smile and I realize that those are tears of joy streaming down her face.

What the heck is going on?

"Is this really true, Alec? You're not playing a prank on me, are you?"

Alec is known to be somewhat of a prankster on the team, but he knows Marissa will kick his ass if he ever pulls something on her. My left leg starts to bounce with nervous energy, the anticipation of finding out what is happening is *killing* me.

"Home," she whispers, and I lean to the side, craning my neck to make sure I'm hearing her correctly. "I can't believe we are going back home."

'Home' is the city of Kelowna in British Columbia, Canada. Two thousand, three hundred and forty-two miles away. Kelowna is where they were before being traded to Nashville.

A startled gasp escapes my lips, causing Luna to look up at me. "What's wrong, Cassie?"

"Um." I look around, scrambling for some excuse to give her since it isn't my place to tell her the news. "I colored outside of the lines." I pick up my piece of paper and hold up the drawing to show her.

"That's okay. I do it all the time, silly goose!" She also holds up her paper and starts to giggle. That sweet sound pierces my heart and the realization that I might never see her and her sister again makes my stomach ache.

"This is a dream come true, Alec. I'm so happy right now!" I turn my attention back to Marissa and watch her start to walk briskly around the kitchen island. "I've got to call my mother. I love you and I'll see you soon?" She nods at whatever he's saying on the other end and tells him goodbye.

"What's going on, Marissa?" I ask as soon as she hangs up. "Did I just hear what I think I heard?" I don't know if Luna understands what the word "traded" means and I don't want to be the one she hears it from.

"Oh, Cassie, it's the best news ever!" I stand up and meet her in the middle of the kitchen where she hands the baby over to me. "We're being traded back to Kelowna. Can you believe it?"

My shoulders slump and I can't hide my disappointment. "No, not really."

Marissa and Alec have been the first family to take me in as a nanny—a profession that was only supposed to pay the bills while I became a famous artist. Instead, I've fallen in love with them and they're like the brother and sister I never had. My art career has taken a back seat and instead, I sell print on demand products of my art on my website when I have free time.

Her smile starts to fade at the sadness in my voice. "Oh gosh, that's right. You wouldn't be able to come with us, would you?"

"You know I can't leave my dad."

My father is my best friend and there's no way I could ever leave him. We've been through so much together with my parents' divorce and my mom's alcoholism. He was and is my knight in shining armor. When I was a kid, he would shelter me from my mother when she was drunk. As an adult, he took me back in when I found my ex-boyfriend having sex with my roommate. He's been the one person who I can always rely on. My moving out-of-state would crush his soul... and mine. We have a special bond and while I do want to travel the world someday, my home is always going to be where my dad is.

"I completely understand." Marissa nods and walks up to

wrap her arms around me and the baby in a group hug. "You know, just because you won't be our nanny anymore, doesn't mean you're getting rid of us. You're stuck with being part of our family forever."

I give her a tight smile, fighting to keep my emotions at bay. It's easy for her to say this now, but we'll see how often I hear from her in six months.

"You need to come out to Kelowna and see how beautiful it is. Oh, I know!" Marissa backs away from us, her brown eyes dancing with mischief. "You can help me and the kids move back and while you're out there, Alec can introduce you to one of his younger teammates. You will fall in love, get married, and live next door to us forever." She claps her hands in excitement as if this is the most brilliant idea she's ever had.

I scrunch up my nose at her nonsense. "No offense, but I would never date an athlete." I've never been into sports, and being part of Alec and Marissa's world has made me even more of an anti-fan. The moving from city to city when traded, all the practices and games that take athletes away from their families, not to mention the psychotic women who try to go after your man just because they're a professional athlete?

No. Thank. You.

"Never say never, Cassie. You can't help who you fall in love with."

"I most certainly will never fall in love with an athlete." I stick my tongue out at her to lighten the mood and she laughs.

"I don't want us to leave Cassie."

We both turn and look down at Luna, who apparently has been listening in on our conversation this whole time. I glance back at Marissa with a raised eyebrow, not knowing how she wants to handle this now delicate conversation.

She walks closer to Luna and squats down to be at eye

level with her. "I know you don't, sweetheart, but Cassie has to stay here with her family."

"I don't want to leave!" Luna crosses her little arms against her chest and stomps her foot against the hardwood floors. Her eyes are narrowed and that cute little mouth of hers is puckered into an angry pout. We are minutes away from a full-fledged temper tantrum.

Marissa glances up at me and my eyes are screaming at her to do something to bribe this kid back into her happy world.

"We are moving somewhere very exciting though! Do you want to know where?"

"Where?" Her little voice is filled with doubt, not really believing her mother.

"We are moving back to where you were born in Canada. To the city of Kelowna where mommy and daddy met and fell in love."

Luna just stares at her mother, showing no signs of being impressed or happy with this news. Can't say I blame the kid because if I were her age, that wouldn't excite me either. I can see the wheels in Marissa's brain turning, trying to come up with something better to cheer Luna up.

"Guess who also lives in Kelowna?"

"Who?"

"Nana and Papa, which means we will get to play with them every day!"

That frown turns upside down and Luna's sweet face lights up with happiness.

"Does this mean we can have sleepovers with them all the time?"

"Every weekend!" Marissa confirms. I press my lips together to keep from laughing, knowing full well she has every intention of hitting up her parents to babysit almost every chance she can get out of them.

"And will Nana make monster cookies for me every day?"

"Well, maybe not every day—" Marissa starts but then changes her mind when Luna's lips start to turn downward. "Maybe every other day."

"I don't know what that means but it sounds like every day to me, so yay!" Luna starts jumping up and down and we both can't help but laugh at her antics.

"Why don't you come with me and we'll call Nana together to tell her our happy news?" Marissa holds out her hand for Luna, who grabs it immediately. I tighten my hold onto Charlotte while we both watch mother and daughter run up the stairs in pure joy and happiness. Luna's giggles ricochet down the stairs back toward us and a fresh wave of sadness rocks me.

I'm going to miss these little girls so much.

And I'll be out of a job.

Loneliness and abandonment start seeping into me like quicksand and before I can push it all away, the voices of my past trauma start blaring in my head.

Of course they're leaving you too.

Your mother left you.

Your boyfriend left you.

Everyone eventually leaves you.

I mentally tell myself to shut up, knowing that I'm being ridiculous right now. This is neither the time nor the place to have my pity party for one. I can do that later in the privacy of my room with a pint of Moose Tracks ice cream.

I watch them until they are out of sight and I hear the door to Marissa's bedroom close. I look down at Charlotte, whose gaze meets mine at the very same time. We stare at each other for a few seconds before her bottom lip starts to quiver. Those mahogany-colored eyes, so much like her mother's, start to water and I know in a few seconds, our brief moment of silence will be shattered by her piercing wails.

"I feel the same way, kid." I gently kiss her forehead and start rocking her, wishing I could cry right along with her.

CHAPTER 3

GUNNAR

Two days later, I'm sitting on the plane, heading to Florida to meet the team at their spring training facility. We only have two more games left on the schedule before the team heads back to Nashville. I study the headshots and bios of the entire Tennessee Terrors coaching and baseball operations staff during my flight in hopes that reading about them and seeing their photos will help me become more familiar with my new team. Once I feel confident that I'll be able to recognize who they are in person, I move on to examining the team's roster. I'm pleasantly surprised to not only see some familiar faces, but also a couple other "old-timers" like myself. I've known Max Murphy, one of our pitchers, for a long time. Not only is he older, but he's also a single father. Knowing I have some things in common with a couple of the guys eases my nerves.

The two-hour flight breezes by and before I know it, we're landing. I turn my phone on when the plane touches down and immediately text my parents and brother about my arrival. We arrive at the gate and with the team putting me up in first class, I make my way out of the plane quickly and head to baggage claim.

Doing my "homework" on the plane immediately pays off when I notice Peter Kelly, Director of Travel Operations, waiting there before he recognizes me. Peter is only twenty-nine years old, but no stranger to baseball since both his father and uncle were famous players.

"Hey, Peter," I greet as I approach him and he startles, not expecting someone to be calling out his name.

"Fuck, you scared me!" He chuckles and shakes the free hand I offer him. "Welcome to Florida, Gunnar. Your flight okay?"

"On time and smooth, just the way I like it."

He laughs. "Those are the best kind of flights." He nods over to the baggage carousel and asks, "How many bags are we waiting for?"

"Two."

He gives me a questioning look. "That isn't very many."

I shrug, not thinking it's a big deal. "We can just buy whatever we need once we're settled in Nashville."

I don't plan on selling my house in Austin, and fortunately, Gavin has a rental house that just became open. Izzy and I will live there until I can find another place. He also has an extra car that I can borrow, which helps me put off car shopping for a little bit longer.

"When will your family be joining you?" Peter asks and I smile at his choice of words. Clearly, he has done his homework and discovered I'm not married.

"My parents and daughter will be arriving the day before Opening Night. They'll stay until we leave for our first road trip. My parents will take Izzy back with them to finish packing up her things and then she'll join me permanently a week later." This will be the longest Izzy and I have been apart. I'll probably handle it worse than she will.

"We have a referral to a nanny agency that a lot of the guys use when they move here. It's listed for you in your welcome packet back at my office."

"Perfect." With my brother helping me out with a place to live and a car, finding a nanny is now my number one priority.

After a couple more minutes of small talk, my bags come into view and make their way closer to where we're standing. We grab them off the carousel and I follow Peter to his car in the parking garage. We put the bags in his truck, get in the car, and drive out of the airport.

"We have a pretty full day planned for you. When we arrive, I'll escort you to meet with Billy and Declan first. Next, human resources will meet with you in my office to go over all the paperwork you need to sign. Fortunately, we got your medical records from the Scorpions' team doctors, so you don't need to have another physical. Afterward, I'll give you a tour of the offices and ballpark. We'll then head to the locker room where you can unpack your stuff, meet the rest of the guys, and get warmed up for practice."

"Sounds great," I respond, happy to hear I'll get a lot accomplished on my first day as a Terror. "I've got a question. Who will help me secure season tickets for my family? I need to pay for four tickets minimum for the season."

"Your brother called as soon as the news broke about your trade and purchased a suite. He told our Director of Ticket Operations that your seats will be with him." I chuckle and shake my head at this news. "No doubt we will have to beef up security for the games he attends, which he has offered to pay for."

My chest swells with pride for Gavin. A lot of people change for the worse when they become famous and start making a lot of money. Not Gavin—his generosity knows no bounds and he's always trying to do the right thing. I know his wife, Aly, has played a huge part in helping him navigate ways to give back to the community. My parents have always tried to keep us both humble and grateful that we get to live such extraordinary lives, since we're both making money from doing the things we love.

Before I can ask Peter more questions, his phone starts to ring. "Sorry, I need to take this," he tells me and answers his phone. While he talks, I stare out the window, taking in the scenery that is Florida. Spring training for me used to be in Arizona, so if I'm here next year, this will be another new adjustment to get used to.

My time in Florida is limited due to spring training being almost over, so I'm not going to dwell on being in a foreign place. I've got a job to do and if I want the Terrors to sign me to a new contract, I need to work my ass off this season.

⚾ 🦇 🦋 🧁

Two days later, I have my first spring training games with the Terrors under my belt and we land back in Nashville. I'm waiting outside the player's entrance of Music City Park for my brother to pick me up. I put his name on the security list and texted him the code to the gate. As I'm scrolling through my phone, I hear my name being called.

"Hey, McNeer!" I look up to see Max Murphy strolling over to me. "Where are you staying tonight?"

"My brother lives in Nashville, so he's picking me up and I'll spend the night at his house."

"Nice. I didn't realize he was done touring."

"He's in between show dates. Gotta catch him while I can." Gavin has one more big leg of his tour to complete and then he'll be home for a while to be present for the birth of his second child and to chill before he starts recording a new album.

"No doubt. Let's plan a night to grab a beer or something."

"I would like that, Murph." Max is a native Tennessean, so I would love to hear his perspective on schools and family life here in Nashville.

A horn honking has us glancing in the direction of a black truck with tinted windows pulling up in front of me. "See you around, McNeer." Max waves goodbye and walks to his car.

Gavin puts the car in park and jumps out of the driver's seat. "I can't believe you're fucking here." He walks around the front of the hood and as soon as I reach him, he pulls me into a tight hug and attempts to lift me off my feet.

"Don't hurt yourself, old man." I joke as he puts me down and releases me. Gavin is two years older and people say the resemblance between us is strong. We both have our mom's sandy colored hair and the famous McNeer green eyes. His face is more chiseled than mine with different bone structure. Gavin is also leaner whereas I'm bulkier with muscle, but we're both in good shape due to our love for working out and being outdoors.

I chuckle as he scoffs at my "old man" comment. "You're light as a feather compared to what I bench press nowadays."

"Oh yeah?" I check out the parts of his biceps that I can see from his short sleeve shirt while we load my bags in the trunk. I can definitely tell Gavin's put on some muscle, but there's no way I would admit that to him. He was the more popular, charming brother, who let all the attention from the ladies go to his head. I always took great pleasure in serving him up a big ol' piece of humble pie. Even though he's not as conceited and cocky as he used to be, it's still my job as his younger brother to bring him down a notch. "Can't wait to see you prove that in the weight room."

His head turns in my direction, narrowing his eyes in skepticism. "You doubting I can do it?"

"I know you can't do it."

"Want to place a friendly wager on it?"

"You know I do," I confirm with a smirk.

"All right then, what am I winning?"

"Times haven't changed, Gavin. You know exactly what you're buying me when I win the bet."

He closes the trunk and looks over at me. "A big bag of chew?"

I nod, happy to see that he remembers. "Only the best kind of chew out there."

Our parents wanted us to be well-rounded kids, so we tried every sport imaginable until we both fell in love with the game of baseball. We learned quickly that chewing gum was a rite of passage while playing ball. There was nothing better than getting our weekly allowance from doing chores around the house and going to the store to buy a bag of Big League Chew. We felt like we were the coolest kids ever, smacking our gum in the dugout, pretending to be our favorite baseball players. We would have contests amongst our teammates to see who could blow the biggest bubbles. We even became competitive with who could acquire the most bags of chew. So naturally it became a tradition that anytime we made a bet against each other, the person who won would get a bag of chew.

We get into Gavin's car and put our seat belts on. "I haven't chewed that gum in years. Can't wait to prove you wrong." He winks at me, and I chuckle at his confidence, but in reality, I secretly hope he does win. Seeing him with the chew will only bring out his competitiveness to wager another bet—who can blow the biggest bubble. He knows I will beat his ass in that category since I still use Big League Chew to this day during every game. It has become a part of my game day ritual. I won't chew it any other day but on game days.

Gavin puts the truck into drive and turns toward the road. "So, tell me how your first trip went with the new team."

"It went really well. The front office seems like a solid organization. Everyone welcomed me with open arms, and I felt that excitement buzzing around the coaches and players that I haven't felt in a very long time. The facilities are nice, and I think Izzy will really like the kid's room." The room set up for families has intricate murals on the wall, tons of toys, and lots of arts and crafts that I know my kid will be playing with every time she's there.

"Speaking of Izzy, how did she take the news?" my brother asks, his tone becoming serious.

Izzy's reaction immediately springs to my mind and I sigh. "She cried at first, but then asked if we could go get ice cream and everything was right in the world. It's good that she's only five, because right now, her life isn't going to drastically change except for not seeing me as much as she's used to these next couple of weeks."

"When are you bringing her here permanently?"

"A week after our first road trip. I need some time to get things unpacked, and I want her room to be all set-up and ready to go. You letting us use one of your rental properties takes a lot of burden off my shoulders right now, so thank you again for that."

My brother shrugs as if it was nothing. "The timing was perfect with our tenant moving out. Besides, I'm happy that the place will be looked after."

"Will you at least let me pay you what your tenants were paying?"

"Fuck no. You're my brother—your money's no good to me. Spend it on my adorable niece."

"That's not hard to do," I grumble because I have no willpower when it comes to saying no to Isabella. All she has to do is bat those long eyelashes over those green eyes and

I'm a goner. "Seriously, Gav, I truly appreciate you doing this."

"You're welcome, but don't get too appreciative yet. You might not like the house or the area."

"Why? I know you wouldn't have an investment property in a bad neighborhood."

"No, of course not, but it's Aly's old house and it's near the colleges. Not the most kid-friendliest of neighborhoods. Nor does it have a gate for privacy. I worry that once people know you're living there, you'll get some unwanted visitors."

"I'm not too worried. Nashville isn't the biggest baseball town like Austin is from what I'm told, so maybe I'll go undetected."

Gavin laughs like I've said the most outlandish thing in the world. "There you go again, thinking you aren't a big deal or anything. This town has been buzzing about signing you since it was made public. Trust me when I say, plenty of people here will know who you are."

I groan, hoping he's wrong and that I can go undetected for a long time...like forever.

"The nice thing about Nashville is that the locals are used to celebrities amongst them and for the most part, they leave us alone. It's the tourists, especially these bachelorette parties that have taken over downtown, that you have to watch out for."

"I don't plan on going out at night, Gavin."

"Oh, c'mon now, little brother. You most certainly need to experience what the nightlife has to offer from time to time."

"No, thank you. I'm perfectly fine staying at home with my little princess."

"Gunnar, you can't stay single forever. Aren't you interested in meeting someone? Someone that might be a good influence on Izzy?"

"Nope." I've thought long and hard about maybe putting myself back out there, and at this stage of my life, I don't feel it's worth it. Dating nowadays is way harder than it was when I was younger. I don't want to bring someone around Izzy who might not have the right intentions and is looking for their next meal ticket in the form of a baseball player—exactly what my ex-girlfriend did.

I met Tasha at a party for one of my former teammates. It was lust at first sight and after that night, we were inseparable. Our relationship was on warp speed, and she moved in with me after only a month of dating. She acted like the perfect girlfriend; making sure I was well fed, helping me take care of personal things while I worked, supporting me by coming to every home game, and even surprised me at some away games. She was wild in and out of bed and at the time, I was addicted to that personality. It was the exact opposite of who I was. But when she started talking about getting married six months into our relationship, for some reason, the idea spooked me. I chalked it up to just not being ready yet. Tasha wasn't happy and took it upon herself to stop taking her birth control. She got pregnant on purpose and when I asked her how she could've gotten pregnant, she blamed it on the antibiotics she had taken for a cold. Thing was, Tasha wasn't the type who liked to take medicine when she was sick. I was suspicious of her answer then, but was still blind to the fact that she might not love me for the right reasons. Tasha assumed that because she was pregnant, I would do the "honorable" thing and propose to her, but I still had this nagging feeling about us. Our relationship was still so new, and I was curious as to how she was going to be as a mother. The first six months of Izzy's life were rough. It was obvious Tasha was suffering from postpartum depression. I tried to help out as much as I could when I was home, but I felt a lot of guilt every time I was on the road for work. I hired a nanny to help Tasha out and both of our families pitched in whenever they could. Yet despite all the help, Tasha grew distant. She seemed unsatisfied with her new life and missed her old, carefree ways. She started leaving Izzy alone with the nanny and my parents more often than I liked. Her late-night outings became more frequent and one time, she didn't even come home. When I confronted her the next day, she told me she slept at her friend's house because she was too drunk to drive home.

I kept believing all her lies, trying to give her the benefit of the doubt that she was just going through a hard time being a new mother, and that she just needed to get things out of her system. It wasn't until I came home early one day to surprise her that I found her having sex with one of the local professional football players—with our daughter sleeping in the other room. I immediately kicked her out of my house and told her she wasn't allowed to take Izzy. Tasha had developed a drinking problem, and I had the good sense to write down every instance of her being drunk around Izzy. I hired a lawyer right away and because of the evidence I had against her, I was able to get full custody and Tasha could only see Izzy under supervised visitations. She didn't even try to fight me on it—she was much more interested in her new life as a football player's girlfriend. When her boyfriend was traded to a new team out in California, Tasha went with him and her only contact with her daughter has been through the phone. Izzy's only form of a "mother" comes from her nanny and her grandmothers.

As Izzy has gotten older, she's been asking more and more questions about why her mother doesn't come visit her. It breaks my heart every time we have the discussion, and that's when I start to have doubts about me staying single. I don't want to just have any kind of woman in Izzy's life. She deserves someone who is going to step up and be the mother she doesn't have, and that's going to take time to find that right person. Time that I am just not willing to sacrifice right now. I still have emotional scars from Tasha—they've just started to finally fade. Izzy is my number one priority, and I want to make sure she gets every single second of my time when I'm not working.

"It's a miracle your dick still even gets hard. When was the last time you used it besides with your hands?" Gavin gives me a side-eyed smirk, and if he wasn't driving right now, I would punch him in the balls.

"None of your business," I tell him just as we pull into the driveway of his rental. It's an old, two-story, brick house that has recently been painted all white on the outside with navy blue doors and shutters. It has a white fence in front of it with a little green space on each side of the walkway.

"Please tell me you've at least hooked up while being on the road?" Gavin asks as we get out of his car.

I shut my door and follow him up the walkway to the front entrance. "No, Gavin. I don't hook up on the road either."

He puts the key in the lock and turns. "God, you sound like a lonely, grumpy, old man."

"Show me the damn house, Gavin!"

He opens the door, and I push him through the entryway. I walk in and am pleasantly surprised at how spacious it is. The house has been completely gutted and remodeled to be more modern, yet has a cozy charm to it.

"This place is beautiful." I walk toward the updated kitchen with all new stainless-steel appliances and beautiful white herringbone tile backsplash between the cabinets and the countertops.

"Thanks. This was Aly's baby, and she poured her heart and soul into the new design of it all. She could sell this house and make a shit ton of money, but Aly has an emotional attachment to it. It was the first house she and her sister bought from their parents as an investment and they both lived here during college and sometime afterward."

"I agree with her. I wouldn't sell this place, especially now after all the work you guys put into it. It's a great rental investment."

The house is deceivingly larger than its outside appearance. The living room is huge, and I can picture Izzy and her toys taking it over. The bedrooms are good sized and I especially love the screened-in back porch with a fenced in yard. The house is perfect for us.

I walk into the room that I designate for Izzy and look around. "I can't wait to get Izzy's room set up. Do you think Aly would help me with that?"

He gives me that "*Are you shitting me*?" look as if I'm a moron. "She would be offended if you didn't ask her for help. You know she loves that kind of stuff."

I sigh in relief because I know Aly will make Izzy's room look like something out of a home decor magazine. "Awesome. Hey, are you sure you guys are fine with us staying here for a bit? Since you refuse to take rent, I feel bad that you're missing out on making money."

He rolls his eyes and groans. "Stop annoying me with this subject. The house is yours for however long you want to stay here."

I nod and a lump of emotions forms in my throat. I quickly swallow it down and find my voice again. "Thanks, Gav. I owe you one."

"You don't owe me anything. You would do it for me if the roles were reversed. You can do me a favor though."

I tilt my head to the side, intrigued to hear what kind of favor I could even do for him. "Oh yeah, what's that?"

"You can start thinking of dating again or at least, letting yourself have some unadulterated fun."

Now it's my turn to groan and be annoyed with the revival of this conversation. "I'll think about it when I'm ready, Gavin."

"When you're ready? That could be when Izzy's in college."

"Precisely."

"What if Aly and I create an online profile for you on that rich people's dating app? We will screen the women for you and meet them first. If we don't approve, then we won't make any introductions."

I bark out a laugh at the absurdity of his idea. "You're ridiculous."

"I'm being serious. I think it's a genius idea. That or one of Aly's friends. I'm pretty sure some of them are ladies in public and freaks in private."

I point my finger at him and give him a stern look. "Do *not* try to hook me up with any of Aly's friends. Just leave me alone and let me focus on Izzy and baseball."

Gavin holds up his hands in surrender. "All right, all right, but we *are* going to have a Welcome to Nashville/Baby shower party this summer. Lots of beautiful ladies will be there for you to meet."

I scoff in exasperation. "I just told you I don't want to be set up with anyone!"

"Maybe it won't be setting you up with anyone. Maybe you'll just casually meet a stranger at this party who you think is beautiful and want to get to know her better."

I laugh at the look of innocence he is feigning, because he's anything but. "I love you, but no to it all."

"You have no choice in the matter. We're having a party and that's final."

"What if I don't show up?"

"You want to purposely piss off my wife? It was her idea."

Fuck, he's got me. "Fine, Izzy and I will be there, but no setting me up, Gavin. I mean it!"

He looks down at his watch, a mischievous smile playing on his lips. "Okay, I won't try to set you up with anyone, but there will be no denying my wife if she decides to play matchmaker."

I groan and throw my head back. I can control my brother,

but my sister-in-law is another story. When Aly gets an idea in her brain, she is relentless, and her thinking she can set me up with someone would consume her during what little free time she has. I'll have to tell her tonight at dinner that I have no interest in dating anyone. I just have to pray she'll listen to me.

CHAPTER 4

CASSIE

I hold my brush tightly between my fingers, concentrating on keeping my hand steady so I can put the intricate details of the highlights in the hair of the woman I'm painting. I get really close to the canvas and squint in order to see if I filled in the lines that I have envisioned to give the hair color some depth. The ringing of my cell phone startles me, and my hand goes adrift, causing me to paint outside of her hairline.

"Ugh," I groan in frustration and toss my brush into a cup of water. Normally, I put my phone on silent when I'm painting, trying to minimize any distractions for the few hours that I get to do this, but I must've forgotten. I look to see who's calling and Grace's name pops up on my screen. Grace Harper is like a sister to me and has been my best friend since high school. Typically, I wouldn't pick up the phone while painting, but I'm just not into it today. I'm frustrated and Grace's phone call is a welcome distraction right now.

"What are you doing?" I ask her as I answer my phone and take a seat in my chair.

"Getting ready to be an adult and go to work. What are *you* doing?"

"I was trying to paint, but I'm just not in the mood. If this is how it's going to be before my next job, then unemployment is going to be a real doozy."

"What are you even talking about?" She scoffs. "You sell your print on demand art, that's technically not being unemployed."

"I told you I haven't sold much yet. Definitely not enough to cover the bills." Fortunately, my only bills are my student loans for art school and my car payment, not to mention food, cell phone and insurance.

"Isn't Marissa paying you to house sit for her?"

"She is, but I was only housesitting to let the movers come in and get everything. The house is basically empty now with just a couple of things left for me to pack up for them." With Marissa and Alec already owning a home in Kelowna, they decided to sell their house here to one of Alec's teammates who is buying it after signing a multi-year contract. The guy and his family move in next week.

"So, you're back at your dad's house?"

"Yeah, just for the time being."

"You can always move in with me," Grace offers, and I smile at her generosity. One of the things I love about Grace is that she's always trying to take care of other people and save them when they need it, which makes becoming a nurse the perfect occupation for her.

"Love you for offering, but I need to live rent free for a little while. Besides, your mom told me she might have another job lined up for me."

Grace's mom, Katherine, owns a nanny agency who caters to celebrities, athletes, doctors, and other high-end clients. She's always treated me like another daughter and when my art career wasn't taking off, she suggested I try being a nanny for the time being. The pay is great, and I usually have time to paint.

"Nice. Did she give you any details yet about who the family is?"

"Not yet, but she said she should know more later this week."

"Well before you go back into full-time work mode, I think you should meet me for a little pow-wow before the blind date I set you up on."

Blind date? Did I hear her correctly?

"I think our connection is breaking up because I could've sworn you said you set me up on a blind date."

She laughs. "That's exactly what I said."

I shake my head and groan, because the audacity of her thinking I would even want to be set up on a blind date is comical. "Why would I ever agree to go on a blind date? You know exactly how I feel about dating right now."

"Cassie, you're a twenty-four-year-old hermit. Do you know how sad that is? You need to get yourself out there and meet new people. I can't be your only friend for the rest of your life."

I roll my eyes at her dramatics. "You're not my only friend, Grace."

"Oh yeah? Name your other friends who you talk to and see on a regular basis?"

I pause for a few seconds and realize I can't name anyone else. Somehow after my breakup with my ex, I stopped talking to our mutual friends. Grace, her mom, and Marissa are the only friends in my life right now.

"That's beside the point." I brush off her comment, refusing to admit she's right. "A blind date is not going out with a friend; it's going out with a stranger. A stranger who could be a serial killer."

She giggles. "You're being ridiculous. A blind date could lead to a new friend if you don't want to be romantically involved with him. Don't worry though, this guy is hot."

I'm already skeptical about this. Grace's taste in men is

questionable at times. "If he's so hot then why don't you go on a date with him?"

"You know I can't do that if I'm supposed to be in this fake relationship with Carter."

"Your 'fake' relationship is the dumbest thing I've ever heard." Grace met Carter Callahan, a pitcher for the Tennessee Terrors, while he was at Nashville Hope Hospital doing charity work. A lot of the baseball players make the rounds occasionally, some for the right reasons, some only for publicity. I haven't figured out which reason Carter was there yet, but if publicity was the goal, he got it and then some. One of the mothers to a patient was an overzealous fan and bothering Carter, so Cassie swooped in and pretended to be his "girlfriend" so the woman would leave him alone. When a video of him kissing Grace went viral, she agreed to fake date him to save both their reputations.

"Yes, you've made your feelings regarding my relationship crystal clear, and I don't need another reminder of how stupid you think I am."

"I don't think you're stupid, I think you agreeing to a fake relationship was a poor decision." I chose my words a little more carefully this time since Grace is being sensitive about the subject. Grace is one of the smartest people I know, but when it comes to good-looking men, she loses all her rational brain cells. This could also be a ploy to save her from the doctor her father wants her to marry, whom she despises.

She clears her throat. "Well, I'm not going to admit you're right, but maybe I should've taken more time to think about the consequences."

I snicker because she basically just said I was right but not in so many words. "I've thought about the consequences of going on this blind date and the answer is no."

"I already told him that you would meet him, so it's a little too late for that."

Now this makes me irrationally angry. "Why would you

do that, Grace? That's pretty messed up. Best friends don't do that to each other."

"I know and I'm sorry, Cassie," she whines in her high-pitched voice that drives me crazy. "But he keeps asking me out and I'm not interested in him that way. I told him I was seeing someone and he just looked so disappointed, so I tried to soften the blow of my rejection by telling him all about my sister from another mister who's even kinder and hotter than me."

"So, you want me to go out with someone who wasn't even interested in me in the first place?"

"How could he have been interested if he didn't know you even existed?"

Fair point, but it's still not cool that she told him I would go before asking me about it.

"I don't know, Grace. You know how I feel about these things. I just don't think this is a good idea."

"His name is Aaron and he's a pharmaceutical rep that supplies the pharmacy inside the children's hospital. He seems like a very nice guy who makes really good money."

"You know that doesn't appeal to me."

"A hot guy making a lot of money doesn't appeal to you?"

"Right now, *dating* doesn't appeal to me."

"Please do this for me, Cassie," she begs, and I can feel my resolve withering. "It's just a drink and possibly a meal. I didn't even tell him your real name."

This amuses me and makes me slightly happy. "What name did you tell him?"

"Amber. I just thought it would be easier to give him a fake name in case you don't want to talk to him again."

"But then what happens if I do end up liking him? How do I explain lying to him about my name?"

"Can we cross that bridge when we get to it, please?"

I sigh and give in like the sucker that I am. "When's the date?"

"Yay!" I hear her clapping in excitement. "It's in three days."

"*Three days?*" I screech like a parrot. "What the heck, Grace? What were you going to do if I refused to go?"

"I knew you wouldn't let me down because you love me, and you hate disappointing people."

"Way to play with my emotions, Grace." My tone is snide and heavy with sarcasm. "I have no idea what I'm even going to wear."

"I'll come over and help you pick something out. We definitely want you to look sexy."

I scoff. "Why would we want that? I'm not having sex with him. In fact, I don't even want him to like me."

"Of course you want him to like you! And it's okay to have casual sex, Cassie. If you are vibing on each other, then why not?"

I close my eyes and pinch the bridge of my nose with my free hand. "This is all becoming overwhelming."

"Now that I think about it, I think that's exactly your problem. When was the last time you had sex?"

I groan, hating that we're having this conversation. My ex was the last person I've been with and that was three years ago. "You know when the last time I had sex was, and I have no interest in having sex with anyone right now."

"You act like a grandma. In fact, I take that back—grandmas are having more sex than you are."

"Shush up, Grace," I tell her over her hyena laughter. "You've already made me ruin my painting by calling me and now you're ruining my day by demanding I go on this date."

"Let's think positive: maybe Aaron will be the one and you guys will fall madly in love."

"Highly doubtful. Plus, you and I have opposite tastes in men so you saying he's hot is debatable."

"I promise you he's good-looking. Hold on and I'll send you a photo."

"Why do you have a photo of him?" I question, thinking about how odd that is.

"I don't, it's from his social media pages." I can hear her clicking on her phone and then my phone dings, letting me know that I have a text. I open up the text and look at the photo. He is good-looking in a very preppy, good ol' boy kind of way.

"So, what do you think?" she asks after I'm silent for a couple of minutes.

"Honestly, he looks like he could be the cousin to Mr. Rogers with the clothes he's wearing."

"Cas, that's so horrible of you to judge someone by their clothes. This guy could be your soulmate and you're going to make fun of what he's wearing?" She *tsks* at me and I feel like I'm being scolded by my elementary school principal. "You know better than that, young lady."

"Good lord, thanks for the epic guilt trip and making me feel like a shitty human."

"You're welcome," she responds cheerfully, and I know she's enjoying every minute of this. "So, can I confirm with him a time and location for you to meet? I was thinking you guys can meet at Uncle Choy's in the Gulch. It's a nice restaurant with a great bar, so at least you'll get a good meal out of it."

"You can't assume that he's going to pick up the tab, Grace." I've heard Marissa talk about Alec taking her on a date there, so I know it's going to be pricey. "That's a very expensive restaurant and not what my budget can afford right now."

"I'll give you money," she offers. "You deserve to go somewhere nice, Cassie."

"I don't want your money."

"It's the least I can do for setting you up without your permission."

She's right—she does owe me for taking one for the team. "That is true. Fine, give me your money."

"Awesome, it's a date!" She squeals in such giddy excitement that I can't help but laugh.

"What the heck am I going to do with you, Grace Harper?"

"You're going to love me forever."

I snort at that because if she keeps these shenanigans up, I sure won't be. "We'll see. I better not be stabbed and thrown in the back of a pick-up truck and dumped in a landfill."

"I've got eyes on you all the time since we can see each other's locations on our phones. I expect a play-by-play of the action, including any sexy time that might occur."

"Yeah, not happening."

"You're such a party pooper. Hey, listen, I need to get going. I have to pack a bag to change at work for Carter's opening night tonight. You will need to come to some games with me."

"No, thank you. It was bad enough I had to sit through some hockey games. Baseball is even more boring."

"When you go to a game with me they aren't."

I laugh. "I bet they aren't."

"I'll call you later. Love you and thanks again."

We hang up and I put my phone on my desk. I look over at my painting and sigh, my conversation with Grace playing over in my head. She's right that I should be getting out more and meeting people my age. I know it's not healthy to hole myself up at home, but it's my protection mechanism. Not meeting people keeps my heart from getting re-broken. I know that's an unhealthy outlook and I need to not believe the worst in people. It's something that I've been working on and going on this date is a step in the right direction.

I stand up, grab a paint brush out of the cup, and squeeze it with a towel to absorb some of the excess water. I start to hum, feeling a little bit more optimistic. Maybe this date won't be so bad after all.

CHAPTER 5

GUNNAR

I can hear the muffled sounds of the crowd anticipating our entrance as we stand in the tunnel, waiting to walk to the dugout. Our team manager, Declan, just made his opening night statements to us in the clubhouse, and we're ready to go out there. Batting practice was fun, but now with a sold-out crowd and being moments away from starting, my body is buzzing with adrenaline. I bounce up and down and swing my arms to keep everything warm and focus on the things I need to do tonight.

Keep your eyes on that ball, Gunnar.

Focus and follow through.

Keep calm and don't get anxious.

"Are you ready for this, McNeer?" Tripp Nash, our team catcher, asks me. "Home crowd is going to go crazy seeing you in Terrors black and white pinstripe."

"Looks better on you than that white, red, and blue boring shit you used to wear." I shoot Damien Donovan, our first baseman, a smirk at his words and he laughs.

"I'm looking good and feeling good, fellas. I'm fired up and ready to get our first win at home." I don't lie when I tell them I'm fired up, but my stomach is also in knots. This is the first time in thirteen years I'm starting an opening night with a different team. I have mixed emotions about it. I'm excited to be with a team that has the potential to win it all, but I'm also nervous and wonder if this might be my last year in the league. I have one more year left on my contract that the Terrors took over. Will I perform well enough for them to want to re-sign me? The few spring training games I've played with them went well, but there's still a lot to get used to with my new teammates and coaches.

"Then let's do this!" Tripp turns around and I follow the boys to the dugout. I can hear the roar of the crowd as I walk out onto the field. I raise my hand and wave, and the crowd gets louder. I see signs with my name welcoming me to Nashville. I point and give thumbs up to every sign that I can see while I jog to my position to start warm-ups. I quickly glance up at the suites and I'm able to locate Izzy holding up a sign reading "Go Daddy!" in bold black letters. I chuckle and wave at her and my parents before focusing on warm-ups. After taking a couple of catches and practicing some plays, I feel the sweat piercing through my skin, signaling that my body is loose and ready. I jog back to the dugout and drink some water before its time to line up on the foul line. Once both teams are in position, the announcer welcomes everyone to Music City Park and player introductions commence. I try to tune it all out and use this time to center myself and my emotions, but when my name is called and the crowd jumps to their feet, it's hard to ignore my feelings. My chest gets tight at the standing ovation I'm being given. I take off my ball cap and salute the crowd in acknowledgment.

"That's what we're talking about, McNeer!" Chase Thorne, our third baseman, yells out at me while clapping along with the crowd. It makes me proud knowing that my team and the local community are excited for me to be here.

Don't let them down, Gunnar.

Once introductions for both teams are finished, it's time

for the National Anthem. "Ladies and gentlemen, please rise and remove your hats as we honor our nation and those who protect our freedom. We are honored to have two-time music award winner Gavin McNeer with us to sing our national anthem."

My head whips around to see Gavin running out onto the field to the microphone. I had no idea that he agreed to sing the national anthem, but I'm not surprised he didn't tell me. I would've told him no, not wanting the team to keep bothering my famous brother with "favors" now that I'm here. I know Gavin is a big boy and can tell them no whenever he wants to, but it still rubs me the wrong way that they asked him without my permission.

He gives me a wink before the music begins and then he starts singing. I can't stop my eyes from getting a little bit teary watching him perform. That little bastard was blessed with such a beautiful voice, and every time I listen to him, I'm in awe of how far he has come in life. Fireworks start shooting off from the scoreboard as he sings the lyrics about the rockets and bombs bursting, the crowd *oohing* and *awing* over the colors in the night sky. I look back up at the suite and my family is all standing there. I get a little choked up from the emotions of being in this moment with them and my teammates. Before I know it, Gavin hits the end notes and slays one of the hardest songs in our country's history to sing. As soon as he finishes, he runs over and gives me a big hug. "Go fucking kick ass tonight. I love you, Brother," I hear him tell me over the thundering noise of the crowd.

"I love you," I tell him before he lets me go and runs off the field to go back up to his suite. The music starts blaring AC/DC's "For Those About To Rock" and I start getting pumped up. The opposing team's batter makes his way out of their dugout, and I walk out to my position at shortstop.

"Let's fucking go," I yell out to the guys as we get the game started.

cNeer!" My teammate, Carter Callahan, calls out three hours later while we're walking back to the clubhouse after defeating the California Comets. "That was fucking incredible! What a game you had. Congratulations!" He pats me on the back and other team-mates echo his sentiment.

"Everyone kicked ass tonight," I tell the guys who are around me as we enter the clubhouse. The coaches follow us in, and we all gather around Declan for his speech.

"Great game tonight, fellas. You kept the momentum going for nine straight innings. You stayed calm when we were down. We had some bombs hit out of the park and incredible catches were made by our boys in the outfield." He points at Kelton James, Jake Reynolds, and Evan Parker. "You guys saved our asses tonight, along with some phenomenal pitching." We start clapping for our pitchers, Max Murphy and Carter Callahan. "I'm going to hand it over now to Coach Wayne to do the honors of giving out the Golden Louie."

I watch Chris Wayne, one of our hitting coaches, grab a yellow kid's wiffle-ball bat from his cubby. I cross my arms over my chest, curious as to what this is all about. "All right boys, I think we all can agree on who deserves to win the Golden Louie tonight. With two home runs and three assists in his first game, the Golden Louie goes to Gunnar McNeer!" He hands me the bat and I start chuckling, not knowing what the hell to do with this thing.

Coach sees my questionable look and laughs. "Sorry, McNeer, you only get this bad boy for one night unless every game for you is like tonight."

"Speech!" Eric Wiseman, our second baseman, yells out and the whole team starts chanting.

I shake my head and chuckle. I walk toward the middle of the room, and they all start clapping. Since I wasn't prepared for a speech, I think of something short and sweet. "Gonna be honest, boys. Tonight was emotional and at first, I wasn't sure how to feel. You all have made me feel like I've been part of this team since the beginning. Having my family here and you guys behind me made tonight that much sweeter. It's an honor to be with this club and I look forward to many more W's on the books. Thanks, guys." Everyone claps and I walk back to my locker.

Declan then continues on, "All right, fellas. We have two more home games before we hit the road. Go shower up and get some rest. We'll see you tomorrow at 12:30 p.m."

I start taking off my uniform and throw it into the laundry bin for the equipment managers to wash before I head to the showers. I finish quickly so I can see my family, who's waiting upstairs in the suite. Once I'm dressed, I start walking out of the clubhouse but stop short because I momentarily forgot which way to go.

"You lost, Gunnar?" Murph notices me looking around in confusion and I laugh.

"I don't know where the fuck I'm going, and I need to meet my family in their suite."

"I'm heading the same way, so follow me." We take the elevator up to the suite level and as we walk, he points out signs to help me remember how to get there in the future.

"You killed it tonight. We need to go out and celebrate. When can you get a night out? I know your daughter's not here permanently yet, but we definitely need to grab a bite to eat sometime."

"I would like that. Izzy leaves with my parents on Saturday afternoon, so after the game would actually be perfect."

"Let's make it a night then." Murph confirms.

"Sounds great." We shake hands and I thank him for

helping me get to the suites. I walk in and everyone starts cheering.

"Daddy, Daddy, Daddy!" Izzy yells and runs to me. I catch her and give her the tightest hugs.

"What did you think of the game, Isabear?"

"It was so much fun, and you did so good, Daddy!"

I chuckle, not believing she really understands my stats for this evening. "I love you, Iz. Thanks for being here tonight."

"I can't love anybody more than I love you, Daddy." She wraps her little arms around my neck and kisses me on the cheek. When she says those things, my heart turns to a big pile of mush. She's such a sweet, caring little girl and I know my mom has influenced her by teaching her proper manners and empathy. I hate that she's growing up without her own mother, but Tasha has made her own choice and poor decisions.

"Proud of you, Son. I know tonight was difficult and you literally knocked it out of the park." My dad walks up and gives me a hug, followed by my mom.

"That's what I'm talking about, Brother!" Gavin claps my hand before pulling me in for a one-armed hug. "Your two-run dinger was sick. I have no doubt it was a big FU to Texas?" Gavin asks and I have to laugh because I was thinking exactly the same thing while I was running around the bases.

"You know it." I smirk. I put Izzy down and watch her run off to her cousin. "Hey, it means a lot that you all are here tonight. You didn't have to buy this suite, nor did you have to sing the national anthem. I know you're busy and have so many other things to do, like spending time with Aly and Austin." He leaves to go back on tour tomorrow and the fact that he and his family are still here this late at night makes me feel guilty.

"There's nowhere else I'd rather be." He squeezes my

shoulder, and I gulp down the lump forming in my throat. "Get used to seeing us here."

Aly comes up behind Gavin and gives me a hug. "We will be here as much as we can to support you and Izzy. You're not alone, Gunnar." She gives me a warm smile and I kiss her on her cheek. Gavin hit the lottery when he met and fell in love with Aly. His relationship with her is the only thing I'm envious about when it comes to his life.

I hear Izzy's laughter as she runs around the suite chasing after Austin, and a sense of belonging washes over me. This is where we needed to be.

This is our new home and it's starting to feel right.

CHAPTER 6

CASSIE

I rummage through my closet, analyzing every single article of clothing that I own and hating them all. I hate having to dress up and go out. I'm a jeans and T-shirt kind of gal and dread the idea of any kind of glam. This is one of the many reasons why I have no desire to go on this date tonight. Nothing in my closet is suitable and my mood is quickly turning into one of doom and despair.

"Knock, knock," I hear someone say outside of my bedroom door and before I can tell them to come in, Grace enters.

"Oh, hey! Sorry, I didn't realize you had arrived."

She shrugs. "No big deal, your dad let me in. I've come bearing gifts." She's holding a huge pile of clothes that she immediately dumps onto my bed.

"Thank you because I really don't have anything to wear." I start picking through the pile and quickly get discouraged by what I see. "Grace, why are these all dresses? Not only do I hate wearing a dress, but we're not even the same size."

"Fear not, grumpy pants. I only brought you my best cutesy and demure dresses, some of which are A-Line."

I give her a *what the heck* look and she rolls her eyes in

frustration. "C'mon, you're an artist. Surely you know what an A-Line dress is?"

"I work with paint, not fabric."

She huffs, grabs a dress off the bed, and holds it in front of her. "Look at the bottom half of the dress. See how it flairs out like the shape of an 'A'?"

I nod. "I see it, but I still don't think these dresses will fit me. I have no boobs and big hips."

"You have the perfect hourglass figure and I would kill for the size of your boobs. Stop being so pessimistic and try them on. Here, these three are my favorite." She throws the dresses at me and they all bounce off my face and into my arms.

I look down at the colors of each dress and balk. "Red? I can't wear a red dress with my hair color."

"Your hair is dark auburn, not bright red. Trust me, the dress will be fine."

"Trust *me*, it won't."

Her eyes narrow and she points to my bathroom. "You're starting to annoy me. Get in there and try the dresses on now or I'm leaving you with nothing!"

"Lord, you're bossy today," I scoff and start making my way to the bathroom.

"And make sure you come out so I can see you in each dress. I will be the judge of which is the final winner."

I shut the door and quickly change out of my clothes and try on dress number one. It's a black, long sleeve V-neck dress that hugs every curve of my body. I absolutely hate it and if she says this dress is the winner, then I'm going to have to sneak another dress in my bag to wear when she isn't around.

I walk out of the bathroom and try to keep my face neutral. It only takes her three seconds to decide. "Too baggy in the top and too tight in the hips. I can see the outline of your granny panties."

"Oh, thank god," I mutter and turn around to go back to the bathroom.

"You know you're not leaving this room without wearing a thong, right?"

I spin back around and glare at her. "I hate those things. It's dental floss for the anus. I don't want to be picking at my ass all night long."

She starts laughing so uncontrollably, she's soon snorting. "Sorry," she wheezes in between giggles while trying to catch her breath. "The mental image of you picking at your ass all night was too much for me." She wipes the mascara away from underneath her eyes. "Gah, thanks for that. I really needed it."

"So happy to entertain you at my expense, Grace," I grumble sarcastically and go back to the bathroom.

"But you're still wearing a thong tonight."

I shoot her the bird before slamming the door. I hear her laughter and smile, loving our honest friendship.

The next dress I try on is a bright red, long-sleeved maxi wrap dress. Grace studies me for a long moment, the tip of her finger tapping against her lips. "Hmm, there's something off about this dress."

"Yeah, it's my hair."

"No," she pauses. "I think the color of the dress washes you out."

"I told you this color red with my hair and pale skin wouldn't work." When it comes to clothes, I usually can't wear red, but I sure can rock it on my lips.

"All right, noted. I will never buy you any red clothes in the future."

"Thank you."

The final dress is an emerald green, long-sleeved mini dress with a square neckline. I stare at myself in the bathroom mirror, amazed at how the color transforms my eyes.

"Winner, winner, chicken dinner! You look smoking hot." Grace exclaims when I exit out of the bathroom. She makes me twirl for her and then I stand in front of my full-length mirror to see the full effect.

"You don't think the dress is a little too short?" I ask, trying to pull the hem down. The dress is barely covering my thighs and the amount of leg I'm showing makes me uncomfortable.

"Are you kidding me? You shouldn't hide those killer legs. Seriously, Cass, you look incredible. What do you think?"

I study my appearance, and I hate to admit it, but this dress not only elevates my appearance, but makes me feel confident and sexy. "I do think I look pretty." I turn from side to side, studying myself at every angle. "Okay, I'll wear it."

"Hell yeah you're wearing it!" She reaches into her tote bag and pulls out a pair of pointed black heels with ankle straps. "Here, these are perfect to go with that dress."

"Ooh, I like these!" I go to grab the shoes, but she snatches them out of my reach.

"You can't have them until you get a proper thong and bra out of your drawer and put them on."

I start to pout but do as she commands. "Now look who's the annoying one."

"You love me," she practically sings with a sugary, sweet smile.

"I sure do," I tell her sincerely, because it's true. Grace is the sister I never had and I'm so thankful for her friendship. "Thank you again for coming to my rescue with clothes and shoes."

"You're welcome. I wasn't going to let you go be your true authentic by showing up in your uniform of jeans and a T-shirt." She winks at me and I laugh.

"If someone doesn't like my normal state of not being glammed up, then to hell with them."

"Amen, sister!" Grace pumps her fist in the air. "C'mon, I'll help you with your hair and makeup."

I stop myself from following her in the bathroom as I question whether or not this is a good idea. "Please don't make me look like a hooker."

Grace yells from the bathroom, "I can't make any promises on that."

⚾ 🧤 🦋 🧁

An hour later, Grace and I arrive at Uncle Choy's. We get there thirty minutes before Aaron does so Grace can give me a pep talk. She wants to be here when he arrives so she can properly introduce us to each other. I also think the mother hen in her doesn't want me sitting by myself, waiting for him.

Once we are seated and Grace goes to use the restroom, I take a look around the restaurant. It's a chic, modern, Asian fusion restaurant with elegant lighting. I gaze past the wide area of tables and see a large bar in the back.

Grace returns to the table and hands me a glass. "Here, I ordered you a shot." The small glass contains red liquid that looks like cough medicine.

"This looks disgusting." I scrunch up my nose while examining the contents of the liquid. "You know I don't drink."

"I know, but one shot will take the edge off your nerves." She nods toward the glass, encouraging me to drink it. "Take it now before he arrives."

She's right—I am nervous and need something to calm me down. I take the shot and am surprised to find it doesn't taste as bad as it looks. "I hope this doesn't make me tipsy."

"It shouldn't. Have you eaten anything since lunch?"

I think about it and realize I haven't. "No. We should probably order an appetizer while we wait."

"Good idea. I'm starving and need to eat something before my shift starts tonight." Grace is dressed in her scrubs and plans on going straight to the hospital after Aaron arrives.

Our waitress makes an appearance and we order some scallion pancakes to start with and water. "Listen, I want you to repeat after me," Grace says after the waitress leaves. I give her a skeptical look but agree.

"I'm going to have fun tonight."

I start to smile, already thinking it's silly that she's treating me like I'm a child. "I'm going to have fun tonight."

"I will not be a judgmental bitch."

I scowl at her. "When am I ever a judgmental bitch?"

"All the time. It's the snotty artist in you."

"No, I'm not!" I think if anyone can be snotty sometimes at this table, it's Grace.

She laughs. "This is so much fun. Now please stop arguing and repeat it!"

"Fine!" I huff. "I will not be a judgmental bitch."

"It's okay to kiss on the first date."

I roll my eyes at her. "It's okay to kiss on the first date."

"And it's definitely okay to have sex on the first date if the chemistry is sizzling and I can't keep my hands off him."

I can't help but giggle at that. "Can you shorten that? It's too long for me to repeat."

"I'm not a slut if I want to have sex on the first date."

"I'm not a slut if I want to have sex on the first date… but I probably won't."

"Why not?"

I shrug my shoulders, not really knowing why. "It just seems… wrong, I guess?"

"Why would it seem wrong?" she questions like she's a detective interrogating a murder suspect.

Our waitress returns with our food and I wait until she leaves to answer Grace's question.

"Sex is just so intimate that I feel it should be with someone you have known for at least more than one night."

"Doing it with someone you barely know and have zero connection to can also be very liberating."

"Who are you and what have you done with my best friend?" Her answer surprises me. While I know she has had more experience than I have, she's also not the type that has slept around either.

"Seriously, Cass. The double standard in our world is unfair. Guys do it all the time. Why can't women?"

"I'm sure there are plenty of women who do, but it's just not something I'm interested in."

"How would you know?" She tilts her head and narrows her gaze. "You've only been with one other guy in your life and he was a douche twat."

I laugh at her nickname for my ex. "You're right, I don't know. I feel it would take off-the-charts chemistry for me to consider sleeping with a stranger."

She sighs. "Just promise me that you'll be more open-minded to it if you are hard-core vibing with Aaron," she requests before taking a bite of her pancake.

"I promise."

She points her fork at me. "And if it does happen, you owe me all the juicy details."

"You'll get all the tea." I giggle and dig into my pancake.

"Tea time is the best." She looks over by the door and does a double take. "Oh shoot, he's here."

I grab my glass of water and swoosh the liquid around the inside of my mouth to try to get any food out of my teeth. After I swallow, I carefully dab at my mouth with my napkin so I don't take off too much of my lipstick.

"Here, take this," she whispers, passing me a breath mint out of her purse. Thank goodness for Grace, because my breath is kicking from the scallions and spices in the pancake. I pop it into my mouth as soon as he makes it to our table.

"Aaron, hi!" Grace greets him and we both stand up out of our chairs. I check him out as he greets Grace first. He's wearing a sky-blue dress shirt, unbuttoned far enough to get a peek-a-boo showing of his chest. My gaze travels down his waist to his beige, slim fit pants that almost seem a little too tight for him. His clothes confuse me because his current style is nothing like what he wore in the photos Grace showed me.

"This is my friend, Amber."

My head snaps up to his face and I can't help the blush that creeps along my cheeks from getting caught checking him out. His dark hair is styled in a classic pompadour, with not even one hair out of place. He has a trendy sparingly short beard and warm brown eyes. He's definitely a good-looking guy. Out of the corner of my eye, I can see a couple of women looking him over.

He holds out his hand for me to shake. "It's so nice to meet you. Grace told me you were beautiful and boy, she wasn't lying." He squeezes my hand hard while blatantly checking me out, licking his lips as his eyes come to rest on my legs.

I gulp down the sick feeling bubbling up my throat. "Nice to meet you as well, Aaron."

"Well, I need to get to work. You two kids have fun." Grace hugs Aaron goodbye first and then wraps her arms around me.

"Don't leave," I whisper in her ear.

"Have fun!" she whispers back and turns to leave.

I watch her walk out of the restaurant and then glance back at my date with an awkward smile.

"Come, sit down and let's get to know each other." He pulls out my chair and I say a little prayer that tonight goes better than what I'm fearing.

CHAPTER 7

GUNNAR

"'m going to kill you."

The words startle me into taking a step back and put me on alert as I view my surroundings. There is no one standing in front of the door to the men's bathroom, so I'm confused as to where the woman's voice is coming from.

"Why? Because this guy is a total creeper!"

Where is that voice coming from? I walk fully out of the men's bathroom and glance to my left and I finally see her. She's facing the wall, hovering in the corner and cowering into herself. It's not a safe position; anyone could come up from behind without her seeing them. Part of me wonders if I should stick around to make sure she stays safe. Not that she's in any real kind of danger, but we are at a loud restaurant which is turning into a bustling bar as the night wears on. I came here tonight with Murph to grab dinner and shoot the shit. He just left to go home, so it's not like I have anywhere to be since Izzy left with my parents this afternoon. But I also don't want to frighten her if she turns around and sees some stranger standing here, listening to her. I look up and down the hallway but can't find a more conspicuous space to hide. *Stop being paranoid, Gunnar! She'll be just fine.*

I shake my head and start walking away, annoyed with myself for becoming so pessimistic and cautious about the world since having a kid.

"Seriously, Grace. There's something wrong with this guy. I don't feel safe."

That stops me dead in my tracks. There's no way I can leave this girl alone now. I don't care if she gets weirded out that I'm standing here, eavesdropping. My conscience won't allow me to leave until I know she'll be okay.

"No, don't come down here. You can't leave work in the middle of your shift. I'll figure out a way to get rid of him. Thank goodness you didn't tell him my real name."

I quietly chuckle at the fake name antics women use, but in this case, it was a smart idea.

"Listen to me loud and clear, Grace. You're *never* allowed to set me up on a blind date *ever* again. I should commit you to the psych ward for thinking I would be attracted to this guy's personality. He's a slimy Rico Suave."

I can't contain my burst of laughter, which causes her to whirl around. My breath is momentarily knocked out of me due to the sheer magnitude of her eyes. The color is a blue that reminds me of the Caribbean Sea. They are mesmerizing and I bet she hypnotizes men within seconds of looking at them. With her dark, red hair, pale complexion and red lips, she's a complete knockout. I try not to let my gaze wander down her body because I can already tell by the look of annoyance on her face that she's not happy to have someone of the male sex within her vicinity. I smile at her and hold up my hands in surrender, hoping that she sees I mean her no harm.

"I've got to go. I'll call you later." She hangs up, slips her phone into her purse, and crosses her arms against her chest. She narrows her eyes in disdain and it's pretty obvious that she has no idea who I am, which is refreshing.

"I'm sorry, but I couldn't help but overhear your conversation," I start but she immediately interrupts me.

"You mean you were eavesdropping."

"Technically, yes, but only because I was concerned for your safety when you said you felt unsafe."

She looks at me with skepticism and I can't say I blame her if the roles were reversed. "I promise you I just want to help you. I have a daughter and if she was alone at a bar, having this conversation right now, I would hope someone would stop to offer her help."

"You don't look like you're old enough to have a kid my age."

Her tone is cynical and she keeps glancing behind me, probably trying to figure a way out. She's in total fight or flight mode and her grit is fucking sexy. I give her one of my best smiles, hoping it comes off friendly and not sleazy in any way. "You're right, I don't. She's five."

"Oh."

"I promise you I'm not some psycho trying to trick you."

"That's exactly what a serial killer would say."

I laugh at her quick wit and smartness. "You're probably right, but you're just going to have trust that I'm not. Honestly, I really just want to help you get to safety."

She bites her lip while she thinks about my offer. *Do not stare at her lips, Gunnar.* My gaze can't help but flicker down and my mind wanders to what it would feel like if she was biting *my* lips. My pants start to feel uncomfortably tight and I mentally chastise myself to get a grip.

I see her body start to relax when she says, "Okay, but how do you plan on helping me?"

"I saw this on a television show once, but what if I pretend I'm your ex-boyfriend?"

She scoffs. "Uh-huh, like he would believe that."

"If we're convincing enough, he will."

"Why an ex-boyfriend? Why not a cousin or friend?"

"Because an ex-boyfriend would intimidate him enough to leave."

I see the realization of my idea spark her interest and she nods. "All right, ex-boyfriend it is. Continue on with the plan."

My mind races and I start to picture the scenario. "You are going to walk back out there first and create some sort of distraction like…knock over your drink."

She shakes her head. "That creates a mess for the waitress."

I smile, liking her empathy for the wait staff. "Don't worry, we'll leave a very generous tip." She bites her lip again and I have to will myself to look away so I can focus on the task at hand. "The commotion will give me the excuse to come over to say hi. I'll introduce myself to him, we will start talking about us, how much I miss you, and how breaking up was a bad idea."

"No cheating," she firmly states and my brow furrows in confusion.

"Excuse me?"

"I don't want the reason for us breaking up to be about cheating."

"Gotcha and no problem with that since I've been cheated on and it fucking sucked."

She looks at me in surprise. "Someone cheated on you too?"

"Yeah. I'm assuming you as well?"

She nods. "My ex-boyfriend did."

"Does your date know?" I wonder, because that just makes the story we're trying to concoct much more complicated.

She sighs. "I'm not sure what my friend has told him about me. He's done most of the talking about himself tonight."

What a douche.

"Let's not worry about this. Hopefully, he'll get the hint that I'm not leaving when I sit down with you guys."

"But what if he asks you to leave?"

"You'll have to play this game with me and pipe up to say you don't want me to leave."

"Okay." She glances down at her watch and grimaces. "I need to get back out there. I've been gone a while." She starts to go but suddenly stops. "Wait, what's your name?"

"Um—" Fuck, I can't think of any good names and I say out loud the first thing I think of. "Lewiston."

She scrunches her nose in disgust. "What the heck kind of name is Lewiston?"

"I don't know," I laugh at how silly it sounds. "I'm sure it's just as good as your name." I raise my eyebrow at her and it earns me a smirk.

"My name is Amber."

"But is it really?" I ask and I have a hunch that it isn't.

"It is for tonight at least." She takes a deep breath and clutches her hands nervously.

"Hey." I gently grasp her elbow and give it a reassuring squeeze. "Take a deep breath and don't worry. We've got this."

She gives me a small smile, not looking very convinced. "Thank you for wanting to help me. I really hope this works."

"It'll work," I tell her.

She nods and sidesteps around me to leave. I turn around and watch her walk back out to her table. I stand there for two more minutes and then I leave the hallway. I walk the perimeter of the bar toward the front where the tables and booths are stationed. I stay close to the farthest wall behind him and watch as Amber swings her arm, causing her glass of wine to go crashing to the ground.

"Oh no!" She exclaims loud enough for most of the patrons dining to glance in her direction. "I'm so sorry," she tells the waitress who squats down with some towels to clean up the mess.

"Don't worry about it. It happens all the time," the waitress responds, and more staff come out to help clean the mess.

I wait until everything has been cleared and figure now is the perfect time to make my move. I put my game face on and casually walk up to their table.

"Amber?" I question in hesitation and when she looks up, a beautiful smile lights up her face and eyes as if she really is excited to see me. I'm so entranced by how stunning she is that for a moment, I forget what I'm supposed to be doing.

"Lewis!" I like how she shortens my name to make it sound more normal. "What are you doing here?"

"I was grabbing a drink with a friend, but he just left. I thought that was you when I looked over at all the commotion. I felt the need to come over and say hi." I bend down and kiss her cheek. I hear her gasp in surprise and I regret not discussing physically touching her beforehand.

"Aaron, this is my ex-boyfriend Lewis. Lewis, this is Aaron."

"Nice to meet you." I shake his hand and notice he's staring at me, his head tilted to the side in thought. *Oh shit, I think he recognizes who I am.*

"You look familiar. Do I know you from somewhere?"

"No, I don't think we've ever met before."

"Hmm." He narrows his eyes and rubs his chin. "You look like someone famous."

Crap. I need to diffuse the situation. "Oh, I know." I snap my fingers and point at him. "You think I look like that professional baseball player, don't you? The one who just got traded here."

His eyes light up in recognition. "Yeah, that's it," Aaron confirms with a smile on his face.

"Yeah man, I get that all the time. It's like he's my doppelgänger, but we have zero relation whatsoever."

"Really?" His voice is laced with doubt as he looks me up and down. "What do you do for a living?"

"I'm a personal trainer," I tell the lie easily, thinking it would make sense with my physique. I turn toward Amber and smile. "How have you been? I've been thinking about you a lot lately."

She blushes and I love how her cheeks grow pink. "Been doing well. Just working a lot. You?"

Shit, I never asked what she does for a living. Hopefully that doesn't come up in the conversation. I'm about to answer her when Aaron interjects.

"When did you guys break up again, because Grace said you've been single for a long time."

"We broke up about six months ago. Our relationship wasn't very serious since we were both busy with our jobs, so the break-up was amicable." She turns to look at me for confirmation and I smile at her quick thinking and excellent answer.

"Yeah, there are things that I look back on that I definitely would have handled differently." I stare at her, not that it's hard to do with how gorgeous she is.

"What would you have done differently, Lewis?" She locks eyes with mine and I can feel my hand automatically grabbing the back of the empty chair next to her, pulling it out and sitting down as close as I can to her.

"I would've never let our careers get in the way of us. I would've made sure you were my number one priority."

She swallows yet we never lose eye contact. For some reason, it's starting to feel like it's just the two of us and I continue to try to think about all the things I would tell her if I was trying to win her back.

"I want a second chance, Amber. Will you give me one?"

"Dude, we're on a fucking date," Aaron angrily responds, breaking our trance. "If you wanted to be with her so badly, you should've called her before now, but you haven't and it's your loss. She's out with me tonight, so it's time for you to leave."

The asshole has a point, but I choose not to respond to him. I focus my attention back on Amber and grab her hand. Time to go all in and not hold back. "I'm sorry I haven't called, but I think fate brought us here to the same place tonight for a reason. I miss you and want to try again. Do you miss me at all?" I give her hand a squeeze, encouraging her to speak up.

"Yeah," she says softly. "I really miss you too, Lewis. Seeing you here, expressing your feelings really changes things for me. Not to mention, you look really hot. I forgot how handsome you are." I slowly smile at her, loving the fact that she likes how I look…at least I hope that part was real. Not that it matters since this is all supposed to be an act.

"You guys are unbelievable," Aaron scoffs. I turn to look at him, throw my arm around the back of her chair and smile, hoping he gets the hint to get the fuck out of here. He narrows his eyes and turns to Amber. "Amber, c'mon. You're not really going to fall for this bullshit, are you? This guy is totally playing you."

"I'm sorry, Aaron, but I don't want to lead you on. I think I want to see where things go again with Lewis."

"You're not even going to finish our date? We haven't even ordered dinner yet."

"I'm sorry, but I'm not hungry." She turns in her chair to grab her purse. "Let me pay for my drink."

"I've got it, Sweetheart." I grab my wallet from my back pocket, pull out a fifty-dollar bill and lay it on the counter.

"I don't need your fucking money. This is my date and I'll pay for the drink she spilled." Aaron grabs my money and throws it at me. He's got a wild, crazy look in his eye and I'm glad she's not alone with him anymore. Amber has great intuition—there's something off with him. He rakes his hand through his hair and takes a deep breath. "Don't go,

Amber. Let's get to know each other and just be friends if you want."

"I'm sorry, Aaron, but I don't think tonight is going to work out."

"Okay, then let's get together another night. I promise you; you're missing out on a good time with someone who's going to treat you like a princess."

"Aaron, I think Amber is trying to be polite here, but there's not going to be a next time for you because I don't plan on ever giving her up again. So it's time to take the hint and leave."

"Fuck you," he yells, his tone of voice causing people to stop talking and stare. "How dare you try to humiliate me. I'm not leaving. In fact, I see plenty of available ladies at the bar who would kill to go home with me tonight. You want to leave so badly, then get the fuck out of here."

I stand up and help Amber out of her chair. I grab her hand and quickly notice how perfectly it fits in mine. I start to pull her toward the front door, but she stops and turns back to Aaron.

"I'm so sorry, Aaron. I don't mean to be rude. This was just quite an unexpected surprise." She feels bad about our deception, but I personally don't feel she has anything to apologize for. The guy is showing signs of unstable and possessive behavior. Instead of walking away amicably, he threw a fit like a whiny little baby.

"Apology not accepted. Grace is going to hear exactly what I think about you and your unexpected surprise."

"Let's go, Amber." I wrap my arm around her waist and guide her to the door. As we get closer to the exit, I whisper in her ear, "Don't turn around and look back at him. Let's walk outside and go to the left." She does as I say, and as soon as we get outside, I look back through the window and see him watching us with a crazed look on his face.

We need to be more convincing so he doesn't follow us

and I do the only other thing that comes to mind. I yank her to my chest and say, "Follow my lead," before crushing my lips to hers. She gasps in surprise but plays along and kisses me back. Her lips are warm and I get caught up in their softness. She slightly parts her lips and I take that exact moment to slide my tongue against them. She moans, wraps her arms around my neck and opens more for me. Damn, she tastes so good. Better than anyone I've ever kissed. Soon I forget why we're here and give in to how incredible holding her in my arms feels. Time seems to stop and all I want to do is hug her tighter, kiss her harder, and bury myself deep inside her. Her soft moans and whimpers are making my dick hurt with need, but I can't stop kissing her.

"Get a room," someone yells, shocking us both back to reality. We pull apart and stare at each other, our chests heaving as we suck in air. I look around to re-focus and see Aaron's murderous face in the window.

"We need to get out of here," I grab her hand and we start to run down the street.

CHAPTER 8

CASSIE

What in the heck is happening? I ask myself as I try to keep up with Lewis while we walk briskly down the street. He's still holding my hand, but his legs are a lot longer than mine are, so I have to double my steps in order to not be dragged along the road. Thank goodness we stop running so I can catch my breath but also collect my thoughts.

The kiss was a complete surprise, but my reaction to it was even more shocking. I've never been kissed that way in my entire life. Sure, I would get butterflies in my stomach when my ex kissed me, but nothing close to what Lewis just made me feel. His kiss was the earthquake that sparked a tsunami of desire inside of me and it dissipated before it had the chance to make landfall. He lit my panties on fire just from the mere touch of his tongue and I practically humped him right there in public. The whole time we were kissing, I felt like I couldn't get close enough to him. Am I that hard up because it's been so long since I've been physically touched by a guy or is he just that good?

I press my free hand to my swollen lips, which are still tingling from being devoured so harshly, so deliciously. Is that what a true kiss is supposed to feel like? Because if so, I've been completely missing out or maybe, I just haven't been with the right person who knew what they were doing.

And apparently Lewis knows exactly what he's doing.

I take this opportunity to finally get a good look at him. I saw how handsome he was earlier when he overheard my conversation with Grace, but I was skeptical of his intentions when he offered to help me. His award-winning performance at being my ex and wanting me back was so convincing that I got caught up in the moment of how good it felt to be wanted again.

"Crap, I don't know where I'm going." The frustration in his voice brings me back to reality. We stop walking and he drops my hand while he looks back to where we just came from. I immediately miss his warmth and the strong grip of his fingers against mine. *I wonder what else those fingers could do.*

"What do you mean?" I ask, needing a distraction from where my thoughts are heading.

"I just moved to Nashville, so I don't know where else would be a good place for us to go."

I look around and know this area of the town well. "There's an Irish pub just a couple blocks up."

"Perfect!" He grabs my hand again, causing me to bite my lip to suppress my smile of satisfaction. We walk in silence for a couple moments until we get to O'Toole's Irish Pub. Lewis opens the door and we're greeted by the host, who has to talk loudly over the raucous crowd. Lewis asks if we can be seated in the back, away from everyone. Fortunately, they still have some booths available, and we follow the host to the back of the restaurant where it's quieter. We sit down next to each other and he hands us our menus.

"Your waitress will be right with you. Enjoy and welcome to Nashville," he says to Lewis and walks away. Lewis quickly looks over at me and smiles when he sees my puzzled expression.

"Do you know him?" I ask because if he does, then it's weird that he didn't even acknowledge him.

"Never met him before," he responds, deciding to browse the menu instead of looking at me.

"Then why would he welcome you to Nashville if he didn't know you just moved here?"

Lewis lifts his gaze to meet mine and shrugs. "You know how sometimes you mean one thing, but say another? I think he meant to say, 'Welcome to O'Toole's' but said Nashville instead."

I think about it for a moment. "Ah, that makes sense. I do that sometimes."

He chuckles. "Me too. I think it was just an oversight. Are you hungry?"

I'm ferociously hungry, but I'm not sure it's really the food I want.

"Yeah, I can eat," I tell him while I stare at his lips. Thank goodness he's looking at the flyer with the specials on it.

Who are you right now, Cassie? I can feel my cheeks turning red, so I look down at my menu and try to focus on food. These naughty thoughts over a man I just met are so not like me. There's no way I can be tipsy from the one shot I took hours ago. I feel like I'm drunk on lust, and I don't like this unhinged chaos inside of me that he created with one damn kiss.

"Hey, listen," he says, and I look up from the menu. "I'm sorry about kissing you without asking for permission."

I'm not sorry, not one damn bit.

"It's okay," I respond quickly, not wanting him to feel bad but also hoping he will stop bringing it up because it keeps rewinding in my brain, making me want a repeat performance.

"No, we should've had a better game plan. I just saw

Aaron watching us and I thought maybe him seeing me kiss you would deter him from following. I'm not really sure if he did, but we're just probably going to have to stay out for a little bit longer to play it safe. Is that okay with you?"

"Fine by me," I agree, not really wanting to go home anymore. This man has me intrigued and I would love to find out what his story is.

"I feel you're being way cooler than you should be about this. I had no right to just grab you like that and invade your personal space."

If he only knew how much more personal space I wanted him to invade.

I feel bad that he's agonizing over this because he clearly looks bothered by his actions. "Lewis, it's truly fine. I understand why you did it and if we're being honest here, I actually kind of liked it." *Lies, you more than liked it.*

"You did?" My eyes are immediately drawn to the devilish smirk he's giving me, and I groan inwardly, appreciating how sexy he looks right now.

What. Is. Wrong. With. Me.

Focus, Cassie. I lock in on his vibrant green eyes and will myself to not look away. "I'm the one that is grateful to you for coming to my rescue. I'm sorry if I wasn't very friendly to you at first."

"Nothing to apologize for. I would've been on alert as well, especially since you already were feeling anxious about Aaron. You were smart to listen to your intuition. There's something wrong with him."

"It makes me feel better that you agree with me. I'm going to kill my friend Grace for setting this up. Oh shoot, speaking about Grace, do you mind if I text her back real quick to let her know I'm okay?"

"Of course. Do you know what you want to eat? I can order for us while you text her back." He catches the eye of our waitress and waves her over to begin our order.

"Let's just share some appetizers if that works for you. You pick." I grab my phone out of my purse to find ten missed messages from Grace.

"Do you want anything to drink besides water?"

I look up from my phone and debate whether or not I want a cocktail. I'm not a big drinker due to my mother's history, but I think one drink won't hurt.

"I'll take a vodka tonic with a lime, please," I tell the waitress as she collects our menus, and I resume texting Grace back. I don't bother reading her messages and instead, I tell her that I'm fine, having drinks with my gorgeous savior, and I'll fill her in about everything later. I put my phone back in my purse and immediately feel it vibrate with back to back texts. I know leaving her that little easter egg without details is killing her right now.

Serves her right.

"The incident with Aaron will make things a bit awkward for Grace at work, but fortunately, she only sees him on the days he's at her hospital."

Lewis's mouth drops open in shock. "Please don't tell me that guy is a doctor or a world-renowned surgeon?"

My lips twitch. "No, he's a pharmaceutical rep who supplies drugs to the pharmacy inside the hospital."

"Oh, thank god." We laugh because that would be pretty bad if he was some famous doctor.

"You said earlier you just moved to Nashville? How long have you been here?"

"I've only been here for a few weeks," he chuckles. "It's been a little bit of a whirlwind."

"Where did you move from?"

"Austin, Texas. Ever been there?"

"I can't say I have but that explains the adorable accent," I smirk. "I figured you were southern, but I just didn't know from which state."

"I'm a true Texan, born and raised. My brother and I love

Austin so much he named his first-born child after our birth city." He laughs at his happy memories and the sound of it makes me smile. "My parents still live there and Nashville actually kind of reminds me of Austin in some ways. What about you?"

"I was born down the street at Vanderbilt Medical Center. Pretty rare to find a true Tennessean these days with so many transplants moving here."

He raises an eyebrow as if he doesn't believe me. "Where's your twang then?"

I giggle at his stereotyping. "Both my parents are from Wisconsin. They moved here before I was born. If you love Austin so much, why did you leave?" I decide to switch subjects, not really wanting to discuss any further details about my mother.

"Work purposes." Our waitress arrives with our drinks and when she leaves, he doesn't elaborate any further.

"Are you liking it here so far?"

"Honestly, this is my first night out and so far, I'm *really* liking it." With the way he's staring at me, his innuendo that he is liking *me* is loud and clear. Warmth spreads throughout my belly and I give him what I hope to be a sexy smile.

"What a memorable first night out—saving some girl from a psycho." I laugh. "You probably will never go out again after this...unless you do this often and have a hero complex."

He grins and shakes his head. "No, this is my very first time saving a damsel in distress. I'm actually not very fond of the nightlife." His smile turns sheepish as if he's embarrassed and shrugs. "I rather be chilling at home, watching a movie with my daughter."

It's so refreshing to hear how much he loves his kid. "That's right, you have a daughter..." my voice trails off and a horrific thought occurs to me.

"Oh my God, are you married?" I practically shriek loud

enough for people to look over at us. I immediately look down at his ring finger, something I should've done the first time I met him.

He starts laughing, "Nope, not married. Remember I told you my ex-cheated on me?"

My shoulders sag in relief. "I didn't realize you were referring to your ex-wife."

"We were never married."

That piques my interest. I wonder what prevented him from wanting to marry his baby mama.

He grabs my hand, his thumb starting to rub circles over the top of my skin. The gesture sends little shock waves down my spine. "Let's not talk about our past tonight. I really prefer all my attention to be focused on you."

Our gazes are locked, and it isn't until we hear the waitress putting down our food that we break eye contact. Lordy, it's getting hot in here, and I know it isn't because O'Toole's has the heater on. I take a big sip of my drink and almost choke on the overabundance of vodka I taste in it.

"Is there anything else you need, sir?" The waitress gives Lewis a once over, her eyes gleaming with appreciation. I quickly glance around and notice a lot of other women looking and whispering about him. Can't say I blame them; it definitely boosts my ego knowing he's choosing to be here with me.

"No, thanks." He doesn't even look her way as he hands me my silverware and plate. Lewis ordered boneless wings in sweet chili sauce, some fried pickles, and beer cheese dip with pretzels. I strategically grab a couple of fried pickles, spoon some beer cheese onto my plate with some pretzels and leave the wings for Lewis. I dip a pretzel into some cheese, take a bite and moan at the perfection assaulting my tastebuds. I grab another one, slather it in even more cheese and start going to town on it. I can feel the cheese all over my lips and I start to lick them, not wanting to waste good cheese on my napkin. I look over at Lewis and immediately stop. My eyes grow wide as he's staring at me with raw hunger.

"You've got cheese all over your mouth."

My tongue automatically darts out and I start licking my lips. I continue lapping around trying to get every morsel, fascinated with watching his eyes grow dark with desire at my actions.

"Did I get it all?"

He shakes his head. "Let me help you." He wraps his hand around my waist and pulls me to him, while his other hand rests against my jaw. He moves his thumb and swipes it against the corner of my mouth before sliding it across my bottom lip. My lips automatically part and my tongue flicks out lightly to touch his thumb.

"Fuck," he growls before replacing his thumb with his mouth. *Yes*, my brain screams in victory at getting another taste of him. Our initial kiss was not a fluke—he's masterfully moving his lips and tongue against mine sending electrical currents straight to my core that has me clenching my thighs together. I moan, sliding my hands into his hair so I can keep him as close to me as possible. *How can someone kiss like this and be single?* I think before my mind is taken over by the need and desperation erupting inside of me. If this is how Lewis makes me feel with his kisses, I think my heart would stop beating if we had sex.

He breaks the kiss and begins nibbling up my jawbone to my ear. "We can't keep doing this here," he whispers right before he starts kissing my neck. I squeeze his shoulder with one of my hands while he sucks over a sensitive spot. I don't even care if I have a hickey tomorrow. My hand moves down his arm, past his waist to his hip. I can feel the indentation of his hip flexors through his clothes. My fingers slide over his upper thigh to his groin where I feel his desire pushing against his pants. He moans as I lightly rub against him, and he crashes his mouth back onto mine again. I don't know what has come over me, nor can I explain my wanton behavior, but I can't make myself stop.

I don't want to stop.

"We need to make a decision." He stops our kiss suddenly and pulls back to search my eyes. "We either end the night now and I walk you to your car or we take this somewhere private."

I don't want this night to end, but I'm also a little apprehensive of having sex with a complete stranger. My conversation with Grace earlier this week about casual sex comes to mind. I know there's nothing wrong with it, but I think what's holding me back is my lack of experience.

"I don't want to go home," I whisper. "But I've also never gone home with a stranger before."

"We don't have to do anything that you don't want to do, but we can't keep kissing each other in public. People are starting to watch." I glance around and I realize he's right, people are staring. I pull back from him, completely embarrassed.

"It's your call, Amber. I don't want you to feel uncomfortable. Trust your intuition." He laces his fingers through mine and gives my hand a squeeze.

I'm not sure I can trust my intuition at this moment because everything just feels so good, so right, and it's a feeling that I'm not ready to give up yet.

"Let's go somewhere private," I tell him and squeeze his hand back.

"Are you sure? You don't have to decide right away. We can sit here and eat our food, but we just can't look at each other," he jokes and I laugh, because we both know that's going to be impossible to do.

"I'm sure," I confirm.

He waves over the waitress and gives her his credit card without looking at the bill. "Here's for the check." She takes his credit card from him, but not before she gives me a nasty look. He presses his lips against mine and whispers, "Remember, you're in control of everything we do tonight. I just want to spend time with you."

Before I can respond, the waitress returns with his credit card and check to sign. He grabs his card, puts it back in his wallet, and scribbles illegibly on the receipt. "Let's go," he commands and helps me out of the booth. He grabs hold of my hand and leads us out of the restaurant.

"Where are we going?" I inquire because there's no way I can take him back to my house. He looks around once we're outside the restaurant and points behind me.

"We're going there." I follow his gaze and see The Omni Hotel. At first, I wonder why he's not taking me to his place, but then I remember he just moved here and his house will be his daughter's home, so I can understand not wanting to take a stranger there.

"Lewis, The Omni is really expensive, and I only know this because my former employer had friends come into town and we would help book the hotel for them," I explain because I don't want him to think I've done this before so I know how much hotel rates are. "There's plenty of other affordable hotels around here."

"I'm not taking you to some cheap ass hotel. Consider this a staycation for both of us. Besides, if you decide you want to leave and go home, then at least I know I will have a very comfortable bed to sleep in for tonight."

When he puts it like that, how can I refuse? "Okay," I agree as we briskly walk toward the hotel. The closer we get, the more anxious I feel with the anticipation of what might come.

We get to the hotel and Lewis walks to the front desk while I wait in the lobby. I watch him talk with the receptionist and within a couple of minutes, he receives a key to a room. He walks slowly toward me, my gaze appreciating how incredibly good-looking he is. His clothes can't conceal his strong body, and my mouth starts salivating at the thought of exploring it.

He stops within inches of me and holds up the keycard to the room. "You still want to go upstairs to hangout?"

I grab the card and lace my fingers with his. "Let's go," I tell him, and I'm rewarded with a heart-stopping, panty-melting smile.

Whatever happens tonight is going to be life-changing. Our chemistry together is too off the charts for me to back away. This might be a one-time thing, but for tonight, I'm done letting life slip me by.

CHAPTER 9

GUNNAR

'm breathing heavily by the time we make it up to the top floor of our room. With no one else in the elevator, I pushed Amber against the wall and continued my exploration of her mouth. I can't seem to quench this overwhelming need to touch and kiss her, but I also don't want to scare her. I don't want her to think I'm just here for the sex. I'm going to let her control what we do tonight, even if all we do is talk until we can't keep our eyes open anymore. Regardless of what happens, this is still going to be a night I know I'll never forget. I get to be around a beautiful woman who not only seems smart and sweet, but also doesn't have a clue as to who I am. She wants to be with Gunnar, the person, not Gunnar, the baseball player, and fuck if that doesn't make me want her even more.

I slide the keycard into the lock and hear it click, the light on it turning green signaling for us to enter. I open the door and push it to the wall so she can walk in front of me. Once we're both in, I shut the door and lock it.

"Wow, this place is really nice," she comments while taking in her surroundings. I got a corner suite that has a living room, dining room, and kitchen that's separate from the bedroom with a killer view of downtown Nashville. The curtains are wide open, the city lights casting a glow inside the dark room. I watch her walk to the windows to look outside. I take off my jacket and hang it on the back of one of the chairs and join her.

"Would you like something to drink?" I ask, wanting her to feel comfortable and at ease.

She turns to me and smiles. "I'll just have some water." I nod and walk to the kitchen. I open the refrigerator to grab a bottle of water and notice there's champagne and chocolates inside. The receptionist told me they had a last-minute cancellation of their love and luxury suite, so I guess that was included with it.

I take them out of the refrigerator and show her. "Someone's cancellation is our gain. Would you like some?"

"I will never say no to chocolate."

I grab two pieces of chocolate with some bottles of water and walk back to her. I hand her the chocolates and watch her take a bite, her eyes closing with the first taste of the sweet treat.

"Hmm, that's amazing." I gulp at hearing her moan and take a swig of my water, telling myself to calm down.

"Want some?" She holds a piece out for me. I nod and before I can grab it from her, she has it in front of my lips. I stare at her while I open my mouth and let her slip the chocolate inside. I close my lips around her finger and suck the remnants of chocolate off it. She gasps when she feels my tongue lick her finger and she slowly pulls it out.

I chew on the piece that is in my mouth and swallow. "You're making it very difficult for me to be a gentleman right now."

"Who says I want you to be a gentleman?"

I smirk at her brazenness. "Tell me what you want, Amber?"

She breathes out a shaky breath. "I want you to kiss me again. Isn't that why we're here?"

I cup her face with my hands. "Hell yeah it is."

I start our kiss slowly this time, wanting to savor the feeling of her lips. Our kisses are gentle and sensuous, but soon she flicks her tongue against my bottom lip, demanding I open wider for her. I groan with desire, those all-consuming carnal feelings of need start to build, and I deliberately slow our kisses to a stop and step back.

Her lips are swollen, and her hooded eyes are glazed over with passion. I rest my forehead against hers and take a deep breath. "It's been a long time since I've been intimate with anyone."

"Me too," she whispers.

"So you understand that if we keep going at this pace, I'm not going to last very long."

She gives me a smirk that makes me want to spank that lovely ass of hers.

"I want tonight to last for us both, so will you do me a favor?" She nods, her gaze becoming wide, alert, and eager.

"Good girl," I tell her. "Now turn around and go to the window."

She narrows her eyes at me with a hesitant smile, but does as I say. Once she's there, she looks over her shoulder at me.

"Look forward and place your hands against the window."

She swallows and turns to look straight ahead at the view of the city.

I slowly come up behind her, my one hand resting gently on her left hip while my right hand sweeps her hair to the side, exposing the nape of her neck. I start pressing soft, feather-like kisses along her skin while the hand that was on her hip wraps around her waist, pulling her against me. I move my mouth along to the bottom right side of her neck, flicking my tongue against her sensitive spots. Her breath starts to hitch, and I nip once at her earlobe before sucking it into my mouth. She moans and drops her hands from the glass to wrap her arms around me.

"Keep your hands on the window," I demand in her ear. She huffs but places them back on the glass. As I kiss back down her neck to suck on the exposed skin of her shoulder, my hands roam her waist until I move them to her breasts. Gently, I squeeze while my thumbs circle around her nipples. She pushes her ass into my erection and starts to move, the friction making my cock throb against my slacks.

"You're playing naughty," I growl because I'm not done teasing her, but I'm also aching to be inside her. I take a small step back and remove my hands from her breasts, sliding them down her waist to her hips, then to the top of her butt cheeks. I lift up her dress and squeeze her ass. I start to squat while my hands glide down the back of her shapely thighs to her calf muscles. I wrap my hands around her ankles and slowly massage my way up the front of her legs, standing back up as I go underneath her dress and walk my finger to the inside of her thighs. Once there, I lightly graze against her clit and I can feel how damp her panties are. I groan, my fingers itching to touch her.

"You're so wet and we're just getting started." I run my hands up underneath her dress to her hips and grip the sides of her thong. "Let's remove these to let them dry." I push the material down and watch them pool around her high heels. I help her step out of them and flick them away so she doesn't trip. My hands make a slow, agonizing journey back up her legs to her core.

"Please," she begs while straining her hands against the window. She continues to rub against me, so I grip her hip with my left hand to hold her still while the fingers of my right hand find her clit and start to rub.

"Please, what?" I press harder against her bud and slowly move against it, entering her ever so slightly.

She drops her head, resting it on her arm. "Please get inside of me."

I take two of my fingers and move them back and forth against her, getting close enough to her entrance, but pulling back right before. Her frustration grows with need and she begins bucking against me.

"Ahhh," she moans as I finally give her what she wants and slide both fingers inside of her.

"Fuck, you're so tight." I lay my forehead against her shoulders as my left arm again wraps around her waist and clutches her to me. Her hips are thrusting against my fingers, her ass moving along my erection.

Her whimpers are getting louder, and I can feel her walls pulsing around me. If I don't stop, she's going to come soon and selfishly, I want that to happen around my cock. I stop rubbing and remove my hand.

"No, please, don't stop," she whines, making me snicker, and I love the fact that I'm the one making her delirious with desire.

"Soon, baby, but for now, we need to remove some clothing." I grab the zipper that's in the middle of her back and bring it down. She hastily removes her arms from the sleeves and the dress falls to the floor. She kicks the dress away and I turn her around and push her against the glass, her ass on display for everyone outside to see. Fortunately, we are high up and the lights are not turned on. I lift her up and she wraps her arms and legs around me. My lips slam into hers, our tongues dueling with one another.

I can barely feel her nipples through the confines of our clothing, so I break my lips away from hers, and start kissing along her neck while my hand pushes down her strapless bra. I grip her breast, lower my head and pull her nipple into my mouth. I lash my tongue against it, her hand gripping my head closer. While I continue to tease her, my left hand snakes behind her back and manages to unhook the bra. I rip it out from behind her and move my mouth across her sternum to give her other breast the same attention.

"I need to feel your skin," she pants. I pull back from her slightly, grab the fabric at the base of my neck with one hand and pull my shirt over my head.

"Yes," she moans when her nipples touch my hot skin. "So much better, but you still have too many clothes on."

"I agree, so hold on. It's time to take this into the bedroom." She grips me tighter and I carry her into the bedroom and lay her down on the bed. I disconnect our lips to stand up straight to remove my clothes. She sits up on her elbows and watches me as I unhook my belt, unbutton my pants and pull down my zipper. My cock springs free as I push my pants and briefs down my hips. She licks her lips while she stares at my cock, and I groan.

I fist myself and start moving my hand up and down against my shaft. "Are you sure you still want to do this?" I give her one last out, because I know as soon as I get inside of her, I'll be a goner.

She nods and suddenly a thought occurs to me. "Shit, I don't have any condoms." I'm not the kind of guy who carries a condom in my wallet since I normally don't randomly hook-up with anyone. I was so consumed with Amber that I didn't even think to stop somewhere to pick some up.

She sits up and holds a finger up. "I think I do." She stands up and walks around me to the living room and rummages through her purse. "Ah-ha." She pulls a strand of four condoms out. "Please believe me when I tell you that I did not put these in here."

"Let me guess, Grace did?" She saunters back into the room, rips one from the strand and tears it open.

"Yes, and while I kept handing them back to her, I can now say I'm grateful she was persistent and put them back in my purse." She pulls the condom out of the wrapper and starts kissing me. Once again, I quickly get lost in our kiss, so I inhale sharply when I unexpectedly feel her cover the tip of my cock and roll the condom down my shaft. I clutch her tighter to me, my kisses becoming more demanding as the anticipation of being inside her builds.

She walks me backward and the back of my thighs hit the bed. I sit down and she straddles me. She wraps her arms around my neck and continues devouring my mouth. Her hips start to gyrate against me, but I'm not yet inside of her. The feeling of her heat and wetness is too much for me to bear. I maneuver us around so that she's pinned beneath me. She immediately opens her legs for me to settle in between them. I grab my cock, bring it to her entrance and rub the tip back and forth against her clit.

"Lewis, please," she pleads, and I know exactly what she needs. I line myself up with her opening and slowly push in. She's so incredibly tight that for a moment I stop so she can get used to me.

"Are you okay?" I ask in a strained voice. I don't know how much longer I can keep still, my body vibrating with the need to move.

"You feel so good," she moans. She lifts her legs to wrap around my hips, making me plunge deeper inside of her. We both groan at how incredible it feels.

"I'm not going to be able to go slow," I murmur as I start thrusting in and out of her.

Her hands move down my back and grip my ass at the same time she clenches around me. "Harder," she demands and my hips start rocking faster against her. Our breathing gets heavier, our panting faster, and I know I'm seconds away from having the best orgasm of my life.

"I'm coming," she mewls, and I feel her entire body pulsing around me as she clenches me to her and screams.

It only takes me two more thrusts before I completely

explode and feel as if my world has been completely turned on its axis.

☯ ✿ ✾ 🧁

'm jarred awake by the vibration of my phone alarm against the nightstand. I pick it up to see that it's seven-thirty in the morning. If I was home with Izzy right now, this would be considered sleeping in, but since I'm kidless and have barely slept due to multiple rounds of sex, waking up at this hour is brutal.

I turn on my side to see if Amber is awake. She's laying on her back with her face tilted toward me, still asleep. I'm tempted to take a photo of her because she looks so angelic and beautiful but decide against it. Izzy sometimes goes on my phone to take photos. It would be hard to explain to her why there's a photo of a strange woman sleeping on my phone.

Despite my exhaustion, I can't seem to go back to sleep. This would be the perfect time for me to get dressed, leave Amber a note of thanks for the incredible evening, and slip out of here, but I'm not that kind of guy. I want to spend what little time I have this morning with her. Today, we travel for some away games, so my time is limited, and I need to go home and pack.

I frown at the thought of this being my last time seeing her. I would like to see her again, but how do I bring up the subject of maybe just being friends with occasional benefits? I don't see how that would be fair to her, even though she did mention she also isn't looking for anything serious right now. But does she really mean it? With the way we seem to ignite around each other, I think feelings would develop quickly. I can't have the complications of a relationship in my life right now. I need to focus on Izzy and my new team. Starting a relationship as soon as I arrive in town would be a distraction that I'm not sure I have the time for. Besides, what if it doesn't work out? I don't want to bring this woman into Izzy's life only for her to leave. Despite the incredible time I've had with her, the right thing to do is to just say goodbye with no strings attached.

For some reason, I keep second-guessing myself. *You're just overthinking this due to the phenomenal sex that you haven't had in years. This is a no brainer, Gunnar!* I quietly get out of bed, put my pants on and go into the other room. I find the binder that has the room service menu and flip through it. Since I'm unsure of what Amber likes to eat, I decide to get a bunch of options. I call the room service number and place the order. After I hang up, I grab the remote, sit on the couch and watch some television. I make sure the volume is low so I don't wake Amber. As much as I would love to go back in the bedroom and wake her up with my mouth, I need to start creating some distance.

Thirty minutes later, there's a knock on the door. I pick up my shirt from where I left it last night by the window and put it on before answering. The hotel employee rolls the cart of food in. He meticulously sets everything up on the dining room table. Once he's done, I sign off on the check and give him a tip. I open the door to let him out and try to close it gently behind him.

"Something smells amazing." I turn around and see Amber walking out of the bedroom in a white terry cloth robe that the hotel provides. Even with bedhead, she looks sexy as hell.

"I'm sorry, I didn't mean to wake you up. I decided to order breakfast for us, but I wasn't sure what you like to eat so I got a little bit of everything." I pull off the lids to show her the eggs, pancakes, potatoes and fruit with whip cream.

"Wow, that's a lot of food," she laughs. "Thank you so much. You didn't have to do that."

"I know I didn't, but I wanted to." I pull out her chair and wait for her to sit down before taking the seat across from her. "Coffee?" I ask, reaching for the pot.

"Oh yes, please. Going to need lots of that today." I pour her a cup and hand her the cream and sugar before pouring myself some. We fill our plates and start to eat in compatible silence.

"Mmm, this is so good," she moans and my dick starts to twitch at the memories of what else makes her moan. Her eyes are closed while she's chewing and my gaze trails down to the lapels of her robe that are slowly starting to reveal the valley in between her breasts. Of course she would be naked underneath. My eyes shift to the floor by the window where her dress, underwear, and bra still lay. *Focus on the food, Gunnar,* I tell myself while I take another bite of my sausage.

"What do you have planned for today?" I ask, curious as to what the rest of her weekend will be like.

"Laundry, errands, and I'm sure Grace will show up on my doorstep, demanding to know what happened last night."

I put my fork and knife down and push my plate away. My appetite for food dissipates as I stare at her. "And what are you going to tell her?"

She brings her coffee cup to her lips and smiles. "I'm going to tell her I was rescued by a handsome stranger."

I smirk. "Is that all?" I ask, knowing full well it won't be.

She takes a sip and then puts her cup down. She leans back into her chair, causing her robe to open wider. "I don't kiss and tell, Lewis."

"And if you were going to tell, what would you say?" The air thickens with sexual tension and I can feel my heart pounding with anticipation of where this is going to go.

"I would tell her that the handsome stranger gave me the best sex I've ever had in my entire life."

I wish I didn't love her response as much as I do, but fuck if that doesn't make me puff up my chest knowing I can make her feel that way. I quickly glance around at the morning sun streaming in and I know I need to see what she looks like while she comes in broad daylight.

Fuck creating distance between us.

"Come here, Amber," I demand huskily and a coy smile plays on her lips.

"Don't you want to finish your food?"

"There's something else I want to eat."

I love the way her face starts to flush, telling me she knows exactly what I'm referring to. She gets up from her chair and slowly walks around to me. She stops right in front of me and my hands immediately untie the knot in her belt. It loosens and my hands push apart the robe to reveal her beautiful body.

I look up at her as I kiss my way around her abdomen. I move her hips back so she is leaning against the table. I reach over and grab a spoonful of the whipped cream off the berries. She jumps and giggles at the coldness of the cream when I cover her right nipple with it. I spread the cream around her breast and then I do the same thing to her other one.

"Mmm, now I'm fucking hungry again," I growl and start lapping up the cream from her nipple.

She inhales sharply and moans when my mouth suckles her hardened peak. Once the cream is all licked up, I move to her other breast and give it the same attention. I then proceed to drop dollops of cream all over her body and lick, kiss, and suck it all up until I make my way down to her mound.

"Lay down on the table." I stand up and help her push the dishes of food to one side before hoisting her up. I stand in between her legs and slam my mouth into hers. She tastes like maple syrup and coffee, the sweetness causing the ache in between my legs to deepen.

I start kissing my way down her neck and to her breasts, forcing her to lay back on her elbows. My appetite for her is insatiable and I quickly get down on my knees. Without giving her any warning, I fuse my mouth to her clit and start licking.

"Oh my god," she pants while she watches me. I watch her lie all the way down and her hands start coursing through my hair, gripping tightly as waves of pleasure start to roll through her. Her head is thrown back, her mouth open as if she's gasping for air. I grab her hips and pull her closer to me, burying my tongue deeper inside of her.

"Please," she begs, her back arching off the table. Her hands tighten their grip on my head, holding me in position to where she likes it. My tongue thrashes harder against her bud and I feel her inner thighs shaking.

"Yes, that's it," she encourages as I continue my assault on her and within seconds, she screams out her orgasm and convulses all over me. Her arms and legs fall limp, freeing me to stand up. I watch her chest rise and fall as she comes down from that incredible high. Fuck, if that's not the sexiest thing I've ever seen. I could never get tired of making her come.

"That was...wow." I help her sit up and softly kiss her on her lips. She places her hands on my chest and moves them up to wrap her arms around my neck. "Now it's your turn."

She hops down from the table, grabs my hand and starts leading me toward the bedroom. I pull off my shirt and get out of my pants, my cock standing at attention and ready to go. We're just about to get into bed when a loud sound from my phone blasts from the coffee table in the living room.

"Shit, my alarm." I run out of the bedroom to grab it to turn it off. I check the time and realize if I don't leave now to go home and pack, I will miss the team flight. "I've got to go."

"Wait, now?" she asks, walking into the living room.

"I'm sorry, but I've got to go to work." I grab my articles of clothing and hastily put them back on.

"You work on the weekends?" I glance up at her to see she's wrapped back up in the robe again. Such a pity.

"Yes, I'm sorry." I grab my jacket off of the chair, put it on, and pat my pockets to make sure my wallet and keys are in there.

"You have nothing to apologize for." She shifts on her feet and nervously pushes a piece of her hair behind her ear.

We stare at each other in awkward silence. I don't know how to say goodbye because I don't want to leave her. "Give me your phone number," I blurt out against my better judgment.

She gives me a sad smile and shakes her head. "Lewis, I think it's best just to leave this as we intended it to be—one night only."

"But I want to see you again." Telling her that wasn't as hard as I was expecting it to be. In fact, it feels right. I *do* want to see her again. "We need more time together."

She walks toward me, grabs my hands and squeezes. "You just moved here, Lewis. You need time to get acclimated and your daughter settled."

I give her a pointed look. "This isn't my first time to Nashville. My brother has lived here for years and I've visited him often."

She chews on her bottom lip in uncertainty. I grab her face and kiss her hard. "Give me your phone number, Amber."

"We barely know each other—"

"And we can get to know each other better if you give me your phone number," I interrupt, getting frustrated as to why she just won't give it to me.

"How about we let fate decide."

"What do you mean?" I ask in confusion.

"Nashville is not that big of a city. If fate has us crossing paths again, then we exchange phone numbers."

I stare deeply into her blue eyes, not understanding what is happening. This is the first time in years that I've asked a woman for her phone number and she's rejecting me? This seems so not like her, but then again, what do I know? She's still a stranger. I shouldn't care as much as I do right now. I don't even want to get into a relationship. The only logical thought is that maybe she would catch feelings quickly if we kept this physical. I drop my hands from her face and sigh. While I don't like her suggestion, I also can't force someone to give me their number.

Maybe it's for the best, Gunnar.

I give her a tight smile and a peck on the cheek. "I'll respect your wishes and stop asking."

She grabs my hands again and rests her forehead against my chest. "Don't be mad at me," she mutters and then raises her head to look at me. "Fate might have us seeing each other tomorrow."

I scoff and shake my head, keeping to myself that I will be in a different city tomorrow. "I've got to go. Check-out isn't until eleven, so why don't you take a nap before you leave."

She smiles, but it doesn't reach her eyes. "Thank you for being the most amazing fake ex-boyfriend, Lewis," she whispers softly, before leaning up and kissing me gently on the mouth.

She pulls back but I grab her biceps and crush her to my chest for one more scorching kiss. She sighs in contentment when my tongue invades her mouth and she wraps her arms tightly around my waist.

The kiss is starting to get out of control so I break apart from her delicious mouth and rest my forehead against hers to catch my breath. I close my eyes, inhaling her scent one more time.

"I'll see you soon, Amber," I tell her confidently and with that, I turn around, open the door and will myself not to look back as I walk out.

CHAPTER 10
CASSIE

watch the door close behind him, a dull ache of sadness starting to form in my chest.

Why didn't you give him your phone number, dummy? my brain asks.

Because he has the power to obliterate us, my heart responds.

I don't consider myself to have an addictive personality, but he could've turned me into a sex addict with what I've experienced within the last twenty-four hours. I know for a fact it was because of *him*, not because I haven't had sex in years. I've never had a night of passion like that before and I know without a doubt I would become emotionally attached to him. Besides our physical connection, he seems to be the perfect kind of guy for me—smart, career-driven, good-looking, and a gentleman with a wicked mouth. He checks all the boxes for my dream guy, but who knows if this would just be a friends with benefits type of relationship and I honestly don't think my heart could handle that.

I stare at the door for a couple moments longer, almost willing him to come back. But he isn't going to, and I just need to hold on to the memories that I now have. I sigh and turn around to pick my clothes up off the ground before heading to the bathroom to take a shower. I hate to wash off any remnants of him, but my body is sticky from the whip cream.

While in the shower, my mind wanders back to Lewis and replays our conversations together. He's in no position for a relationship right now. How can he be with having just moved here and with a daughter to raise? I'm not even sure if he shares custody with his ex. So many questions left unanswered and at this point, it doesn't even matter because the more I think about my life, the more I'm determined that not having any contact with him is for the best. I need to get my own life in order. I'm jobless and trying to build my art career, which is going to take time and a lot of effort on my part. I need to focus on painting more and finding a full-time job that pays more money than what I'm currently earning with selling print-on-demand.

But what if you do happen to see him again soon?

While I do believe in fate, karma, and manifestation, I also can't think about the what ifs that may or may not happen.

I turn the water off, step out of the shower and put the hotel's robe back on. I use the blow dryer to dry my hair and as soon as I shut it off, I hear my phone vibrating in the bedroom. I walk over to the nightstand and retrieve my phone. I have over twenty missed texts from Grace and a couple from my dad. *Oh shit, I never told him I wasn't coming home last night.* While living at home rent free is a huge perk, having my father worry about my whereabouts when I'm not around is getting inconvenient. I know this conversation is not going to be fun, so I call him first to get it over with.

"Not like you to not come home and at least text me about it." His voice is tense with anger when he picks up and I immediately feel guilty.

"I'm sorry, Dad," I respond softly. "I know I should've texted you back, but I was distracted and… was having fun,"

I stutter because I don't want to lie to my dad, but he doesn't need to know what I've been doing.

"You don't owe me any explanations. You're twenty-four years old and an adult. I sure don't want to know what you were distracted by. As long as you're safe and happy, that's all I care about, but in the future, please text me back so I know you're okay."

"I promise this will never happen again," I tell him.

"Okay, kiddo. I love you."

"I love you too, Dad. I'll see you soon."

As soon as I hang up with him, I breathe a sigh of relief that the conversation is over. I lather my body with the lotion the hotel provides and put my clothes and shoes back on. I walk out to the kitchen and sit back down at the dining room table. I look at the table and feel my cheeks redden from the memory of what just occurred on it. I take a photo of the table as a keepsake memory and eat the untouched fruit.

My phone vibrates again, and I see it's Grace leaving me another text message.

> Grace: You better be sleeping off a night of drunken sex and not dead in a ditch somewhere. Wait, that's actually not funny at all. Why have you been at the Omni Hotel for 12 hours?!? Damn you, Cassie, pick up your phone or I'm coming down there!!

I grin at her message and decide to put her out of her misery by calling her back.

"Are you okay?" The phone didn't even ring and her voice is frantic with worry.

"I am fine, just tired and sore from too much sex."

She screams out in frustration. "I hate you for keeping me in suspense! But seriously, I was actually getting super worried. You can't do that to me ever again."

"I'm really sorry, Grace. You're right, I should've texted you again to let you know I was okay."

"Yeah, you should've. Also, you made me lie to your dad and that isn't cool."

I scrunch up my nose in confusion. "First off, I never told you what to say to my dad and secondly, why were you even talking to him?"

"He called me this morning when he saw that you never came home and asked if you slept at my house. I couldn't lie to him. He's like a second dad to me so I told him no, but I reassured him that you were fine, even though I had no idea if you were or not."

I sigh, feeling ashamed that I made the two people who love me the most in this world worry for my safety. "I'm sorry I put you in that position, Grace. Thank you for not lying to him. I called him this morning and talked with him."

"What did you tell him?"

"I told him I was distracted and having fun. Considering he knew I was out on a blind date, he probably knows exactly what I was doing." I groan and cover my face with my hand. It's going to be pretty awkward seeing my dad when I get back home.

I've got to get out of his place.

Grace laughs. "Poor Papa Warner. Now he has visualizations of his daughter distracted by dick." She cackles at her own joke, and I shake my head.

"That isn't even funny, Grace."

"Yes, yes, it is. Anyhoo, get your butt over here. I need the play-by-play details of what happened last night. I've already received a text from Aaron, telling me how rude and inconsiderate you were for ditching him for your ex-boyfriend. Carter almost had to do the Heimlich Maneuver on me because I started choking on my food."

Oh crap, I didn't even think about Aaron saying something to her about Lewis. "You didn't tell him Lewis wasn't my ex, did you?"

"No, I played along and pretended that was out of character for you."

"Everything about last night was out of character for me," I mutter, still in disbelief over everything that has happened. It feels like a dream—a hot, wet, naughty dream.

"Wait, is he still there with you right now?"

"No, he had to go to work."

"What does he do for a living that he works on the weekends?" she asks, and I can hear the suspicion in her voice.

"He's a personal trainer."

"Oh," she pauses. "I guess that makes sense. Get over here because I've got to hear this story face to face"

"Okay, I'll see you in about thirty minutes."

I hang up with Grace, grab my purse and take one final look around the suite.

"Thanks for the memories," I say out loud, which is silly to say to a hotel room, but I think it's safe to say I will never forget this place.

⊘ 🎀 🦋 🧁

stopped to get some more coffee and a scone for Grace before pulling into her apartment complex. I walk up the stairs to the second floor and knock on her door.

She opens it immediately and gives me a once over. "The walk of shame never looked more beautiful," she snickers.

I laugh and follow her inside to her kitchen. I take a seat on one of her barstools and hand her the paper bag. "I brought you a scone and your favorite latte as an apology."

"You owe me way more than this." She sits next to me,

takes a bite of her pastry and with her mouth full of food says, "Start talking."

I tell her everything that transpired, starting with my date with Aaron and how I ended up in bed with Lewis. "Wowzers, I can't believe you popped your one-night stand cherry."

I tilt my head and give her a weird look. "Not sure if that's really something to be proud about. I really wasn't planning on having a one-night stand."

"Most women don't, unless you're a groupie of some sort, but who cares about that?" She waves her hand around. "Give me some dirty details like how big was he?" She wiggles her eyebrows up and down and I blush at the memory of him.

"Let's just say he is very, very talented and knows how to use his appendage very well."

She gives me a *what the fuck* look and I giggle. "It's not about the size, but the motion of the ocean."

"So you're saying he had a small penis?"

I snort and shake my head. "No, he definitely didn't have a small penis. It was perfect. He was perfect. He was selfless in the bedroom and made everything about me." I pause, because there are so many more wonderful things to say, yet I'm completely failing at describing how incredible last night was for her to even understand. "I can't explain it, Grace, but every time he kissed me, I felt like I was about to combust, and the sex was just out of this world. I don't think I'll ever have sex like that again in my life."

She props her head up with her hand, giving me puppy dog eyes, sighing. "Sounds like it was an incredible night. You're welcome, by the way."

"For what?" I ask in confusion.

"I basically manifested last night for you by giving you a pep talk on one-night stands and putting condoms in your purse."

"'Thank you, by the way, for those. We used all of them." I feel my cheeks get hot after admitting that to her.

She has a smug look of satisfaction on her face. "Again, you're welcome." I laugh and roll my eyes at her. "So, when are we seeing Prince Charming again?"

I shrug. "No clue. Might be never."

Her coffee cup makes it halfway to her mouth before she stops and gives me an incredulous look. "Please tell me you exchanged numbers."

"Nope," I tell her, popping my 'p'. "He wanted to, but I told him it was best if we didn't."

She slams her coffee cup down and thank goodness there is a lid on it or else there would be coffee all over her countertop. "What in the hell is wrong with you?"

"He's a single dad who just moved here for his career. I don't even know what the hell is going on in my life. I just don't feel it's good timing."

"You're not marrying the guy, Cassie. It's just dating or even less complicated and you can be friends with occasional benefits."

I shake my head at her. "I'm not wired that way, Grace. From the way I feel just after one night of sex, I know I would want to spend twenty-four hours, seven days a week with him. He would have the power to make me fall in love with him quickly. I can't risk my heart shattering all over again."

Just then my phone vibrates and I look down to see her mom calling. I show her the screen and she nods, knowing I'm going to take the call.

"Hi, Mrs. Harper. I'm actually here with Grace at her place and you're on speakerphone."

"Hi, Mom," Grace says with a cheerful voice filled with love. Sometimes I'm envious of the close relationship Grace has with her mom. It makes me wish my mom fought harder to stay sober for her family. That's why I enjoy being a nanny

—I get to be the present and stable motherly figure to these kids that I never got.

"Hi, girls!" Mrs. Harper greets. "Cassie, honey, good news. I have three interviews lined up for you next week."

My eyes go wide with excitement. "Three? Wow, that's amazing! Thank you so much."

"I will email you the dates and times of each interview. Let me know if you have any schedule conflicts."

"Pretty sure I don't," I respond with a laugh.

"Just double check and make sure. Once you confirm, I can let you know the locations of the interviews and a little bit of background information on each family."

Due to her high-end clientele, we normally are not told their names or their professions until the day of the interviews. Sometimes we meet them at their homes, oftentimes in an office, or they come to the agency's office.

"Sounds good, Mrs. Harper. I will look over my calendar as soon as I get home."

We talk a little bit longer with her before agreeing on a lunch date for all three of us and then saying goodbye.

"See, good things are on the horizon for you!" Grace salutes me with her coffee cup and takes a sip.

Knowing I have three interviews next week fires me up. "This motivates me to get my shit together. I need to add a couple more photographs of some of my paintings to my website and I need to call the Germantown Art Crawl and purchase a booth."

"That's my girl!" Grace cheers. "You've got this! And listen, I understand why you didn't want to exchange phone numbers with Lewis. I might not agree with it, but I get it."

"Thanks, Grace." I stand up out of my chair and give her a hug. "I better get going while I have the energy to complete my to-do list before my body remembers that I haven't slept for more than five hours."

I exit Grace's apartment feeling a renewed sense of hope and confidence about my future. I can't have any distractions in my life right now if I'm going to accomplish my dreams of one day making a living from selling my art and seeing it hung on walls around the world.

CHAPTER 11

CASSIE

This week has been a whirlwind of getting everything on my to-do list accomplished and going on two of the three interviews Mrs. Harper had lined up for me. The first interview was with a personal assistant to a famous musician. They wanted me to go on tour with them and that was an easy pass. While some might think touring sounds glamorous and exciting, I have no desire to travel every week to a different city, live in and out of suitcases and hotels, and think of ways to entertain two young children while on the road. Thanks, but no thanks.

The second interview was with a neurosurgeon and while I thought the interview went great, apparently my age was an issue for him, since he told Mrs. Harper I was too young and didn't have enough experience. Today is my third interview and the only thing Mrs. Harper has told me so far is that it's another athlete who is a single father. I'm supposed to call Mrs. Harper on my way to the interview for more details.

I check myself out in the mirror and debate whether or not I should change again for the umpteenth time. I always make sure I dress up and look professional, but I just don't feel like myself in my interviewing clothes. I'm wearing a sleeveless, fit and flare, houndstooth plaid dress with a black cardigan to cover my arms and black ballet flats. My hair is pulled back in a ponytail and I'm wearing minimalistic make-up and jewelry.

"Gah, just get on with it, Cassie," I mutter to myself in frustration and decide what I'm wearing is fine. I spray on some perfume, grab my tote bag and leave for the interview.

Once I get into my car, I enter the address I was given into navigation. I'm happy to see it's only fifteen minutes away from my dad's house and appears to be close to the universities in midtown. I pull out of my driveway and when I get on the road, I call Grace's mom.

"Okay, Cassie, let's go over the final details that I can now reveal to you. The family you're meeting today is the McNeer family. Does that last name ring a bell to you?" she asks.

I frown at the name being unfamiliar. "No, it doesn't. Should it?"

"Only if you like country music and follow baseball."

"That would be a no to both," I answer with a laugh. "Is that going to be a problem?"

"It shouldn't be. If anything, I think they will like that you don't know who they are. Gunnar McNeer plays professional baseball for the Tennessee Terrors and is the father you will be interviewing with, but only if his sister-in-law, Alyson McNeer, likes you. She will be the one you meet with first and if you get the job, she will be one of your main points of contact when Mr. McNeer is out of town. Her husband, Gavin, is a famous country music singer and songwriter."

Now that she's said his name, it does sound vaguely familiar, but only because I've heard his brother mentioned on the radio.

"If Mrs. McNeer thinks you are suitable for the job, she will then have you meet with Mr. McNeer." She pauses and I can hear the sound of papers rustling. "Do you have any other questions?"

"Since I've never watched a baseball game in my life, how does their schedule differ from hockey?"

"Baseball has more games than hockey. I'm pretty sure it's almost double."

"*Double?*" I question in shock because that just doesn't seem possible.

"Yes, a regular season in baseball has one-hundred and sixty-two games compared to hockey's regular season of eighty-two games. That doesn't include spring training and post-season either."

That many games hurt my brain. "So he will be on the road a lot then?"

"Yes. You would be a full-time, live-in nanny and your days off will be sporadic due to his schedule. Because he's a single father, you will be compensated very well for your time and help. Even more than what you made with your last family."

That's music to my ears. "Will I be dealing with the child's mother at all for the days she has custody?"

"Mr. McNeer has full custody of his child, and I was told the only other person you will be in contact with is Alyson McNeer and some other members of his family."

My mind can't help but wonder what kind of woman the child's mom is for him to get full custody. Either she's a career driven woman who didn't make the time to share custody or she has addiction issues. Whatever the case may be, it's none of my business unless Mr. McNeer wants to tell me.

"One other thing I need to warn you about," she says and I stiffen in my seat due to the tone of her voice. "Gunnar and Gavin McNeer are big names in their respective industries, so you might come in contact with some unwanted visitors."

I groan, knowing exactly what she's referring to. She's warning me that I might be dealing with either paparazzi or psychotic fans, usually the female kind who are determined to bag a celebrity.

"Noted, thanks for the warning. Anything else I need to know? I'm almost at their house." I glance at the navigation and it says I'm two minutes away from my destination.

"I think that's all for now. Just be yourself and they're going to love you like we all do."

I smile at the warmness in her voice. "Thanks, Mrs. Harper, and thank you again for setting up these interviews for me."

"You're most welcome. Go kick butt and call me later."

I end the call and a minute later, I arrive at my destination. I double-check the address just to make sure I've got the right house because this is not at all what I would expect for a famous baseball player to live in. It's an adorable two-story brick house that appears older and looks as if it has been remodeled. What surprises me the most is the lack of security. There was no community gate to get into the neighborhood and there's no gate protecting the house either. There's just a white picket fence as the first line of defense. Most athletes that I've come across, which have only been hockey players, either lived in gated communities or high-rise apartment buildings and condos that have front desk security that visitors or guests have to check-in with.

I turn off my engine and check my reflection in the rearview mirror. I examine my teeth to make sure they're clear of food and apply my lipstick. I throw it back in my purse, take a deep breath, and count to ten.

You've got this, Cassie. Just be yourself.

Once my mental pep talk is done, I get out of my car, shut the door and head up the walkway to the front door. I ring the doorbell and within a few seconds, a beautiful brunette with the cutest baby bump answers.

"Hello!" I greet with a wave and a smile. "I'm Cassie Warner. I'm here to interview for the nanny position."

"Hi, Cassie! I'm Aly McNeer, Gunnar's sister-in-law." She offers me her hand that I immediately shake. "Please come in." She turns to the side and stretches out her arm, indicating for me to enter. I walk in and take in my surroundings.

A candle is burning in the distance that makes the whole place smell of citrus and vanilla. The house is deceivingly bigger than what its outside appearance perceives one to believe. The front hallway is long and leads into an open concept living room, dining room, and kitchen.

"Please, come this way." She walks me to the dining room and motions for me to take a seat. "Would you like something to drink?"

I shake my head. "I'm fine, thank you."

"No problem." She sits down and examines the papers in front of her. "I reviewed your résumé and it's nice to see that you've worked with a family in sports before. I called Marissa Fitzgerald and she raved about you. Can you tell me a little bit about your time with them and what it entailed?"

"Sure." I nod and clear my throat. "As you know, Mr. Fitzgerald is a professional hockey player so my main focus was helping Mrs. Fitzgerald with their children during hockey season, especially when he was on the road. When I first started off with them, they only had one child, so I was more of a part-time nanny. When they welcomed their second child, I became full-time. I lived with them during his road trips and stayed overnight if they had any special events that they needed a sitter for."

"Would you go to any of his home games?" Aly asks after she writes down some notes on her papers.

"I did attend many home games, but not all due to the baby. The ones I did attend, we would often leave during the second intermission if it was a night game. If it was an early afternoon game, we would stay for its entirety and go out to dinner after."

She chuckles. "Got to love those afternoon games." Afternoon games were my favorite, but they are few and far between in hockey. "What about during the off-season?"

"If they stayed in Nashville, then I worked for them full-time. If they went home to Canada, then I was off. Sometimes I would go on vacation with them, but never to Canada since they had family there to help them."

She nods while writing everything down and once she's done, she looks up and smiles at me.

"Excellent, so your past experience is somewhat similar to what my brother-in-law needs, but he needs a full-time, live-in nanny, even when he's home. He's a single father, so there will be no one else living here to help him. Were you made aware of that?"

"Yes," I nod with a smile. "That won't be a problem."

"Great. Now, tell me what your days off were with the Fitzgeralds during the season?"

"There were barely any home games on Fridays and Sundays, so those were my consistent days off when he was home. But if he was leaving for a road trip or did have a game, then we would negotiate different days during that week. Those were few and far between though."

"Unfortunately, baseball's schedule is more inconsistent than hockey's. I think it's going to be difficult for you to have designated days off during Gunnar's season. If you get the job, that's something that you and Gunnar will work out. My husband and I will help out whenever he needs it during your days off."

I love seeing how involved they are in his life. "I understand that there might be some weeks where I have no days off and I'm fine with that."

She shakes her head. "That won't happen. You deserve your days off. We will take our niece on those days."

"It's really great to see how close you all are. Some family dynamics are not like that." I think back to my own childhood when my father was left alone to take care of me while my mother was out partying and staying out until the early hours of the next day. If she came home at all. "Your niece is a lucky girl to have an aunt and uncle who love her so much."

"We're really excited that they're here in Nashville. Gunnar is an amazing father, but his parents were his support system back in Texas and while we will try to help out as much as we can, we have our own growing family as well." Her mentioning Texas takes my mind back to Lewis and I wonder if they are both from the same area. What if they know each other?

Focus, Cassie! Do not think of Lewis. He probably doesn't even know the McNeers; the state of Texas is big!

"Not to mention," Aly continues talking. "When Gavin tours, we go on the road with him. He's actually currently on the road right now and our son and I flew back here this week to help Gunnar with these interviews." She stops and gives me a questioning look. "Wait, were you even aware of who my brother-in-law was before today?"

"No, I had no idea until—" I quickly glance at my watch and calculate the time."—thirty minutes ago who Gunnar McNeer was." She laughs and I sag my shoulders in relief that she doesn't seem mad about that. "I also have no clue who your husband is either. I'm sorry, but I'm not a huge fan of sports or country music. I hope that doesn't offend anyone or disqualify me for the job."

She waves her hand and rolls her eyes. "Trust me, it offends no one. In fact, it will help keep my husband's ego in check." We both laugh and I really like Alyson McNeer. She seems intelligent, kind, and genuine. "Gunnar absolutely despises being in the public eye but loves giving back to the community. That, along with being a kick-ass baseball player, makes him a fan favorite. It's fine that you had no idea who he was, but I must warn you, you might have to deal with some enthusiastic fans. I'm assuming you're used to that?"

"Yes, Mr. Fitzgerald has his share of, um, 'loyal' fans." I

use air quotes when I say loyal and she giggles, knowing exactly what I mean by that.

"I'll be honest with you; I do worry about them being here in this house with the lack of security. This was actually my old house before I met Gavin and we kept it as an investment property. Gunnar only has one year left on his contract the Terrors took over so who knows where he might be next year."

"So, wait, this move might not even be long term?" I question and immediately feel disappointed when she nods. I don't know if I want to take a job that might only be for a year.

"Because of the uncertainty of where he will be next year, he doesn't want to commit to a house, which is understandable. We'll see how long it takes for the neighborhood to figure out they have a future hall of fame baseball player as their neighbor and how they handle it. Are you from the area?"

"Born and raised, so I know the locals usually don't bother the celebrities."

She nods. "That's right and we're so thankful for that, but living in my gated community with our security does give me peace of mind. Due to his schedule, he won't be around much, so hopefully no one will notice." She sighs and takes a deep breath. "Do you have any other questions for me?"

"As of right now, no."

"Okay, well, let me tell you a little bit about Izzy." I perk up in my chair, excited to hear about her. "Her full name is Isabella, but we all call her Izzy. She's five years old and the cutest child outside of my own." She laughs and I love how her eyes light up when she talks about Izzy.

"She's a sweet, funny, precocious child. For the most part, she listens and does what she's told, but lately it seems like she's having a hard time not seeing Gunnar like she normally does during the season. My in-laws have told me she's been acting out lately."

"I feel that's normal under the circumstances she's currently in," I tell her. "She'll get better once she's here with him and has a consistent routine."

"Exactly. Kids need structure and her daddy is her security. She's a very smart little girl, who loves arts and crafts and prefers to be outdoors."

"Those are two of my favorite things as well, so it sounds like she and I will become best friends."

"Walk me through what a typical week would be like for you and Izzy when Gunnar is on the road," Aly asks, and I reach in my bag and take out a mock schedule that I had prepared. Her eyes light up as I go through each day and I'm relieved to see she's impressed with my schedule.

"Will Izzy be starting school in the fall?" I inquire, because that will change what our daily routine will look like.

Aly looks stumped and takes a moment before she answers. "That's a great question. I don't think Gunnar has had a chance to think about what he wants to do when school starts in August. If they were still back in Texas, she would be attending private school, but he might decide to hold her back for a year to wait and see where they end up."

"That's understandable. Regardless, I'll plan on including daily teachings of what she needs to know for kindergarten."

"Wonderful! I know Gunnar will be very happy to hear this. Did you homeschool with your other family?"

"No, they weren't of age yet, but Luna was a super bright child for a four-year-old and already knew most of the required sight words for kindergarten. We read a lot, and she was great with memorization. I just feel any way we can get ahead makes it easier on the child when they transition to school. It's also a great opportunity to discover if the child has any learning disabilities so we get them the help they need before starting school."

"I one hundred percent agree with you. So far, my mother-in-law has been working closely with her and doesn't see anything of concern." She looks down at her notes and then back up at me. "I think that's all I have at the moment. What other questions do you have for me?"

I pull out the list of questions I wrote down and quickly check off the ones she already answered. "Do Izzy and Mr. McNeer have any dietary restrictions or are they allergic to anything I need to be made aware of?"

Aly shakes her head. "Neither one of them have any known allergies."

"That's great, it makes things easier for me." I quickly scan down my list and check off the other questions she answered. "I think you've answered all my questions so far."

She claps her hands. "Wonderful. Well then, I think it's time for you to meet Gunnar. Let me just tell him I'm bringing you into his office to meet him." I put my questions away while she types on her phone. I'm relieved to see I passed her test and am moving on to the next part of the interview, which will be the hardest part.

"He's ready for us, so please follow me." We get up from our chairs and I follow her out of the dining room. My palms start to sweat, and I wipe them down my dress. I'm nervous to meet who I'm hoping is my future employer. I can only pray that he likes me enough to hire me.

She stops in front of a black door, looks back at me with a smile and knocks. I hear a husky voice tell us to come in. She slowly turns the knob and opens the door. I follow her in with a big smile on my face.

Then I see who Gunnar McNeer is and feel like I was just suckered punched in the gut. This might be the cruelest joke that's ever been played on me.

Fuck you, Fate.

CHAPTER 12

GUNNAR

t feels like time is standing still as I stare at the woman who has been haunting my dreams since I met her last week. This can't be Cassie Warner, the woman who's interviewing to be Izzy's nanny. This woman looks exactly like my Amber. She has the same beautiful face, same red hair, and those same blue colored eyes that hypnotize me like a moth to a flame.

But her name never really was Amber, was it?

Flashbacks of when we first met come racing back to me and I feel my shock start to turn into disappointment. My emotions must be playing all over my face because Aly steps into my line of vision, giving me a look of concern.

"Gunnar, are you okay?" *No, I'm not fucking okay* is what I want to say, but I clamp my jaw shut, needing to calm down before I speak.

The woman whose name was never Amber, but Cassie, steps forward and clears her throat. "Hi, I'm Cassie." I look down at her outstretched hand and back up to her face. Her eyes are pleading with me to play along, to pretend we don't know each other, and I give in.

"Gunnar McNeer," is all I can muster. I take her hand into

mine and gently squeeze, wishing I didn't remember how smooth the touch of her skin felt. I quickly drop her hand, needing to get as far away from her as possible. Her scent has already permeated my nasal passage and has made its way down to my dick, which is hardening as it takes a joy ride down memory lane. I walk back behind my desk, but don't sit down.

"Thanks Aly, I'll take it from here," I tell my sister-in-law, who's looking at me as if I've grown two heads. I know she's going to be questioning me as soon as Cassie leaves, but I can't focus on that right now.

"I'll just be in the kitchen if you need me." Aly gives me a *what is wrong with you* look before walking out and closing the door behind her.

We stand in uncomfortable silence, both of us not even knowing where to begin. I grab her resume off my desk, reading it one more time. *She told me she was an artist. Was that a lie?* I look down at her schooling to see she did graduate with an art degree. Then I look at the year she graduated and start doing the math in my head of how old she is.

No, that can't be right, I think and do the calculation again.

Holy shit, I think I'm going to be sick.

She clears her throat and I look at her in shock. "Wow, when I said we can let fate decide if we ever see each other again, I never imagined it would be like this." She laughs nervously and shifts uncomfortably on her feet. She's wringing her hands while she stands there, and I somehow manage to find my voice.

"You're twenty-four?" My voice is hoarse and sounds foreign even to me.

She narrows her gaze and I see something ignite in her irises. "Yeah, so?" Her voice is defensive, as if I'm starting to piss her off.

I drop her resume to my desk and rub the back of my neck

before looking at her in utter disbelief. "Jesus Christ, I'm eleven years older than you!"

Her pupils widen and she places her hands on her hips with an angry stance. "That's what you're focused on? My age? Not the fact that you had me in positions you only see in pornos and yet here I am seeking to be your nanny?"

Fuck. I rub my hands down my face, wishing she never said that because all I can see right now is her naked body riding me hard, her tits bouncing in a way that is forever embedded in my brain.

"Which is precisely why you being my child's nanny is a horrible idea," I growl out in frustration.

She scoffs. "It was just one night of sex. Just because it happened once doesn't mean it will happen again."

Are you fucking kidding me? I walk toward her and get within inches of her face. She stands her ground and doesn't move, but I see her swallow. My gaze lobbies between her eyes and those damn, addictive lips of hers.

"You don't think now that I've had a taste of you, I wouldn't want more? I can't stop thinking about you or that night." She sharply inhales, causing me to solely focus on her lips. "So yeah, you being my nanny and living under my roof is a *terrible* idea."

Walk away before you do something stupid, Gunnar, like kiss her. I ball my hands into fists to refrain from grabbing and crushing her to me. I go back behind my desk again. This time I do sit down because I can't let her see how she's physically affecting me. The air is thick with emotional and sexual tension. I need to stay away from her.

Do not leave this chair, Gunnar. Sit here, ignore her and hopefully she'll take the hint and depart.

But instead of leaving, she walks forward and sits down in the chair in front of me.

"We're both adults here and can be professional." She

folds her hands in her lap, and I'm amazed at how composed she looks on the outside.

"You're barely an adult." The words are out of my mouth before I can stop them, but I don't care. I can't get over the fact that I'm eleven years older than her.

She rolls her eyes but ignores my comment. "I agree that hiring me might be awkward in the beginning, but I'm here for your daughter, not you." For some reason, that stings, and pisses me off even more that I'm hurt by it. "We can pretend that night never happened."

Good fucking luck! "I haven't been able to get the scent of your perfume out of my nostrils since that night, so there's no way if I see you every day, can *smell you* every day, that I'm going to forget. And guess what?" I really need to just stop speaking my mind, but I can't. Her indifference to the situation has made my anger explode like lava out of a volcano. "I *don't* want to fucking forget!"

She closes her eyes and takes a deep breath. When she opens them back up, her gaze is filled with desperation. "I need this job; you need a nanny. I'm more than qualified to take care of your daughter. Please don't let what transpired between us prevent you from giving me a chance."

I shake my head, not wanting to hear anymore. "It's not going to work, Cassie. I'm sorry to have wasted your time, but you need to leave."

She hangs her head in defeat and nods. She gets up from the chair and starts walking toward the door. She stops and turns around to look at me. I groan inwardly, my resolve about to snap in two at the sight of her.

"Good luck, Gunnar. I truly wish you nothing but the best." She opens the door with her head held high and walks out.

I lean back in my chair and close my eyes. I have this urge to run after her, but what the hell would I say? I *can't* hire her. She's the distraction I can't have in my life right now, plus I have to think of Izzy. I don't want to bring a new person in her life and me fuck it all up for her to lose them. She's already lost so much not having her mother.

I can hear Aly's voice asking if Cassie's okay, but her response is inaudible. I listen for the front door to open and it's only when I hear it shut that I release the breath I didn't realize I was holding.

I hear footsteps getting closer to my office and know Aly's upset by how heavy they sound against the hardwood floors. Within seconds, she enters over the threshold into my office and marches straight up to my desk.

"How do you know Cassie Warner?"

I knew Aly was too smart to ignore the look of recognition that passed between us when we saw each other.

"Technically, I don't know her." I rub my eyes with the heels of my hands, a headache forming at the base of my skull.

"What does 'technically' mean? Don't lie to me, Gunnar. All I know is that girl was barely in your office for ten minutes and left here with tears in eyes."

Shit, I wish Aly never told me that. I hate myself right now knowing that she was upset enough to cry, but telling her to go was the right decision. "I didn't mean to make her cry."

"I left your brother's tour to be here to help you. Don't bullshit me and tell me the truth."

"It's a long story, Aly." I remove my hands from my face and look at her wearily. With my adrenaline depleted, I'm left feeling tired, disappointed, and not in the mood to have this discussion.

"I've got nowhere to be, Gunnar." She sits down in the chair that was just vacated by Cassie. She leans back into the chair, folds her hands and places them on the top of her baby bump.

"Don't you need to get back to Austin?" I suggest, trying to stall telling her the truth.

"Valerie and Rowan are watching him." Valerie is Aly's sister and Rowan is her husband. They live in a small town called Murfreesboro just southeast of Nashville. "Don't piss off your pregnant sister-in-law or Gavin will kick your ass. Tell me what happened so I can try to help fix it."

I shake my head, a sad smile playing on my lips. "There's nothing you can fix. The damage is done."

She rolls her eyes at me. "Damage? What damage? Stop being dramatic. Are you hiring her or not?"

"No, I can't hire her."

She narrows her eyes at me. "Why? She's perfect for Izzy."

"You can't tell someone's perfect for one another until you get to know them better." Not sure if I mean Cassie and Izzy or Cassie and me, but regardless, it's the truth.

"Cut the shit, Gunnar. Why are you not hiring her?"

"She's too young?" It's more of a question, not a statement, and it doesn't fly with Aly.

She sits up and slams her hand against the desk. "Gunnar, you're really upsetting me and it's not good for the baby. Please," she begs and I know it's time to cut the shit. "Tell me how you know Cassie."

I take a deep breath and for the next five minutes, I tell her everything that happened between Cassie and me. When I'm done, she grabs a tissue from my desk and dabs at her eyes.

"Why are you crying?" Fuck, I've made another woman cry. I think I'm developing an ulcer from the stress of it.

"The entire thing is just so sad," she sniffles and proceeds to blow her nose loudly.

"Sad for who?"

She throws her hands up in the air in exasperation. "Sad for you both. Gunnar, what if Cassie is your one true love?"

This must be the pregnancy hormones talking because

that's just crazy. "Let's not get carried away here, Aly. This isn't one of your romance books, you know."

"You said you can't stop thinking about her."

I shrug. "Yeah, but that doesn't mean I'm in love with her. I just haven't had sex in a very long time."

"No, because if it was about popping your dry spell, you would've continued hooking up with psycho groupies on your road trip this past week." I snort at her theory. After what happened today, I'm definitely done with one-night stands.

"I still think fate brought her here today for a reason."

I sigh in exasperation. "It's just a fucked-up coincidence, Aly."

She shakes her head. "No, it's a sign that you should hire her."

"Aly, it's a *bad* idea," I tell her sternly.

"Why?"

I love my sister-in-law, but I can't hide my annoyance at repeating this subject. "Because I probably won't be able to keep my hands to myself."

"That's the dumbest reason I've ever heard. You're an adult, Gunnar! If you don't want to start a relationship with her, then keep your hands to yourself. If you can't stop thinking about her, then date her. This isn't a life-or-death situation here."

"If it goes bad, then Izzy is the one who suffers again, and I refuse to let that happen."

"Is that the real reason or are you just afraid to let someone back in again?"

I take a moment to think about what she's asking. "Maybe it's both."

She gives me a sympathetic smile. "You can't continue living your life in fear of getting hurt again. You don't deserve to be alone, Gunnar."

I lean over the desk and grab her hand. "The smartest

thing my brother ever did in his life was marrying you, Aly. Thank you for loving me and my family. I truly appreciate it. Don't worry about me, I'm doing just fine being alone."

The lie comes smoothly out of my mouth. I'm hanging on by a thread being a single dad in a new city, but she doesn't need me to admit that. I know everyone is worried about how I'm going to handle things once Izzy arrives here permanently, but they don't need to live my life for me. They all need to concentrate on their own lives. Gavin and Aly will soon have a newborn again and my parents are getting older. They need to enjoy each other and their retirement and not be my permanent babysitters. Getting a nanny is the right thing to do, but it can't be one who I lust after and who consumes all of my thoughts.

"I'll always worry about you, Gunnar." She slips her hand from underneath mine and puts her business face back on. "Let's not change the subject here. Are we hiring Cassie or not?"

"Not and the answer is final."

She stands up and points her finger at me. "I think this is a mistake, Gunnar. She's perfect for the job."

I give her a knowing look. "I'm confident that there are other candidates out there who are just as perfect."

She harrumphs. "Your penis had to go screw everything up."

Her comment is so unexpected that I bark out a laugh. "My penis and I apologize for this inconvenience."

She sighs and rubs her belly. "I'll go call the agency and ask for more candidates." She pauses before turning around. "They're going to ask for a reason why Cassie wasn't considered. What do you want me to tell them?"

The only logical reasoning that they would believe is her age. "Tell them I prefer someone with a little more experience who's older."

She nods but does so with a scowl. "Stupid men," she mutters loud enough for me to hear while exiting my office.

I don't disagree with her, because I feel like the dumbest asshole on the face of the planet. I also feel horrible about how things ended with Cassie. I glance down at her resume and find her phone number. I could call her and apologize for how I handled things...

No, Gunnar! You need to leave her alone.

Annoyed with myself for even thinking of reaching out to her, I take her resume and run it through the shredder to avoid any temptation. Cassie Warner needs to be deleted from my brain forever. No more distractions! My family and my baseball team are the only people I need in my life right now.

CHAPTER 13

GUNNAR

"Hey, McNeer!" I hear my name being called amidst the chaos in the locker room and turn around to see Peter coming toward me. We just defeated the Montana Mavericks for the third night in a row in front of their home crowd, so players are celebrating. "Your dad called during the game. Said it wasn't urgent, but he wanted you to call him as soon as the game ended."

I frown with concern. It's not like my dad to call during games unless it's an emergency. "Okay, thanks." I go to my locker, grab my cell phone and walk out of the room to find somewhere quieter to take the call.

"Hey, Son," he answers on the first ring. "How did the game go?"

I ignore his question and go straight to the point. "What's going on, Dad? You never call me during a game. Is Izzy okay?"

"Don't worry, Izzy's just fine and is already asleep for the evening," he reassures me in a calm voice. "Your mom wasn't watching where she was going and stepped in a pothole. She fractured her ankle bad enough that she needs surgery."

"Oh, shit. When's her surgery?"

"Fortunately, they can get her in on Thursday morning, so her ankle will stay wrapped up and in a boot for tonight and tomorrow."

My mind races as to what I can do to help my family. "I'll ask the team to put me on the family medical emergency list and I'll be there tonight. We can figure out how long I need to be out there after mom's surgery."

"Son, calm down. We don't need you to do that. I called Gavin and he said he didn't need Sosie to stay on the road with him since they only have a couple more shows left, so she's on an airplane right now to help out." Sosie is our cousin, who Gavin employs as his personal assistant, and she travels with him for work. "She'll watch Izzy while I'm with your mom during her surgery. She'll stay for a couple of days after the surgery to help mom get settled and pack up Izzy's remaining things. She's agreed to accompany Izzy back to Tennessee, but you need to call her to discuss those details."

I shake my head, not liking that it's still so much on him having an injured wife to take care of. "Dad, it's no problem for me to be there to help you."

"I appreciate the offer, Gunnar, but I'll be fine taking care of your mother by myself." Both my parents keep themselves in great shape, so I have no doubt my dad can take care of my mom. "Sometimes there are too many cooks in the kitchen. No offense, but having you, Sosie, and Izzy all here would drive us crazy."

I chuckle because I can see his point.

"I just feel bad that Izzy has to leave earlier than expected. We're going to miss her."

"Don't feel bad, Dad. I'm so grateful to you and Mom for keeping her this past month and traveling back and forth from Texas to Tennessee so I can see her. I know it's been a burden on you both and I'm sure you're exhausted from entertaining a five-year-old constantly."

"Our grandchild is never a burden. We're happy we could

help out, but I do worry about you. Izzy will be there by next week and you need to concentrate on playing ball. Did you find a nanny yet? Aly said she met the perfect one for you, but you had issues with her?"

Damn it, Aly! "Don't worry about a nanny, Dad. We'll be just fine," I sigh, not wanting to even think about my non-existent nanny situation, nor discuss with my dad why Aly's "perfect" nanny is anything but. "Are you sure I can't come out there to help?"

"No," he answers firmly. "Now, tell me how tonight went."

"It was a solid game. I went 3 for 3 with 2 RBIs and a run scored. Overall, great road trip." I hear some voices behind me, so I look over my shoulder to see some of the guys dressed and rolling their suitcases to the bus. "Dad, I've got to get going or the team is going to leave me behind. I'll call Izzy in the morning."

"Sounds good. Love you, Son. Be safe."

"Thanks, Dad, you too."

I hang up with my dad and race back to the locker room to get showered and dressed.

Fifteen minutes later, I make it on the bus and grab a seat next to Carter. "Hey man, is everything okay? We were getting worried that you were kidnapped by a groupie and not coming home with us."

I laugh. "Nope, I just had a family emergency to deal with but everything seems to be under control." I tell him what happened with my mom and how Izzy will be here sooner than expected.

"Oh shit, that's a lot. Did you find a nanny?"

I shake my head. "No. Do you know of anyone? I know you don't have kids, but maybe you know a friend who can babysit until I find someone more permanent?"

He tilts his head to the side to think about that. "No, but my girlfriend has a best friend who's a nanny."

I sit up straight, hope starting to fill me. "Really? Do you think she's available?"

"I'm not sure. Let me text her." He pulls out his phone and starts typing on it. "I know she used to work for a Nashville hockey player, but the guy just got traded."

And just like that, I deflate right back into my seat, suspicion overtaking me as I know who he's referring to. "Her name wouldn't happen to be Cassie Warner, would it?"

Carter's eyes light up. "It sure is! Did you already interview her?"

I scoff at the irony of it all. Cassie did warn me that Nashville was a small town at heart. "Yeah, I did and it won't work out."

He frowns in confusion. "Why not? Grace says she's amazing with kids."

"Let's just say, Cassie—and probably Grace as well since their friends—hates my guts."

"What did you do?"

I proceed to tell Carter a condensed version of what happened with Cassie. "I'm surprised Grace didn't tell you."

He blows out a breath. "Yeah, me too, but that shows you how loyal she is to Cassie."

"Excuse me," Tripp interrupts and peeks his head around the side of my seat. "I couldn't help but overhear you ladies gossiping. Can I give you some unsolicited advice?"

I smirk at him calling us 'ladies'. "I'm sure you will whether I ask for it or not," I answer him dryly.

He gives me a cocky grin. "Sure will! So here it is: stop whining about how you won't be able to keep your hands off her because of how incredible the sex is, blah, blah, blah." He rolls his eyes in annoyance. "Grow some fucking balls by keeping your dick in your pants and then you won't have any issues. This is a business transaction. Treat it as such. You obviously are in a desperate situation to find someone and your kid should be your first priority."

"Of course Izzy's my first priority," I growl, not appreciating anyone questioning me as a parent.

"Then hire the qualified nanny so you can relax knowing your kid is being taken care of when you're on the road."

"This advice is rich coming from someone who has no children and is younger than me," I huff out, wishing he kept his mouth shut and minded his own damn business.

"Which is exactly why you should be listening to me. You're welcome." He gives me a salute and sits back in his seat.

"Tripp is right," Murph responds from the seat across the aisle. "You need a nanny ASAP, so stop being a jackass and close the deal. Call the agency now and see if she's even still available. Qualified nannies are hard to come by."

Just then Carter's phone dings and he reads his texts. "You're still in luck. Grace says she is available and wants to know why I'm asking?"

I take my phone out of my pocket and look up Katherine Harper's cell phone number. "Tell her you'll talk later about it."

The guys are right. With Izzy potentially being here in as little as five days, I'm desperate enough to hire Cassie. I'm thirty-five years old—of course I can be professional and keep my hands to myself if Cassie becomes our nanny.

If she would be even willing to at this point. I have a lot of groveling to do.

I find Katherine's number and dial her up. I'm prepared to leave her a voicemail but am relieved when she picks up after the second ring.

"Hello, Mrs. Harper. This is Gunnar McNeer. I'm sorry to bother you so late, but I've changed my mind and would like to hire Cassie Warner for the nanny position."

CHAPTER 14

CASSIE

pull up in front of Gunnar's house, park the car, and turn off the engine. I look out the window and sigh, wondering what the hell I'm doing here. I mean, I know *why* I'm here, but this just feels like it's a bad idea.

When Mrs. Harper called me last night saying Gunnar had changed his mind and wanted to hire me, I was shocked and then angry. He acted like a jerk the last time I saw him, so a tiny part of me wants to tell him to go to hell. I was devastated when I discovered he was Lewis and not even a personal trainer, but an *athlete*. After the surprise of it all simmered down, I tried to make light of the situation, but him freaking out over our age difference annoyed the crap out of me. Just because he's eleven years older, definitely doesn't make him smarter. During his little temper tantrum, I willed myself to turn off my emotions and act like *that* night was no big deal and we can just forget it ever happened. Was I really going to be able to forget our phenomenal night together? Of course not, but I assumed he would. I thought I was going to be just another notch on his belt and he would forget about me when his next conquest came along. Isn't that how most guys are?

Why would you think that about him, Cassie? You don't even know the guy except for how good his dick feels inside you.

I groan and rest my forehead against my steering wheel. I almost didn't agree to come here today. Mrs. Harper said his mom broke her ankle and won't be able to take care of Izzy anymore, so this is an emergency situation for him. I felt bad and my need to help people has me giving in. He asked for me to come over to "talk" about the position and his expectations. He's even offered a five thousand dollar signing bonus if I can start tomorrow. I technically have not said yes to the job, and I know Mrs. Harper thinks I'm crazy for not jumping on it, but she also doesn't know the real reason why he didn't want to hire me in the first place. Only Grace knows and I've sworn her to secrecy.

You can do this, Cassie.

Don't think about that night.

Don't think about how he told you he never wants to forget about it.

You need this job.

I nod at my mental pep talk and step out of the car and walk to the front door.

He opens it within seconds of me ringing the doorbell. I hate how my heart starts to pound at the sight of him. I can't stop my gaze from traveling up his body to those gorgeous green eyes; I lose myself in their depth. Damn him for looking so good in a white T-shirt and jeans.

"Hey," he greets in his stupid sexy voice with that stupid sexy accent. "Come on in." He pushes the door wider for me to walk past him and I get a whiff of his Irish Springs soap that he must've just used in the shower. The butterflies in my stomach start to flutter and it pisses me off even more. I might have to wear a mask if I agree to take this job.

"Is Izzy here?" I inquire while glancing around for her. My pulse is racing and there are things I feel I need to say to him. Things a child does not need to hear.

"She is out shopping with her cousin." I whirl around and watch him close the door. My gaze follows those strong fingers twisting the lock and I gulp. I remember exactly what those fingers did to me and it makes my core clench with need. I want those damn fingers inside me again.

No, Wanton Cassie! Focus on why you're here.

"We need to lay down some ground rules if I'm going to accept this job," I blurt out, deciding to just rip the band-aid off. He crosses his arms across his chest, making his biceps bulge against his cotton shirt.

Eyes up, Cassie! Do not remember how amazing it felt to be held in those strong, sculpted arms.

I give my head a little shake to clear my lustful thoughts. "Rule #1: What happened last week can never ever happen again." My silly, romantic heart cries out in protest, while my brain is fist pumping in victory at laying down the law like a badass.

"You're damn right it will never happen again," he growls in a menacing tone with a sour look on his face.

"Well you don't have to say it like that!" I angrily place my hands on my hips, hurt that he seems so revolted about one of the greatest nights of my life. Clearly, he's had time to turn off his sensitivity chip or maybe this is his way of hurting me back after the other day in his office.

"Like what?"

"Like it was the most disgusting thing you've ever done. Like you… regret it." My voice lowers and I look down at my feet, not wanting him to see me get emotional. I feel a wave of my abandonment issues start to rise inside of me.

Not now, Cassie! Get it together. You will not be weak in front of him.

I fight to control my emotions, mentally chastising myself for letting a stranger trigger my past trauma.

I look up when I see his feet moving closer to me. My eyes

widen in surprise at the stormy look on his face, his jaw clenched tight and ticking.

"On the contrary, Cassie." He stops mere inches away from me and I can smell the fresh spearmint on his breath. "I have fucked you in my head and in my hand every night since our time together. My only regret from *that* night is I wish I met you under normal circumstances because I still can't stop thinking about you and it's fucking with my mind."

My mouth drops open in shock from his bluntness. His gaze darts from my eyes to my mouth and I watch those jade eyes go dark with desire.

"Close your mouth," he demands in frustration. "Now all I want you to do is suck me off. Damnit, this isn't going the way I was planning." He turns around, places his hands behind his neck and looks up at the ceiling.

I snap my jaw shut and my eyes pop in astonishment. Images of me with my mouth around his cock make my blood start to bubble with lust. Lord, this man and his dirty mouth might be the death of me and any professionalism I have left.

"This is a bad idea," I whisper, wishing our night together was not playing on repeat in my brain.

He turns around and scrubs his face with his hands before jamming them in his jean pockets. "Yes, we've already established that, but I'm in desperate need of a nanny and you seem to be the only available one who can start right away. So let me lay down some ground rules of my own."

He takes a deep breath and continues, "I didn't choose to move to Tennessee, my job made me, and while I'm here, I'm going to make the most of it. I'm going to play the best baseball of my career, take the best care of Izzy that I can, and spend time with my brother and his family. What I won't be doing is getting into any relationships."

I give him a confused look. "Okay…what does that have to do with me?"

He points to me and then back to him. "You and I will not be getting into any romantic relationships."

I cross my arms against my chest in annoyance. "Who said anything about a relationship? I sure don't want one and no offense to you and your profession, but I would never date an athlete."

He frowns. "Why not?"

"You're surrounded by temptation to cheat all the time."

His spine stiffens and I can tell I've offended him. "I've never cheated on anyone in my life."

"Good for you. I hope you keep that streak going."

His eyes widen at my sass. "How quickly you've forgotten that I was cheated on too."

"Oh, I remember, but it doesn't mean you won't one day make a poor decision."

He scoffs at me. "I would never cheat on a woman I love."

I shrug, wanting to get off this topic and not go down the rabbit hole of my trust issues. "If you say so. Now that we've established that we won't be romantically involved, what are your other rules?"

"My other rule is that we have to start over."

I narrow my eyes on him. "What does that mean?"

"It means we keep the past in the past and start afresh. Let's pretend today is your first interview instead of last week." He holds out his hand for me to shake and plasters a fake smile on his face. "Hi Cassie, my name is Gunnar McNeer and I'm a single dad who just moved here from Austin, Texas. I'm hoping you will help save my ass by becoming my new nanny."

I bite the inside of my cheek, trying hard to refrain from giggling at his ridiculous antics. "Nice to meet you." I place my hand in his and know instantly it was a mistake from the jolt of electricity I feel when our palms connect. I yank my hand back and ball it in a fist at my side. Rule number three should be no touching.

"My five-year-old daughter is named Izzy and she will have you wrapped around her little finger within an hour of meeting her." I can't help but smile as I realize if she's anything like her father, then I'm going to be in *big* trouble.

"I can't wait to meet her," I tell him. "Will she be home soon?"

He glances at his watch and nods. "Should be any moment. So, does this mean you will accept the job?"

"That's the fastest first interview I've ever had," I say dryly. "What are your expectations of me as your nanny?"

"To keep my kid happy and alive."

I burst out laughing but stop when I see he is quite serious. "Of course my plan is to keep her happy and definitely alive. But what else do you expect out of me?"

"I want you to love and nurture her but I also don't want you to be her best friend. She's five—she will try to walk all over you and take advantage of your kindness if you let her."

I'm impressed that he acknowledges this about his own daughter. "I'm not afraid to discipline, but rest assured, I don't believe in spanking. There are other ways to get your point across without physical touch."

He nods. "Excellent. I also expect you to be brutally honest with me, even if you feel it's something I won't like to hear."

"Noted. I can do that." It's easy for parents to say they want to hear it all, but I'm interested in seeing if I do have something negative to report about Izzy, how he realistically will respond.

"While this will be your home away from home, I ask that you don't bring anyone over without my approval first."

"The only people who might want to come visit me are my dad and my best friend, Grace."

"Ah, yes, the infamous Grace who is dating one of my teammates, Carter Callahan." He gives me a knowing look and I almost blurt out that they're really not together but bite my tongue and nod. Grace would absolutely disown me as a best friend if I told her secret.

"I have no issues with your father and Grace coming over, but anyone else, please ask me first."

"Of course. Is there anything else?"

"Aly left me very detailed notes about you from your previous interview, so I really don't have any questions on my part to ask. Why don't we resume this meeting in my office so I can give you my schedule to look over. I have a feeling the schedule will prompt a lot of questions from you." He turns around and I follow him to his office.

Last time I was here, I was too preoccupied to get a good look around. It's a well decorated, modern office. The walls are painted a navy blue with light wood floating shelves that are littered with keepsakes, awards, trophies, and photos. I sit down in the chair in front of his desk as he walks around, sits down, and opens a folder. He pulls out a piece of paper that has a lot of black and gray colored boxes in a calendar and hands it to me.

"This is my regular season schedule. The black boxes indicate the home games, the gray are the away games." I study the schedule and I'm alarmed to see not only all the back-to-back games, but also some away games immediately following a home game the next day. "I prefer for you and Izzy to attend most of my home games, but you don't have to stay for the full duration when we play at night."

"I'm not a sports fan, but this schedule seems a little too crazy to me. When do you get a day off?"

He points to the schedule. "The white boxes with nothing written in them are the off days."

"Oh. Duh." I roll my eyes at the obvious, making him chuckle. "How does your body handle this grueling pace?"

"Fortunately, baseball is not as physical as hockey is. We can handle back-to-back games because of that. Don't get me wrong, it's exhausting and very tough on my body at my ripe old age. I do tend to sit in an ice bath after most games and do a sauna to try to maximize recuperation."

"I didn't know your season was so long."

He nods at the piece of paper. "That schedule doesn't even include spring training and post-season if we make it."

My eyes widen in shock. They only get about three months off if they make the postseason. "How do you relax when your off-season is so short?"

He shrugs. "You just make the most of it. Having a child makes the off-season go by very fast."

I look back down at his schedule. "So would your days off be mine as well?"

He winces and nods. "Yeah, and I realize that it's not many. When my brother comes back into town from touring, he and Aly can take Izzy off your hands for some days off. They've already offered, so it's just about letting them know which dates."

"But isn't she about to have another baby?" There's no way Aly should have three children on her hands to watch. Her own children will be a lot to handle.

"I already told them I refuse to be a burden, but they're insisting that Izzy needs to spend time with them and her cousins. I'll have to take them up on some of their offers because even on my days off, we might have community events that I will want to attend. Some of the events are fun for Izzy and she can go with me, but I would like for you to go with us just in case I'm needed elsewhere during the event. It would make me feel better knowing that you're around to watch her."

"It won't be a problem. We'll figure everything out."

"I really appreciate you being so accommodating." He smiles and then gives me a shy look. "So, what do you think?

He passes another piece of paper across his desk and I see it's a non-disclosure agreement. I raise an eyebrow at him in question. "I know your agency has you sign an NDA, but I also have my own for you to sign."

I grab the NDA and start to read over it. It's your standard non-disclosure agreement, the same type I signed with the Fitzgeralds. Signing this would mean I'm agreeing to be his nanny though. I pause and bite my lip to think, which causes him to groan and close his eyes. "Can you try not to do that in front of me?"

I huff in frustration. "Sorry, but sometimes I can't help myself and it's a natural reaction."

He opens up his eyes and holds up his hands. "You're right, I'm sorry. I need to control how I react every time you do something sexy. It's unprofessional and unfair."

I sigh. I don't know about this. He must see my hesitation because he clasps his hands together as if he is praying and pleads, "Please, Cassie, I'm desperate for help here. Will you please be our new nanny?"

For some reason, the fact that I'm back here because he can't find someone else bothers me. I need to let it go and just take this for what it is—a job that I need. But he's right in the sense that he has to stay professional with me because I *will* cave in to his charm and to his touch. And if he can't control his reactions toward me, how are we going to be able to stay away from each other? What if we fail at keeping this strictly business and have sex again? Would I get fired? Could I do casual sex?

I just don't know if this is worth the risk. For my mental sanity, I should not accept his offer.

"Okay, I accept." The words rush out of my mouth before my brain has a chance to stop them.

You're a freaking idiot, Cassie.

"Oh, thank god!" His shoulders sag with relief and he stands up. I sign the NDA and hand it back to him. He takes it from me and puts it back into the folder. "Thank you, Cassie. I promise you, you won't regret this."

I smile and nod, already regretting it.

CHAPTER 15

CASSIE

Less than twenty-four hours later, I'm once again pulling up to Gunnar's house, but this time, I come with my stuff to move in. Today is my official first day as his nanny and even though I met Izzy last night when she came home, I'm still a tad nervous. The real question is what am I nervous about—starting a new job with a new family or being under the same roof as Gunnar?

I learned quickly that Isabella McNeer is definitely not a shy five-year-old. When Gunnar introduced us, she commented on how much she loved my hair and then grabbed my hand to show me her room. She proceeded to tell me how much she loves butterflies and then took out every article of clothing she owned that had them on it—including her underwear. She made me laugh within the first two minutes of meeting her and I can tell we're going to have a fun time together.

Sosie McNeer was more guarded and reserved. She had no problems letting it be known that she was sizing me up. I wasn't offended by her; she's protective of her family and I can appreciate that. She watched me closely while I interacted with Izzy and right when I was leaving, she smiled and told me she looked forward to getting to know me better.

Once I left Gunnar's house, I called Mrs. Harper and told her I accepted the job. I drove to her office and signed my contract. Grace was working one of her shifts, so I went home, had dinner with my dad and then proceeded to pack up the everyday items I would want to have at Gunnar's house. I tried to get a decent night's sleep, but I kept tossing and turning into the early hours of the morning. With Gunnar having to leave for the road immediately after his game tonight, I'm being thrown right into the deep end of seeing how Izzy handles a new nanny who's practically a stranger to her without her father around to intervene.

Please let this go smoothly and don't let me do anything that gets me fired on the first day on the job.

I step out of my car and grab two rolling suitcases out of my trunk. I throw a tote bag over each shoulder and walk up to the front door. I take a deep breath to calm my nerves and ring the doorbell.

"She's here!" I hear a little voice scream in excitement with running footsteps that stop right behind the other side of the door. The lock unbolts and the door swings open by Izzy, who is standing there with her hair a wild mess wearing unicorn pajamas.

"Good morning, Izzy," I singsong with a smile.

"Hi, Cassie!" She giggles while jumping up and down in excitement. It settles my nerves seeing that she's happy I'm here.

"Isabella Elizabeth McNeer, what have I told you about opening the door by yourself?" Gunnar comes up behind her, clearly not happy that she opened the door without him. I can't say I blame him since I didn't see her look out the window next to the door to see who it was.

She turns around and looks at him. "I wasn't alone, Daddy. You're right here with me."

"I wasn't when you initially opened the door. We've talked before about not opening the door for strangers."

"But Cassie isn't a stranger."

"Yes, but you didn't know it was her at the door," he points out in frustration.

"You said it was her when the doorbell rang," she grumbles with a scowl matching one I've previously seen from her dad.

I press my lips together to refrain from laughing while I watch these two spitting images of each other argue. If this is happening while she's five, her teenage years are going to turn Gunnar's hair gray. He will probably look even more handsome in ten years too.

Stop thinking about him like that, Cassie! He's your boss, nothing more. You probably won't even be her nanny by then.

He sighs loudly in irritation and looks at me. "Good morning. Here, let me help you with your things." He reaches for one of my suitcase handles and our fingers graze in the exchange. I inhale sharply and try to act nonchalant, but there's nothing normal about this man's touch and the electricity that shoots up my body from it.

"I wanna help," Izzy says, looking up at me expectantly.

"Thank you so much for offering to help, Izzy. Why don't you carry this tote bag for me?" I slide the straps off my right shoulder and hold it out for her. "It shouldn't be too heavy for you." She grabs hold of the straps and instead of holding up the bag, she lets it fall straight to the floor. It rolls to its side and my arts and craft supplies fall out. She gazes up at me with one of those *uh-oh* looks and I smile to reassure her it's okay.

"Ooh, what's this?" She sees a coloring book peeking out of the bag and decides to start taking everything out to see what else is in there. "Are these mine?" she wonders and I squat down to the floor to get on her level.

"They are for both of us to color together." She takes out

the bags of colored pencils and markers, lays them on the floor by her little legs before diving back into the bag and grabbing a thin, long tin that contains paint brushes.

"You're making a mess, Izzy. Put everything back in the bag and take it to Cassie's room," Gunnar tells her and then glances at me. "I can get your other things from the car," he offers and before I can respond, he turns around and walks out the door.

I help Izzy put everything back in the bag and follow her to the first-floor guest room. I place my stuff on the media console and decide to leave them there to unpack later. Izzy has already run out of the room, so I hustle to keep up with her.

"Did you eat breakfast?" I ask her as she bounces her body against the couch while watching cartoons.

"I was eating cereal," she answers and that explains the ring of chocolate around her mouth.

"Why don't you go finish your breakfast while I help your dad get everything else out of my car?" She doesn't answer but walks back to the kitchen table and sits down at the island where she left her bowl.

I wait for Gunner to return, not wanting to leave her alone. When he comes back through the door, he has my other suitcase, another tote bag over his shoulder, and his hands full with my easels.

"Wow, you got most of it." I run over and grab the easels out of his hands to help. We walk back to my room and I place the rest of my stuff where I left my other things. When I turn around, I catch him staring at the bed with a look of longing before turning his gaze on me. We stare at each other for a moment before he blinks, turns on his heel and walks out of the room.

Was he imagining me in bed? His bedroom was not part of the tour yesterday and I think it's the door right across from Izzy's room upstairs. Thank goodness it's nowhere near mine.

It's inevitable that I'll see his room and I won't be able to stop thinking about him in his own bed.

Imagine all you want, Cassie, because that bed is forbidden just like he is.

I go back out into the living room at the same time he's walking back into the house with my blank canvases. "I shut your trunk for you but go ahead and pull your car into the driveway so it's not in the street."

"Okay, thanks," I tell him while he walks past me to put away my things. I pull out my car keys from my pocket and go move my car. When I'm finished, I walk back into the house to see he's in the kitchen helping Izzy rinse out her bowl. I watch him show her how to put the bowl in the dishwasher, impressed that he's teaching her at such a young age to clean up after herself.

"Where's Sosie?" I ask, feeling slightly awkward and not knowing what to do with myself while he's here.

"Sosie has her own place."

"Oh, really? I didn't realize she lived in Nashville as well."

"Yeah, Gavin moved her here from California years ago to be his assistant and fortunately, it's been a good fit for both of them."

He helps Izzy get down from her step stool. "Izzy, go get dressed for the day," he instructs and Izzy goes racing by me to her room.

"Does she need help?" I ask, wanting an excuse to not be alone with him because that's when my thoughts start to turn salacious.

"No, she can do it on her own. By the way, Sosie will be here later today to escort you to the game. She's going to show you where to park, how to get your badge identifying who you are for security purposes, and how to get to the suites and the family room by the clubhouse."

I nod with a fake smile plastered on my face, but on the inside, I'm dreading going to his games. I felt the same way with the Fitzgeralds. All those people in one place with the noise and the drunkenness of others makes me uncomfortable. It unfortunately brings flashbacks of my childhood when my mother would take me to bars with her so she could get drunk with her friends. I know it's not fair to compare the two different experiences and at least at Gunnar's games, we'll be sitting in a suite, which should be a more pleasant experience. Marissa liked to drop her kids off in the family room and sit in the stands at Alec's games. Hockey games are so loud; they became her time to have a couple of cocktails with the other wives. I made sure I was the one driving us back home when that would happen. Most of the time I preferred to be with the kids in the family room, but she wanted me with her in the stands.

He starts to chuckle. "You don't have a very good poker face. I promise you it won't be torturous."

That makes me genuinely smile and I start to feel bad about my negative attitude. "I'm sorry, I've never been a big sports fan and this will be my first baseball game."

His mouth drops open in shock. "Seriously? Your dad never took you to a game?"

I shake my head. "He was more of a football type of guy." I shrug, holding my hands up. "He would watch some baseball, but I never watched it with him."

He blows out a breath. "Well, I hope you won't be too bored at the games. At least Izzy will keep you busy unless she wants to go to the family room. Then you might want to stab your eyeballs out, especially if it's a pitchers' duel."

"What does that mean?" I ask because he's speaking a foreign language to me right now.

"A pitchers' duel is when the pitchers are on fire and runs are difficult to come by. Some fans find the low scoring games to be boring, but I don't think they are. To me, they're exciting and filled with the anticipation of who's finally going to beat the pitcher and get a run."

I smirk at him. "That's because you're the one playing *in* the game and love the sport."

He laughs. "Touché."

"Who else will be in the suite with us?" I inquire. Gunnar already mentioned the suite belongs to Gavin, so it's nice to know that everyone in there will somehow be connected to the McNeers.

"Gavin is still on tour, so it will be you and Izzy, Sosie, and whomever else she invited. Sometimes Aly's sister and her family come as well."

"Can I invite a couple of my friends?" Izzy asks when she comes running out of her room, dressed in a butterfly shirt with matching shorts. I glance at Gunnar in question and he's got a strange look on his face. It appears as if he is struggling with a response since Izzy might not have any friends here yet, so I step in to help him.

"You just moved to Nashville and you already made friends?" I exclaim with an excited voice. "I'm impressed, Izzy! Tell me their names."

"Austin—" she pauses and tilts her head to the side to think. "—and you!" She points at me and giggles with that cute, infectious little laugh. I smile back, happy that she considers me a friend already. That means she already feels safe and comfortable around me. I grab her cute little finger and squeeze, making her laugh harder as she pulls it away from me.

"Austin's with Uncle Gavin and Aunt Aly on the road, so he won't be there today," Gunnar tells her while ruffling up her already messy hair. "I've got to start getting ready. You be the best girl and listen to Cassie, okay?" She nods and he kisses her on top of her head before looking up at me. "Ready to start your official duties?"

I laugh. "I'm here, aren't I?" I wave him off. "Go get ready."

"Thanks," he grins in the boyish way that turns my

insides into mush. He walks away and heads up the stairs to his bedroom.

I turn to Izzy and ask, "Should we make your daddy victory cupcakes?" Her eyes go wide with excitement and she nods while licking her lips. "Okay, let's start baking," I laugh and she follows me into the pantry.

I'm pleasantly surprised to see such a well-stocked pantry with everything I need and then some. I take out all the ingredients and put them on the countertop. I open the refrigerator and grab the rest of the items I need. *How does Gunnar have time to grocery shop*? I wonder and remind myself to ask him when he comes back out.

"All right, Iz. I'm going to measure everything out and you'll get to dump it all in the bowls. Deal?" I look through the drawers and cabinets and take out the mixing bowls, measuring cups and spoons.

She nods and climbs up on her step stool so she can reach everything. "Can I mix it altogether too?"

"You sure can, but we can't go fast or it will make a big mess." She gives me a mischievous grin and I immediately regret telling her that. *Note to self; do not let her mix everything by herself.*

She listens intently to the instructions I give her and tries hard not to spill the contents outside of the bowl. I do the cracking of the eggs myself, but I make sure I explain to her how to be careful so we don't get any of the shell into our cupcakes. When it's time for her to stir the wet ingredients with the dry, I gently place my hand on top of hers and help guide her into mixing the batter properly.

"Do you know where the cupcake tins are?" I inquire, wanting to see how well she knows this kitchen. She goes by the oven into the drawers underneath it and pulls out two cupcake tins. Izzy hasn't lived in this house full-time for very long and already she has memorized where things are. This shows me how intelligent she is and gives me ideas on how to home in on her skills even more.

She helps me grease the tins with butter and I preheat the oven for baking. I grab a ladle out of the drawer and give it to her to do the honor of pouring the batter into the tins. She gets batter everywhere but it doesn't matter because we're laughing and having a good time together.

"What's so funny?" Gunnar asks with a warm smile. I didn't even notice his return to the room with us. My stomach flutters when I notice how handsome he looks in his game-day attire. Alec had to dress up as well, so I'm not surprised to see Gunnar in a suit. He's wearing a collared white button-down shirt underneath a navy blue jacket with matching slacks and a tan belt and dress shoes. This man would look hot in just a garbage sack.

"We're making you victory cupcakes for when you come home with a win tonight." I avert my eyes and concentrate on helping Izzy get the rest of the contents out of the bowl.

"I love that manifestation, but I won't be home tonight, remember? We leave for our eight-game road trip right after the game."

"Oh," I comment, embarrassed that I already forgot his schedule and slightly disappointed that he won't get a chance to even eat one. "Maybe we can bring them with us to the game tonight for the suite?"

"They usually don't allow outside food, but I bet George won't give us any issues if you smuggle them in, especially if you bribe him with one." When I give him a questioning look, he chuckles. "Sorry, George is the security guard at the player/family entrance. Sosie will introduce you to him." He looks over at Izzy and smiles. "I bet they're going to be the best cupcakes I've ever eaten."

Izzy slides her finger against the side of the bowl and licks the batter off her finger while giggling. "Ooh, good idea, Iz." I mimic her and get a big glob on my fingertip. I put my finger in my mouth and suck off the sticky, delicious batter.

"Mmm, it's so good." She nods at me and we both dip our fingers back in the bowl for more. I stick my finger back in my mouth to lick off more when I happen to glance up at Gavin and freeze in place. His eyes have darkened with lust and are narrowed in on my mouth. My mind sends flashbacks of when he licked off whip cream from my breasts and I feel a blush creeping up my cheeks. I quickly remove my finger and busy myself by washing my hands.

Gunnar clears his throat and throws a large, manilla envelope on the countertop. "Inside this envelope is a credit card and discretionary cash for you to use for groceries, supplies, and any outings you take her on." His tone is curt and he refuses to meet my eyes.

That answers my question about who buys groceries. I wipe my hands on a towel and grab the envelope to open it. I take the credit card out and put it in my pocket to put in my wallet later. I open the white, letter sized envelope and gasp at the amount of cash inside of it. "This is a lot of money, Gunnar."

He ignores my comment and walks over to Izzy. "I'm gone a lot. I want you to have everything you need for Izzy. You don't need to be spending your own money on things that involve her. When you use the money or the credit card, just please grab receipts and put it back in the envelope. I will replenish the cash every week."

I shake my head. "That won't be necessary. This will last us a long time."

"We'll see." He turns toward Izzy and spreads his arms out wide. "Give daddy some good luck sugar."

"Wait!" I call out before she can jump into his arms. "Wash your hands so you don't ruin your dad's suit."

"I don't care about the suit, Cassie." He gives her an encouraging look and she jumps into his arms. He sticks his nose in the crook of her neck and proceeds to kiss her up and down, causing her to scream with laughter. I snatch my phone from my back pocket and quickly take a picture of them to send to him. What a lucky little girl to be so loved by her father. It reminds me of the relationship I have with my own dad.

He puts her down and I see tiny fingerprints all over his shoulders. I wet a paper towel and without thinking, I grab his arm and start blotting at the stains. My eyes are trained on the smudges and I don't realize how close I get to him until I hear him inhaling. My fingers stop and my gaze trails over to his face to catch him closing his eyes while he gets a whiff of my scent.

"Please stop," he demands in a gruff voice and I can hear the double meaning behind his words. He opens his eyes and I take a step back, balling the paper towel in my fist. He swallows and takes a side step away from me.

"I love you, Isabear." He grabs his suitcase off the floor and heads toward the garage door. "I'll see you girls tonight."

We both watch him leave and when the door shuts, I blow out a deep breath. Day one of being Gunnar McNeer's nanny has commenced and I feel like I barely made it out unscathed from the scorching fire that are his heated stares.

CHAPTER 16

GUNNAR

Another win is in the books and I'm feeling great despite catching a line drive that knocked me on my ass. It was a game saving catch though and the roar of the crowd was deafening while I was slow to get to my feet. I promised Coach I would have the team doctor check me out and once he gave me the all clear, I quickly got dressed to meet up with the girls. Sosie texted me, letting me know they were outside the family room, so fortunately I don't have very far to go.

"Hey, old man." I look up to see Judd Samson, our rookie pitcher, walking toward me from outside of the clubhouse. "Who's the hot redhead with your cousin, Sosie?"

My mood immediately sours. "None of your fucking business," I growl, knowing exactly who he's referring to.

"Oh shit, sorry! I thought you were single?"

"I am single, but you don't need to know her or even talk to her."

He laughs, thinking I'm joking when my face and tone of voice says I'm dead serious. "C'mon, McNeer. Stop bringing good-looking women to the park for us to inquire about."

"Understand this, Samson." I stand up from out of my

chair and put my jacket on. "Under no circumstances, whatsoever, would you be allowed to date anyone that is part of my family or even associated with me."

"I never said I was interested in dating." He winks at me and laughs, oblivious to the fact that I'm about to punch his fucking face in. Diesel steps in between us and puts his hand on my chest.

"Easy, McNeer. He's just fucking around, but in poor taste." Diesel must've given Samson the *you-better-shut-the-fuck-up-and-apologize* look because Judd side steps around him and holds up in hands in surrender.

"I didn't mean anything by that, Gunnar. I'm sorry."

I lift my chin up at him in acknowledgment, but don't say a word. Sometimes when rookies make the big leagues, they're all about how many women they can bang in a short amount of time. I get it, I was a rookie too once. I don't encourage their behavior, but I also don't tell them what to do with their lives. If they want advice, I'll give it to them. If I see any of them struggling, I will offer it unsolicited. Judd is a good kid, but like all rookies, sometimes gets carried away.

"It's the nanny, isn't it?" Tripp asks with a gleam in his eye. When I only nod at him, his smile widens and he heads to the door. "Glad to see you wised up and listened to me, McNeer. Think it's about time I go meet the woman who wets your dreams."

"Tripp—" I yell out but he's already out the door.

"I'll go make sure he behaves. Besides, we're curious about her too," Murph says with a cocky smirk as he and Evan proceed to follow Tripp out the door.

"Jesus Christ," I mutter. I grab my suitcase to take with me to the bus and leave the clubhouse. When I walk outside, there are multiple children running within a circle of adults containing the kids in one area. I recognize my daughter as being one of those kids playing. I walk up to Aly's sister, Valerie, and her husband Rowan, who were given guest passes to come down to the family area. I give Valerie a hug and kiss on the cheek and slap Rowan on the back.

"Looks like Cassie is the shiny new toy that everyone wants to play with," Rowan comments with a smirk as we watch Cassie being surrounded by some of my teammates and their girlfriends and wives. She smiles as introductions are made, but she seems tense. She hasn't noticed me yet and her eyes keep darting over to watch Izzy.

I ignore his comment, trying to keep my cool while I watch Judd flirt with her. "Glad you guys got a chance to meet her tonight."

"Aly told us all about her, so it was nice to finally meet her in person."

I freeze, hoping he's not insinuating that she told them *everything*. "What do you mean, *all* about her?"

He gives me a weird look. "Meaning how great she is and seems to be perfect for Izzy. Why? Is there something I'm missing here?"

I shake my head. "Nope. Nothing at all."

He narrows his eyes at me. "Bro, you're acting weird."

"I just got knocked on my ass by a line drive and soon will be boarding a plane to go on a nine-day road trip. I'm tired and preoccupied." It's partly the truth, but he doesn't need to know everything that has transpired between me and Cassie.

"That catch was sick." He takes a step back and looks me up and down. "Are you okay?"

"Yeah, I'll just be sore tomorrow."

I glance over at Sosie to see her talking with Delilah Monroe, a country music singer who's dating Diesel. Behind them, Diesel is talking to Scotty Wilkins, another country music singer who is friends with Gavin and Sosie.

"Was Scotty in our suite tonight?" I ask Rowan. Gavin and I suspect something's going on between him and Sosie, but neither one of them will fess up.

"He sure was. Sat next to Sosie the whole time." As if

Scotty can feel us staring at him, he glances over at us and nods in acknowledgment.

"Fucking Wilkins," I mutter. "He better not be messing with her." Sosie's like the sister we never had and we are all super protective of her, especially since she didn't have the best childhood.

"What if Sosie likes him messing with her?" I look over at Rowan, who cocks his head at me in question.

I sigh. Sosie is an adult and can do whatever she wants, despite us warning her not to get involved with someone like Scotty. "If she does, I hope she's making him wear two condoms."

Rowan laughs out loud, which causes the kids to stop playing and some of the adults to look over at us.

"Daddy!" Izzy yells and races over to me. I catch her with an *oomph*, my body protesting at the impact.

"Are you okay, Gunnar?" Cassie walks over, eyeing me with concern. "You had us worried when you didn't get up right away from that catch." My gaze assesses her body clad in a cropped black tank top and high-waisted jeans that hug her in all the right places. Her hair is pulled back in a loose ponytail, with tendrils slipping out to frame her face. Her make-up is light but magnifies those incredible eyes. No wonder Judd was practically salivating over her. She's fucking gorgeous.

Stop eye-fucking her in front of all these people, Gunnar!

I turn my attention to Izzy, who's looking at me with sad, puppy dog eyes. "Daddy's just fine." I kiss the tip of her nose, which makes her giggle. She squirms in my arms and I put her back down. She runs back over to play with the kids.

"Did you enjoy the game?" I ask Cassie and for some reason, I really hope she says yes. I want her to like coming to my games.

"I did, but trying to keep up with all the statistics hurts my brain." I laugh because baseball stats can be very confusing. "Rowan was kind enough to try to explain everything to me, but I might be hopeless at remembering."

"It's a lot to learn for your very first game."

"Wait, this was your first game?" Evan's girlfriend, Christy, asks in surprise.

Cassie nods. "Guess I was deprived as a child, guys." Everyone laughs at her joke and she visibly relaxes.

"Boys, it's time to get on the bus," Peter Kelly announces while he walks by us. I make my rounds hugging everyone goodbye until Izzy and Cassie are the only ones left. I squat down to Izzy's level and pick her up to give her a hug.

"Daddy's got to go play some games in other cities, but we will FaceTime with each other every day." For the first time since she was born, I don't want to leave her. This will be the very first time she'll be left with someone who isn't our immediate blood. This isn't just a three-game road trip—it is the second longest road trip we have on the calendar for this season. Cassie is practically a stranger to her. What if she freaks out and throws a crying fit?

I put her down, but she clings to my leg. "I don't want you to go," she whimpers softly and that sound starts to shred my heart into little pieces. I feel the sweat beading up in the middle of my back from my nerves.

"I know, sweetheart, but Daddy has to." I'm about to give in to her by making excuses not to go, when Cassie sees my struggles and intervenes.

"Izzy, I was talking with Nolan's mommy, Christy, and we were thinking of stopping for some ice cream right now. Would you like to go with me to get ice cream with Nolan? We can invite Sosie too if you want?"

She looks up at Cassie with watery eyes, but a small smile plays on her face. "Afterward, we can go home and start coloring in that special book I brought you. By the time your daddy calls us tonight, we can show him what you colored. What do you say?"

I don't bother mentioning that she should be asleep by the time I land. I hold my breath in anticipation of my daughter's reaction. Cassie holds out her hand and Izzy looks at it for a couple of seconds before giving her a small smile and putting her hand in Cassie's.

I release the breath I was holding and sigh softly in relief.

"We got this, Gunnar." Cassie reassures me, her gaze holding mine and all I see is determination in it. "You have nothing to worry about. Izzy and I are going to have the best time together." She places her hand on my forearm and squeezes. "I will protect your daughter with my life. Now, go get on that bus."

She removes her hand and my skin tingles from her touch. My chest tightens with pride over her confidence and something else I can't quite put my finger on. I have this overwhelming urge to hug Cassie but keep my hands to myself.

"Thank you," I tell her sincerely. I grab hold of my suitcase and quickly kiss Izzy on the head. "I'll talk to you ladies later." I turn around and start walking in the opposite direction, my heart feeling heavy. As I get closer to the bus, I look over my shoulder and see Cassie and Izzy skipping away, and my daughter's laughter puts a smile on my face.

In less than five minutes, Cassie prevented my daughter from having a total meltdown. Right then and there, I know I made the right decision in hiring her. Now all I have to do is make sure I don't screw it all up by falling for the nanny.

CHAPTER 17

GUNNAR

These nine days away from home have been rough and with a loss to end our road series, the team is happy to be heading back to Nashville. Once the plane touches down safely, I text Cassie to let her know I'm on my way. Luckily my house is only twenty-five minutes away from the airport, which means I'll make it home in time for dinner.

I get caught in a little bit of the Monday after work commuter traffic but am pulling into the garage thirty minutes later. The scent of garlic, grilled onions, and other spices weaves its way through my nostrils as soon as I open the door to the house, causing my stomach to rumble with hunger. I walk into the living room and stop dead in my tracks. There's a huge sign saying "Welcome Home, Daddy" hanging from the wall with balloons on each side. Music is playing from the speakers and Cassie is supervising Izzy, who is pouring sauce into a bowl. My chest tightens with emotions while watching them.

Cassie had zero issues with Izzy while I was away and in fact, she made things so fun for her that Izzy barely wanted to talk to me. Cassie was constantly sending me photos of her when they would go on outings and she made sure I talked with Izzy in the mornings and afternoons. It was such a relief to know she was being taken care of so well that I was able to fully concentrate on my job and not worry about things here.

As if she senses she's being watched, Cassie looks up and does a double take when she sees me. "Hi," her voice is raspy with surprise and her smile almost takes my breath away.

"Daddy!" Izzy screams and in her haste to put the sauce down, she spills a good portion of it all over the counter. "Uh-oh," she says, giving Cassie a worried look.

"Don't worry about it. Go give your dad a hug and I'll clean it up." She helps Izzy off her step stool and Izzy races over to me.

I pick her up and hug her tightly to me. "God, did I miss you so much, Isabear." I stick my nose in the crook of her neck and do my usual routine of tickle kisses. She screams so loudly my ear drum rings from potential damage. I put her down before she headbutts me by accident from all her squirming.

"Come see what we've done in the playroom, Daddy." Izzy grabs my hand and pulls me toward the stairs. I glance over at Cassie, who has a sheepish grin on her face, before going upstairs. When Cassie asked if she could make some changes to the playroom, I told her she had free reign since decorating was not my forte.

Izzy lets go of my hand when we reach the top and runs to the playroom. She waits for me inside the doorway and when I reach the threshold, she asks "Are you ready for the surprise, Daddy?"

"I'm ready. Should I close my eyes?"

"Yes. Close your eyes and give me your hand." She grabs my right hand and I cover my eyes with my left. I feel her pulling me into the room. "Okay, stop! Now open your eyes," she demands.

I slowly open them and freeze, my mouth dropping open in shock. In one week, Cassie has transformed this place into a miniature school room. The walls have some of Izzy's art hanging in stylish gold frames, a couple of dry erase boards for Izzy to practice her handwriting, and posters of site words are all hanging up. A long table is by the window and on it are two easels next to each other–one for Cassie and one for Izzy–with the paint supplies in between. One of the corners is set up as a cute reading nook with two small bookshelves overflowing with books that were still in boxes when I left and two bean bags are in front of them. I turn in a circle and see the back wall is bare but as I get closer, I can see a light sketch of stencils etched into the wall that looks like it will be a mural of a fairy garden.

"I texted Aly, asking permission to do a mural with Izzy," Cassie comments from the doorway. I turn to look at her and a blush flushes her cheeks. "I hope you don't mind what we've done in here."

"Are you kidding me?" I walk around the room in awe. "This room is incredible." What Cassie has done is turn a boring playroom into a kid's dream world that will encourage Izzy's imagination.

Her shoulders visibly sag in relief and her smile becomes brighter. "Izzy helped me with everything and picked out what pieces of her artwork she wanted to frame. She's really talented for her age."

I feel Izzy hold my hand and I look down at her, pride shining in my eyes. "I'm so proud of you, Iz. Do you love your new playroom?"

She smiles and nods. "We're going to start painting the wall tomorrow, right Cassie?"

"Tomorrow's my day off, but I promise we will start on Wednesday when I return."

Izzy pouts and I ruffle her hair. "We're going to have so much fun tomorrow that you won't be disappointed about waiting one whole day to paint." I glance at my watch and then at Cassie. "Now that I'm home, why don't you start your day off early? I can finish making dinner."

Her eyes widen in horror and she turns on her heel and runs down the stairs. "Oh my gosh, dinner!"

Izzy runs after her and my tour of the playroom seems to be finished. I follow after the girls and whatever Cassie is cooking smells amazing. "Did you burn dinner?"

"Saved it in the nick of time. It'll be ready in a couple of minutes." She pulls out a casserole dish from the oven and turns over the chicken to make sure it's cooked. "Izzy, grab the plates and pick where we each are sitting at the dining room table, please."

Izzy does as she asked and I feel bad standing here, watching Cassie take care of everything for us while I do nothing. "You didn't have to cook dinner. I could have easily made something for me and Iz so you could start your time off."

She shrugs. "I like to cook. But if you do as well, I promise to stop intruding on your turf."

"God, no. I hate cooking." That makes her laugh and the whimsical melody of it makes me smile. I try to think of something witty to say to make her laugh again but I'm stumped and don't want to sound like I'm trying too hard.

"Why don't you change so you don't get food on your nice clothes?" she offers while straining the noodles from hot water.

"Are you demanding that I take my clothes off?" I tease, but as soon as the words are out of my mouth, I immediately regret them. The vivid memories of her taking off my clothes that night start replaying like a slideshow in my head.

Jesus, Gunnar, you haven't been home for more than ten minutes and already you put the conversation in the gutter. She's going to sue you for sexual harassment and then you'll be out of a nanny. Izzy will be heartbroken and hate you forever.

"I'm sorry, that was really unprofessional of me." I shake my head at myself. "I was just trying to be funny."

She raises her eyebrows in surprise and glances to where Izzy is in the dining room. When she sees she's out of earshot, she responds, "If we were under different circumstances, maybe I would be trying to take your clothes off." She casts her gaze downward and my dick hardens from her response.

Shit, I'm in so much trouble.

"What's next, Cassie?" I hear Izzy's little voice coming closer and it forces me to focus back on her.

"Dinner is ready, so go wash your hands," Cassie tells her and brings the food to the dining room table.

"I'll go change and be right back." I turn and head to my room, needing some distance so I can adjust myself and deflate my hard-on. I change into a T-shirt and sweats and inspect myself in the mirror.

"You are hungry for food, not your nanny, Gunnar," I reprimand my reflection while making sure my sweats don't look too clingy against my semi-erection. I close my eyes and take a couple of deep breaths before feeling safe enough to return downstairs.

Cassie and Izzy are coloring a place mat when I return. I pull out a chair and sit down. I survey the table to see Cassie made roasted green beans, fettuccini alfredo with baked chicken and garlic bread. "Wow, everything looks amazing," I tell her as she puts the crayons back in their tin.

"Hopefully it tastes as good as it looks." She gets up from her chair and grabs a plate that was on the counter. "I already made Izzy a plate and cut things up for her." She puts Izzy's plate in front of her to eat. She then grabs a cup and fills it with water for Izzy.

I make myself a plate and am about to start eating when I notice Cassie is not sitting back down but is starting to clean the dishes she used to prepare dinner. "Why aren't you eating?"

"Oh, I figured it would be nice for you and Izzy to have dinner together."

"But you worked hard to make this food."

She shrugs. "It's okay. I can eat something later after I leave."

For some reason, her response annoys me. I want her to sit down and enjoy the meal she made. "Sit down and eat, Cassie," I demand, giving her a stern look.

"Cassie," Izzy whisper yells. "Come sit down or you're going to be in trouble. Daddy might even spank you." I have to bite the inside of my cheek to refrain from groaning at the image of a naked Cassie, bent over my knee, ready for a spanking. I'm not even into that, so it would be more like me going to town on that beautiful ass of hers.

"Okay, I'll sit down," Cassie squeaks out, her lips pressed together as she looks at me with laughter in her eyes. She grabs a plate and starts loading it up with food.

We eat in companionable silence before I ask her what's on my mind. "What do you usually do on your days off?"

"If there's no art exhibits to go see, then I'm usually painting or networking to try to get my artwork into galleries."

"How does one get their art into a gallery?" I ask, impressed that she's really trying to make a name for herself in the art world.

"You can apply if galleries have open submissions, but you don't want to just be in any kind of gallery. You want to be in one that gels with your style of painting, who has good foot traffic and does a good job promoting your work."

"Interesting. I didn't realize any of that."

She smiles. "Most people don't. When you're just beginning, you're trying to get yourself into any gallery, thinking the exposure will be amazing, but it can be the exact opposite."

"Sounds like you know from experience."

She nods. "The first gallery I was in barely had any events, didn't promote my work and just wasn't the right fit. Now I know which galleries would serve me better, so I've been building up my portfolio and uploading my art to my website."

"What's your website? I would love to see your work." She tells me the name of her website and I grab my phone from my pocket and type it in. It's a very professional looking website, with her paintings available to view almost immediately. I start to scroll and am in awe of the beautiful masterpieces she has created.

"Wow, Cassie, you're really good," I tell her with sincerity.

"I want to see!" Izzy chimes in and I get closer to her and show her some of Cassie's paintings. "Wow, those are pretty."

"Awe, thanks Iz. Keep painting like you do and maybe one day you'll be a professional artist," Cassie says and Izzy nods, her eyes shining with awe.

"If you sell your paintings straight from your website, what's the point in being in a gallery then?"

"Exposure. Good galleries already have a built-up client base who are regulars. Selling on my website doesn't give me the foot traffic or client base a gallery does. Yes, I get to keep the majority of my revenue, but a well-reputable gallery is worth giving them a percentage of your sales due to the exposure they give you."

I nod in understanding. "That makes sense. So, how can I help spread the word about your paintings?" I ask because I really do want to help her.

"That's really kind of you, but you don't have to do that." She gets up from the table and takes her plate over to the sink.

"Leave the dishes, Cassie. I will take care of them. And I'm serious, how can I help you?"

She shrugs. "I guess if you hear of anyone wanting some art, then you can give them my name and website." I make a mental note to send the website to Aly, Valerie, and Sosie to see if they know anyone who wants to commission any paintings.

"Can I have a cookie, Cassie?" Izzy asks her and I sense Cassie is relieved the subject is off her.

"You have to ask your dad."

I look over at Izzy's plate to assess how much she's eaten. "Eat two more green beans and help me with the dishes and then you can have one." Izzy grabs two green beans and stuffs them in her mouth, causing me to blow out a breath in exasperation. "That's too much food at once, Iz. I don't want you choking." She nods her head while chewing and I laugh.

Cassie walks over and starts to reach for my plate, but I grab her wrist to stop her. "You're off-duty, remember? I've got this." Cassie looks down at my hand and swallows. Her gaze then returns to mine and we stare at each other for a few moments. Her skin feels just as I remembered—soft, silky and warm. She nods without saying a word and I reluctantly let go of her. She puts my plate back down in front of me and steps back.

"You guys have fun tomorrow. I'll be back Wednesday morning bright and early." She gives me a small smile before walking over to Izzy and kissing her on the head. We say goodbye and I watch her grab a tote bag from the living room and leave. I look over at Izzy, who looks sad to see Cassie go.

"How do you think we can help Cassie sell more paintings, Iz?" I ask her, curious to see what that smart, little brain of hers comes up with.

"We can sell them on the street with some lemonade," she suggests, and I chuckle at her adorable idea. "Why don't we buy one, Daddy?"

"We can, but I have a feeling she won't take any money from us. Besides, she's painting you a whole wall in your playroom." But Izzy's suggestion forms an idea in my head. I grab my phone to call my sister-in-law. Aly picks up on the third ring.

"Aly, I need your help with something." Then I proceed to tell her my idea.

CHAPTER 18
CASSIE

know every child is different and I shouldn't have "favorites" amongst the children I have watched over the years, but if I did, Isabella McNeer would be at the top. She's so easy to please that it makes our days go by so terribly fast. It's hard to believe one month has already passed since I've joined the McNeer family, yet it feels like I've been with Izzy for years.

Because Gunnar is on the road a lot, Izzy and I have set up a daily routine that he follows on my days off to keep things regular for her. It makes the transition of him being home to going back on the road easier for Izzy if her routines stay consistent.

I've started to enjoy going to the games, especially our game day rituals of baking victory cupcakes and making Gunnar a sign for Izzy to hold while we're in the suite for him to see when he's at bat. Right before he gets into the batter's box, he points his bat straight at our suite to acknowledge her. It's the cutest thing in the world and makes me swoon every time he does it.

Which leads me back to my biggest problem with this job: I'm still horribly attracted to my boss. Trying to stay professional when I'm around him is becoming increasingly more difficult as the days go by and I discover more about who he is as a family man. When he's home, it's hard not to drool over how handsome he is and my ovaries want to explode every time I see sweet moments between him and Izzy. The most torturous of times are at night after Izzy falls asleep. I try to hide out in the playroom and paint until it's time for bed, but even then, I barely sleep. I toss and turn on those nights because my mind wonders about what he's doing in his room, if he's changed his mind and has started hooking up with other women while on the road, and if he still thinks about our night together because I sure do.

All. The. Damn. Time.

When we're at his games, I try to engage with anyone who's in the suite with us, because if I don't keep my mind occupied, I will stare at him all game long, admiring how nice his ass looks in those baseball pants.

Exactly what I'm doing right now.

"Earth to Cassie." I hear Grace call out and I reluctantly remove my gaze from him and focus on her. We had extra tickets for the suite tonight and Gavin has told me I can invite whomever I want when it's not filled, so I've been extending that invitation to my dad, Grace and her parents.

"You really need to act like you're watching the game because if you don't move your head more often, everyone will be able to tell who you're fixated on and the jig is up," Grace says with a wicked grin.

I give her a warning look to *shut the hell up* and she just laughs. "Nothing's going on, Grace."

"I find that hard to believe, but since there's little ears around, we'll have this discussion later." She looks down at Izzy, who is sitting on my lap, her head leaning back against my chest. "She's about to fall asleep if you keep rubbing her forehead like that."

I tilt my head and look down at her. Sure enough, her

eyelids are half closed. "It's almost the seventh inning stretch, so we'll leave then." When we have night games, leaving during the seventh inning is perfect because there's no traffic. We quickly get home and get ready for bed.

"What time do I need to meet you on Saturday for the art crawl?" Grace asks and I smile with excitement. Lately I've seen an increase in sales off my website with both paintings and merchandise, so I put that money into buying a booth at the Art Market in Germantown. Being free to paint at night has increased my portfolio and I'm excited to show it off this weekend in hopes of more sales and visibility. Grace will help with sales and transactions while I network amongst the curators of the galleries that interest me. If they like what they see, then maybe I'll score another local exhibition.

"Aly and Gavin got back last night from his tour, so they said I can drop Izzy off at two in the afternoon for a sleepover. The crawl starts at six, so meet me there at four o'clock to set-up."

"This better prove to you that I still follow the 'hoes before bros' mantra since I'm missing Carter's game to help you." Grace and Carter's "fake" relationship has turned sexual and while she claims she's just having fun with him, I have a hard time believing feelings haven't gotten involved yet.

I roll my eyes at her. "For someone who isn't in a real relationship, you sure act like the doting girlfriend."

"Shh, I don't want my parents to hear." She looks over at them and sees they're having a conversation with my dad. "How else do you expect me to keep up appearances if I don't play the part?"

"I just don't want you to get hurt." I give her a knowing look and she waves me off.

"I won't. Trust me, I know what I'm doing."

I don't believe her for one second, but I let the discussion drop. I look at the scoreboard to see we're one out away from the seventh inning. "I'm going to get Izzy home." I nudge

Izzy to make sure she's awake. "C'mon, Peanut, let's get you out of here." We stand-up and make our rounds saying goodbye to everyone.

"I'll walk you to your car, kiddo," my dad offers and says goodbye to Grace and her parents.

"You don't have to do that, Dad. You could stay to watch the game."

"Nah, I'd rather make sure you get safely to your car. Besides, I'm tired and can watch the rest of the game from the comfort of my own home."

I nod in understanding and we head toward the elevators and take them down to the first level. We walk in comfortable silence until we exit the stadium and then my dad asks, "How is everything going, honey?"

"Really great, actually." He helps get Izzy into her booster seat and buckles her seat belt for her. Once she's secure, I shut the door and turn toward him. "Izzy is such a great kid and we have a fun routine down that she seems to enjoy."

"Good." He moves closer to me and lowers his voice. "What about her father?"

"What about him?" I eye my dad suspiciously, not under-standing why he is asking about Gunnar.

"Is he treating you right? Are you comfortable around him? I was a little concerned when I heard you would be moving in with a single dad."

Oh, if he only knew. "My relationship with him is strictly business, Dad. He has been a gentleman." *A gentleman in the naughtiest of ways.*

"Glad to hear this. Is he dating anyone?"

God, I hope not. "Not that I'm aware of."

He tilts his head toward Izzy's car window. "And what about the mother?"

I shake my head. "Not involved and I don't know why."

"Okay." He nods and pulls me in for a hug. "You know I'm always here for you if you need anything or need to talk."

"You're the best, Dad." I give him a tight squeeze. "I need to get her home."

"Love you, kiddo."

"Love you too, Dad. Get home safe." And with that I get into my car and head back to Gunnar's house.

⊘ ◊ ▽ ☕

'm riding high from the success of the art crawl when I arrive at my dad's house late Saturday night. He helps me unload all my supplies and unsold artwork back into my room and once we're done, he goes back to sleep. I take a shower and get ready for bed. After I do my night-time routine, I slip in between the covers and get settled into bed. Just when I'm about to fall asleep, I hear my phone buzz on the nightstand. I roll over to pick it up and see I have a text from Gunnar. Concerned there might be something wrong with Izzy, I open my messages to read his text.

> Gunnar: How did tonight go?

I blink in surprise, happy to see that he cares enough to ask. It's past midnight, he's got to be exhausted from his game today.

> It was amazing, thank you for asking. I sold a couple of pieces and networked with two curators from very reputable galleries that fit my painting style. They gave me their cards and I plan to reach out to them next week.

> Gunnar: That's wonderful, Cassie. Happy to hear tonight was a success.

Gunnar: What are you doing right now?

I'm in bed. What are you doing right now?

Gunnar: I'm at The Rooftop Replay with a couple of the guys. I wasn't ready to go home to an empty house after our loss tonight.

The Rooftop Replay is an exclusive bar on the tenth floor of the Regency Hotel where the players go to hang out in the VIP area so they will not be bothered. Only the wealthy and the good-looking get in. My stomach drops with disappointment to know he's out right now. I can only imagine all the beautiful women that are there.

I'm sorry you guys lost tonight.

Gunnar: Thanks, but shit happens. There's no crying in baseball, right? :)

Did Izzy have a great time with Austin? I checked in with Aly and she sent me a couple of photos of them playing together.

Gunnar: She was very happy that they were back from tour. That's really sweet of you to check in on her during your night off.

It gives me peace of mind to know she's doing well when I'm not there. Thanks again for letting me take off tonight. Very kind of you to check in. Go have fun with the guys. I'm sure there are some beautiful women vying for your attention right now, so get off your phone, silly.

I hit send and cringe at my message. The last thing I want

him to do is talk to other women, but I have no claim on Gunnar. He's my boss and that's it. If he wants to bring someone home, tonight would be the perfect opportunity. The thought makes my stomach churn and I fight the urge to throw up. I'm about to turn my phone off when it buzzes again with a text.

> Gunnar: The only beautiful woman I want to pay attention to is the one I'm texting with right now.

I close my eyes and sigh with a content smile. This shouldn't make me as happy as it does. I should tell him he's crossing the line, but I don't.

> Gunnar: I'm sorry, I shouldn't have said that. It was unprofessional of me.

> Gunnar: Please accept my apology, Cassie?

> No, you shouldn't have said what you did. It was unprofessional, but...

I wait a moment to torture him for a little bit before I finish my sentence.

> I liked it.

When he doesn't respond right away, I wonder if I'm the one who's gone too far, but then a new text comes through from him:

> Gunnar: Sweet dreams, Cassie. I know who I'll be dreaming about tonight.

I press my thighs together and groan. I walk my fingers down to my core and start playing with my clit. I imagine that it's him entering me, his fingers playing with me and it doesn't take long for me to quietly orgasm.

Within minutes, I'm asleep, dreaming of my sexy, green-eyed boss.

CHAPTER 19

GUNNAR

oday was scheduled to be a day off, but all players had to report to the team's annual charity golf tournament. Cassie arrived to the house early and made eggs and pancakes for Izzy and me. Our text exchange from last night wasn't brought up, but she seemed distant and shy this morning. I need to stop being so freely open with my feelings when it pertains to how much I want her. Aly would tell me I'm playing games, but that isn't my intent. It's crystal clear that we both want each other, but even though we agreed that we don't want a relationship, I can't risk us becoming physical again and having feelings develop.

Stop lying to yourself, Gunnar. Feelings for her have already developed.

Fuck, if that's not the truth. To me, no other woman holds a candle to Cassie. She occupies my thoughts constantly. It's unhealthy to want someone as much as I want her, but I don't know if my feelings are lust at first sight again like they were with Tasha or if this is something more.

I shake my head as I drive home from the tournament. It can't be anything more. She's young and has her whole life ahead of her. I'm only a couple years out of retirement and have a daughter to raise. I don't even know where I'll be after the end of this season. Nashville is where her family and friends are. Texas is my home and once the season is done, Izzy and I will probably head back there until I know where I'm going or until I decide to retire. I don't want to start something with Cassie only to have to end things once the season is over.

The thought just reaffirms that I need to stop behaving like a horny teenager and remind myself when I have lecherous thoughts about her that she's my employee. Nothing can happen between us.

Nothing.

I'm pulling into my driveway when my phone rings. Tasha's name flashes on the screen and my mood immediately darkens. I've been ignoring her calls for the past week because I'm still pissed that she's gone months without calling Izzy. She's left me a dozen voicemails and texts, but I haven't listened or read any of them. There's nothing she can say that will make me forgive her for abandoning our child. Her parents claim she's been in rehab, but they've also lied for her in the past. For years they were in denial of what a terrible mother she was, and it's only been recently that they've apologized to me for enabling their daughter's behavior. I don't know why she's suddenly trying to get a hold of me and quite honestly, I don't care. I send the call to voicemail and get out of my car to go into the house.

"Hello?" I call out, but no one greets me back. I hear the faint sounds of music playing, so I walk to the back windows and that's where I find the girls. They are outside on the back porch and by the looks of it, they are gardening. They are facing each other, dancing and singing the lyrics to the music of Coldplay's "Higher Power". While Cassie in a bikini top and cut off shorts makes my mouth run dry, I'm mesmerized by the sight of my daughter. She's wearing her butterfly one-piece bathing suit, with purple rain boots and a hat shielding her face from the sun. I don't think I've ever seen her radiate this kind of happiness before. I know she loved being with her grandparents, but it dawns on me that she needed someone younger like Cassie, who can match her energy.

When the song ends and a different one begins, they walk over to one of the planters and inspect its contents. I hear Cassie instruct Izzy to get the hose so they can water their garden. Izzy runs over to the side, grabs it and brings it to her. Cassie proceeds to show her how to turn the nozzle and spray the plants. After she's done demonstrating, she hands the hose back to Izzy. *Uh-oh, that's a mistake,* and sure enough, my daughter proves me right by turning the hose on Cassie.

Cassie screams and Izzy's evil giggling has me throwing my head back in laughter. Cassie tries to grab the hose from her, but Izzy gets her square in the face. Cassie turns her body to the side and tries to dodge the flowing water, but Izzy is being relentless. Eventually, Cassie pries the hose out of Izzy's hands and it's payback time. Izzy's screaming, trying to run from Cassie and they're both soaked to the bone. Cassie eventually turns off the hose, scoops up Izzy in her arms and starts to tickle her. She puts her down and holds her upright until Izzy regains her balance and then kisses her on her forehead. The love that shines from Cassie's eyes for my child tightens my chest with emotions I should not feel for my nanny.

I continue to watch them for a couple more minutes and decide to make my presence known. I grab some towels from the laundry room and open the back door. "Can I join in on the fun?"

"Daddy!" Izzy runs straight toward me and plasters her wet body against my legs, my shorts absorbing the water off her body. "Cassie got me with the hose."

I bend down and wrap Izzy's towel around her back. "Yes, but only after you got her first." I look up to say something to Cassie but the words die in my throat as my eyes widen and freeze on the hard buds of her nipples protruding against the fabric of her bikini.

"Looks like you're both excited to see me." Cassie follows my gaze, looks down at herself and gasps. She crosses her arms over her chest, her cheeks flush red with embarrassment. I chuckle and hand over the other towel I brought out for her. She yanks it out of my hands and wraps her body in it.

"Izzy, show me what you girls are planting." I walk over to the planter they were working on when I arrived.

"We made two fairy gardens and planted some flowers that will bring us butterflies," she exclaims in excitement, and I laugh.

"That is very cool. You have to make sure the plants get watered every day so when their flowers bloom, the butterflies will eventually come. Do you think you will remember to do that?"

She nods with a smile. "Uh-huh."

"Why don't we go inside and write it on our daily to-do list?" Cassie suggests while walking toward the door. Izzy runs after her and I follow both girls inside and up the stairs to the playroom. I watch Cassie help Izzy write it on their list that is written on one of the whiteboards.

"Cassie, why don't you take the rest of the day off?" I offer. "Izzy and I are going on a daddy/daughter date to the movies and then to dinner at my brother's house."

"I want Cassie to come too," Izzy interjects and gives me a look of hope.

"I'm sure Cassie has things she would like to do by herself." I glance from Izzy to Cassie, who gives me a small smile.

"Lucky girl that you get to go on a date with your dad! Let's go pick out something fun for you to wear to the movies." Cassie holds out her hand for Izzy, who immediately takes it and they walk out together to get her ready.

zzy looks adorable tonight, Gunnar. Where did you get her outfit?" Aly asks while the adults watch the kids try to catch fireflies in their backyard after we eat dinner.

I look over at Izzy and think for a moment, not remembering buying her the pastel rainbow tulle skirt she is wearing with a jean jacket and white top. Then it dawns on me where she got it from. "Cassie made the skirt for her."

"That nanny of yours is like Mary Poppins, except hotter."

Ain't that the truth.

"Maybe I should introduce her to my brother, Nick," Rowan ponders and the thought makes me scowl. Nicholas Pryor is a good-looking hockey player. No way in hell do I want him to make an introduction.

"She's not looking for a relationship right now," I tell him and can see out of the corner of my eye Aly's know-it-all smirk.

"What does Cassie do on her days off?" Valerie asks.

"Tonight she's having dinner with her dad and then painting. Sometimes she goes to exhibitions to support other local artists."

"Her work is remarkable. I was scoping out her website the other day and I bought one of her paintings for our new offices." Valerie and Rowan own their own CPA firm and are rapidly growing, so they just opened a second office close to downtown Nashville.

"I've already asked her to make something for the new baby's room," Aly chimes in while rubbing her belly.

"But you don't know what we're having yet," Gavin comments in confusion.

"As long as you know the theme and color palette of the room, you can still paint something without knowing what the gender is." She rolls her eyes and I smirk because as always, my sister-in-law is right.

"That's really great of you guys for supporting her. I appreciate it."

"It's so great that you care so much about her and her art," Aly comments back with a sly smile. I narrow my eyes, hoping she can mentally hear me telling her to shut up.

"Don't tell her I'm telling you this, because I don't want to get her hopes up, but I actually know someone who owns an art gallery in New York," Valerie says with a cocky smile on her face.

"Do I know who this person is?" Aly asks.

"Maybe. Do you remember Michael McDermott in high school? He was in my grade but very popular?"

Recognition lights up Aly's face. "I actually do remember. He was hot. All the girls swooned over him."

Valerie nods. "Yup, that's the one. Anyway, he owns a big-time art gallery in Brooklyn, so I reached out to him about Cassie. I sent him her website and he called me right away."

"*Who* is this guy again?" Rowan asks in a demanding voice.

"I went to high school with him and he's gay. Stop being so alpha." She rolls her eyes at him and I chuckle at how the two sisters handle their husbands so similarly.

"What did he think about her paintings?" I ask, dread starting to creep inside my belly.

"He said he will take a look at her portfolio in the next couple of days."

"If he likes her stuff, then what does that mean?" Sosie chimes in with a question.

"It means he might offer her a spot at one of his exhibitions."

I sit up a little straighter with this news. "Wait, does that mean she would have to go to New York?"

Valerie thinks for a moment. "Probably because they'll have an opening night for her."

I slouch back into my chair, not liking the idea of Cassie going to New York. *If she goes to New York and does well, then she might want to stay there forever, leaving you and Izzy.*

"Why do you seem upset by this, Gunnar?" Aly gives me a pointed look. "Is it because you don't want her to leave you?"

"*Izzy* would be very upset if she left us," I emphasize, my eyes warning her to cut it out.

"I don't think Izzy would be the only one upset."

"Alyson, stop!" I growl out, my patience snapping at her meddling.

"Ooh, he called you Alyson." Valerie looks over at her sister with a mischievous grin on her face.

"Don't talk to my wife in that tone of voice." I glance at Gavin, who is giving me a warning look.

I look over at Aly and apologize. "I'm sorry for my tone, Aly, but please stop insinuating things that aren't true."

She scoffs. "What am I insinuating that isn't true?"

I just shake my head at my sister-in-law because she knows she's pushing my buttons on purpose.

"What *is* the deal with you and Cassie?" Gavin asks and I wonder if Aly slipped and told him.

My head whips toward her and I glare at her. "You told him, didn't you?"

"I didn't, asshole, but way to take the bait and oust yourself."

I glance at Gavin and his face confirms it. *Shit, he got me.*

I sigh in resignation. "Something in the past happened, but there's nothing going on now."

"I find that very hard to believe," Rowan pipes in with his two cents. "We all see how you two eye fuck each other. The sexual tension is so high that it rubs off on us and I have to go home and bang my wife. Not that I needed your endorphins rubbing off on me to do that in the first place."

"TMI, Rowan." Aly covers her ears. "I don't want any mental images of you having sex with my sister." Rowan laughs and Valerie hits him in the chest to stop.

"Jesus Christ, what did you do, Gunnar?" Gavin demands in a stern voice and I know I'm not getting out of here without telling them, so I give them the short, condensed version. Everyone's quiet for a moment when I finish the story.

"This is straight out of a romance movie," Valerie sighs and Aly nods in agreement with her.

"Except there's not going to be a happy ending, not for Cassie anyway," Sosie says so matter-of-factly that for a moment, I want to argue that there could be if I was willing to put my heart back on the line.

"Cassie says she doesn't want a relationship, so maybe *I* would be the one to get hurt. Either way, we're not taking the risk of finding out."

"Gunnar, I think she cares about you and if you tell her what you've been doing—"

"Aly, no!" I give her a warning look and this time, she keeps her mouth closed.

This is the perfect time to get out of here. "Izzy, it's time to go." I stand up out of my chair and hug everyone goodbye. "Thanks for having us."

"I'll walk you out," Gavin offers.

"You don't have to," I tell him as I watch Izzy give everyone a hug and kiss goodbye.

"I want to." I inwardly groan, knowing that I'm about to get one of his lectures.

He carries Izzy over his shoulder like a sack of potatoes and tickles her belly as we walk out the front door to my car. He opens her door for her and gives her a kiss after she buckles herself into her booster seat. He shuts the door and walks me over to the driver's side of the car.

"You're an honorable guy, Gunnar. You were dealt a shitty hand with Tasha, but that doesn't mean every woman is going to be like her."

"She's too young, Gavin…" I start but he interrupts.

"Don't bring age into this. Do you like her and I don't mean just as your nanny?"

"Yes, I like her," I groan. "I don't fucking want to, but I do."

"Then either be with her or don't. It's that simple."

"No, it's not that simple," I argue, my voice rising.

"You're the one making it complicated." He jabs his finger into my chest, pushing me against the car. "Do the right thing by her: either date her or treat her as your employee and stop playing games." God, he knows me so well. I haven't even told him half the things I've said to her and I certainly haven't told him about her responses back.

"What if she's the one playing games and leaves me when it's time to move on?"

He looks at me as if I'm the dumbest human on the planet. "Then she wasn't good enough to be your forever if that's how she's going to treat you."

I shake my head. "I just don't want to take that risk if that's going to be the outcome."

"Then I guess you'll never know, Brother." He points to Izzy in the car. "Your little girl needs a mother figure in her life. *You* need a woman in your life. You say you don't, but Gunnar, you deserve to find love and I think this girl makes you happy. I haven't seen you this lively in a long time and I know it isn't just because of your new team."

He walks toward me and pulls me in for a hug. "I love you, Gunnar, but life is a risk and sometimes you have to risk losing your heart again for the one who might be worth it."

He lets go of me, turns around and starts walking back to

the house. "I'll see you in the suite after your game tomorrow."

I watch him walk in and shut the door. I take a deep breath, get in the car and start the engine. I look in the rearview mirror at my beautiful daughter. He's right, she does need someone other than me in her life and I have no doubt that Cassie would be the perfect fit for that role.

If that's a role she would even want.

But the bigger question is: Am I mentally strong enough to handle the rejection of not being wanted again?

I don't know if I want to find that out.

CHAPTER 20
CASSIE

'm sitting at the park, watching Izzy play on the playground when I get a text from Valerie Pryor.

Valerie: You're going to be receiving a call from a man named Michael McDermott with a 718 area code. Pick up the phone when you see that number. Do NOT let it go to voicemail. Trust me."

There's been so many silver linings that have come out of being Izzy's nanny and two of them are my budding friend-ships with Valerie and Aly. I've gotten to know Valerie better from spending time with her at the games and since Aly's been back in town, we've taken the kids together to the zoo and the splash pad. They're both so generous, kind, and fun to be around and I'm grateful that they see me as more than just a nanny.

Okay, but are you going to fill me in on what this call is about so I can be prepared to talk to him?

> Valerie: Let's just say that you get to check
> something off your bucket list.

I frown at her response, trying to remember when we discussed our bucket list items and what I told her. I thought we talked mostly about traveling. She and Rowan went to the Greek Isles for their honeymoon and I know that's on my list of places to see. I don't know what else I've told her that would qualify being on my bucket list besides travel and dreams for my art career. I wish she would just tell me why he's calling, but I guess I will find out soon enough.

I focus my attention back on Izzy and smile when I see her start talking to another little kid at the top of the slide. She's so good at engaging with other children that I know she's going to make lots of friends in kindergarten next year. I look over at the adults on the other side, wondering which one of the adults is this kid's parent. There's a woman with long, brown hair wearing sunglasses sitting across from me on the bench. She's watching Izzy and this child intently, so maybe that's his mom because the couple who are on the opposite end of the jungle gym are playing with their baby.

I continue watching Izzy when I feel my phone vibrate in my hand. The 718 phone number flashes across my screen and suddenly I feel nervous. I swipe to the right and answer the call.

"Hi, is this Cassie Warner?" asks a man with a calm, soothing voice.

"Yes, it is," I confirm, my gaze still on Izzy as I talk.

"Great, my name is Michael McDermott and I'm the owner of McDermott's Art Gallery in Brooklyn, New York." My mouth runs dry and my pulse starts to race as my brain registers the words 'art gallery' and 'New York'. "I went to high school with Valerie Pryor and she sent me your website. From what I've seen so far, I'm very impressed with your work."

"W-wow," I stutter because I'm completely taken off-guard. "Thank you so much for your kind words."

He chuckles. "You're welcome, but I'm just being honest. I know this is last minute, but we had a cancellation of an artist who was supposed to be in our July exhibition. I normally don't take artists outside of the New York area, but because I'm friends with Valerie and trust her judgement, I'm willing to take a chance on you. Would you be interested in the open spot? It's a multi-artist exhibition, so we would only have room for two of your smaller paintings or one large one."

My mouth drops open in shock and I'm at a loss for words. Now I remember telling Valerie that having one of my paintings being displayed in an art gallery in New York was not only on my bucket list, but would be a dream come true for me.

"It would be an honor, Mr. McDermott! Thank you so much for this opportunity." My voice is a higher octave than normal due to the excitement that I can't contain. "What do you need from me to get this ball rolling and confirm my spot?"

"I will send you a contract with our terms of agreement. Read it over and once you sign it, then your spot is reserved. The first thing I will need from you is your headshot and bio so we can put that up on our website for the exhibition. I will send you the dimensions of your designated wall space and you can decide from there if you will be submitting two small paintings or a large one. When you decide which piece of art you're submitting, we will then need a couple of sentences on what your painting is about."

Even though he can't see me, I am nodding like crazy. This is the same process I went through locally with one of the galleries here in town. "Was there any specific painting from my website that you feel would fit best with your gallery?"

"We always encourage the artist to go with the painting

that has evicted the most emotions out of them that they are willing to part with."

I love this advice from him. "The one I'm working on now is the one that's bringing out my vulnerability. I'm halfway done with it. When is the exhibition?" I inquire, praying I have enough time to finish it.

"It's the evening of July seventeenth. Doors open at six o'clock, artist introductions start at seven and it should wrap up around eight. We will need your artwork in house the Monday before the event. Will that be a problem?"

That's less than two months away, but I should be able to finish the painting by then if I drop everything else except for Aly's baby nursery painting. Gavin is having a joint party for her and for Gunnar moving to Tennessee next weekend and I wanted to present it to her then. My mind races to try to recall when Gunnar's All-Star break is, but it shouldn't matter. This is a once in a lifetime opportunity that I'm confident he would want me to take.

"It shouldn't be a problem. I can send you a photo tonight of what the painting looks like so far and what my vision for it plans to be."

"Sounds great. I look forward to seeing it."

"Thank you, again, Mr. McDermott. You are making my dreams come true," I tell him with a laugh.

"It's my pleasure and please call me Michael."

We say our goodbyes and I hang up. Izzy is still playing with the little boy from earlier. They are taking turns chasing each other down the slide and seeing who can make it back up to the top the fastest. I check my watch and see we have about fifteen more minutes until we need to go home and get ready for Gunnar's game tonight. Since Izzy is having fun and we have some time, I call Valerie.

"Do you have good news for me?" she asks as soon as she picks up the phone.

"Valerie! Oh my gosh, I can't believe you did that for me! I don't know how I can ever repay you," I tell her, tears of happiness threatening to spill down my cheeks.

"I didn't do a thing. I only had the connection—you're the one with the talent. Tell me everything!"

I relay my conversation with Michael and she squeals with joy. "I'm so excited for you! We need to celebrate."

She continues talking but I stop paying attention as I watch the dark-haired woman get up off the bench and approach Izzy and the little boy. From the other side of the jungle gym, a man walks around and calls out a name that the little boy responds to. He says goodbye to Izzy and slides down to the man I'm presuming is his dad. The dark-haired woman walks up to the slide and starts talking to Izzy. *What is this woman doing?*

"Val, let me call you right back," I tell her and hang up without hearing her response. I stand up and start walking toward them. As I get closer, I hear the woman say to Izzy, "Do you remember me? I'm your mommy," and I start to run.

"Get away from her!" I yell and stand right in front of the slide to catch Izzy when she slides down. "Izzy, slide down please. It's time to go home." She looks between me and the woman claiming to be her mother and I can see the panic starting to set in on her little face.

"Please, I only wanted to see her," the woman pleads, holding her hands up defensively. She takes off her glasses and places them on the top of her head. Now that I have a good look at her face, I can tell this is her mom. While Izzy has her dad's coloring, her facial structure is mostly her mother's. Aly has mentioned Tasha briefly to me, but I'm still clueless as to why she's not in her daughter's life. She's a beautiful woman and I immediately feel resentment toward her due to how she's treated Gunnar and her daughter.

"Then you should've called to make an arrangement with Gunnar."

"I've tried calling him, but he won't pick up my calls or

answer my texts." She starts crying and I can't stop staring at her. "I know he hates me. I've been a horrible person to him and to her, but I'm trying to be better. I just got out of rehab after six months and she's the first person I wanted to see."

"Cassie?" Izzy's small voice pulls me out of my stare down and I glance up at her. I try smiling at her, but I know she can sense something's wrong.

"Slide down, Peanut. It's time to go home." She hesitates and quickly glances at Tasha before looking at me. "I will catch you. See, I'm standing right in front of the opening." She glances over the guardrail to see where I'm standing and nods. I hear her slide down and as soon as she makes it to the bottom, I grab her and pick her up. She wraps her arms and legs around me and holds on tight. She looks at Tasha with hesitant eyes. I don't know when the last time she's seen her mom was, but I know she hasn't seen her here in Tennessee, nor has she talked to her on the phone.

"Please," Tasha pleads and reaches out, but I step back, not letting her touch Izzy's. "I just want to see my little girl." She starts hyperventilating and there's no way this woman is faking this. "I... want... to... be... in... her...life," she stammers in between breaths. My heart hurts as I watch the tears of pain streaming down her face.

"Go back to wherever you are staying and don't leave," I command in a firm voice. "I will talk to Gunnar and get him to call you back."

"Oh, thank you so much," she clasps her hands together in prayer and nods at me.

"He's going to be very mad at you for just showing up here. Do *not* follow us home," I warn her. "I will call the cops and have you arrested for trespassing and stalking."

"I won't." She shakes her head and wipes at her tears. "Please have him call me." She looks at Izzy and smiles. "I'm sorry if I scared you, honey. I'm just so happy to see you. I love you."

Izzy just stares at her. "You'll be hearing from Gunnar," I tell her and turn around and carry Izzy to our car. I walk as fast as I can and am thankful that I got front row parking today.

"Everything is okay, Peanut," I reassure her while I buckle her into her booster seat.

"I want my daddy." Her voice is soft and she looks scared, but uncertain as to why she should be.

"We're going to call him right now. Hey, why don't we see if Austin can play?" That seems to perk her up a little and she nods.

I shut her door and race around to the driver's side. I get in and lock the doors. I don't see Tasha anywhere, but that might mean she is in her car, waiting to follow me even though I told her not to. If she's a smart woman, she'll go back to wherever she is staying.

Not wanting to take any chances, I call Aly first. "Hey, are you home?" I ask as soon as she answers. I start the car and pull out of my parking space.

"Yes, why? Is everything okay?" Her voice is filled with concern and I know she can hear the panic in my tone.

"Tasha just showed up at the park and even though I told her not to follow me home, I don't know if she'll listen. Since you live in a gated community, I know she won't be able to get through the security guard without being on the list of approval."

"Come over now," she demands with a stern tone. "Does Gunnar know?"

"I'm calling him now. See you in fifteen minutes."

I hang up with her and call Gunnar. I glance at the time on my dashboard, praying he has his phone or his smart watch on him. It's too early for batting practice, so he's either working out or in team meetings.

"Cassie?" he answers on the third ring and I sag with relief.

"I need you to meet me at Aly's house *right now*." I look in my rearview mirror while I talk to make sure I'm not being followed "Your ex just showed up at the park and started talking to Izzy. It was only for a brief couple seconds and then I intervened. I think it's best we don't go to the game tonight and stay at Aly's since I'm not sure if she's following us or not."

"I'll be right there," he growls and hangs up.

I put my phone down and glance at Izzy in my mirror. She is staring out the window with a pensive expression. "Iz, want to listen to our playlist?" I don't bother waiting for her response. I grab my phone, open my music app and start the playlist. "Beautiful Day" by U2 starts to fill the car and I start singing the lyrics, hoping she joins in like she usually does.

"Cassie?" she asks and I turn the music down to hear her.

"Yes, Peanut?"

"Is my mommy coming with us to Aunt Aly's?" I swallow, not knowing how to answer her question.

"No, but your daddy is going to talk to her."

"Will I see her later?" she asks and I wince, hating to hear the hope in her little voice.

"Do you want to see her?" I question, curious as to what is going on in her little mind.

She doesn't answer at first but then says, "I think so."

"Okay, well, we can tell your daddy that when we see him," I reassure her and smile at her in the rearview mirror.

"I haven't seen her in a long time. Why is that, Cassie?"

My heart breaks at her question. "I don't know, Iz, but your daddy is going to meet us at Aunt Aly's house and we can ask him, okay?"

She nods and looks back out the window again. I sing out the lyrics, waiting impatiently for her little lips to start moving in chorus with mine and finally, they do. As if she senses me watching her, she looks in the mirror and smiles. I smile back and continue singing while focusing on our drive to Aly's, but my mind flashes back to the image of Tasha, crying out for her child. *What happened that she hasn't been in her life for a while?*

Gunnar has a lot of explaining to do.

CHAPTER 21

GUNNAR

Rage is brewing inside of me like trapped steam inside a pressure cooker and all I want to do is get to my little girl. I explained to Declan that I have a family situation I needed to attend to and he let me take the night off. I'm speeding to Aly and Gavin's house, needing to see with my own eyes that Izzy is okay.

I can't believe Tasha has the balls to show up here unannounced. How did she even find us? She hasn't called Izzy in over six months and I wasn't going to be the one to remind her that she has a daughter to speak to. Izzy isn't just some convenience she gets to pay attention to whenever she feels like it.

It takes me twenty minutes to get to Gavin's house from the ballpark due to traffic. As soon as I get out of the car, I race to the front door and ring the doorbell.

Gavin opens the door and gives me a hug. "The girls are upstairs playing with Austin in his playroom."

"Thanks for having them over," I tell him while we climb the stairs to their second floor.

"No need to thank me. I'm glad Cassie thought about

coming here instead of going home. The security guard at the gate has reported no followers so far."

"Good."

We get to the hallway and round the corner into the playroom. Cassie and Aly are sitting on the couch talking while Austin and Izzy are playing inside a fort made-up with sheets and blankets. Hearing her little voice puts me at ease and I'm grateful to see she's bossing her cousin around like usual. I put my finger to my lips to signal Cassie and Aly not to announce my presence. I grab the hem of one of the sheets and quickly yank it up in the air.

"Boo!" I yell and the two kids scream in fright.

"Daddy!" Izzy crawls out of the fort and hugs my legs. "You scared me."

I pick her up and hold her tightly to me. "I'm sorry for scaring you. I was just playing around."

She pulls back and fists her hands on my chest. "I saw mommy today at the park!"

I swallow and muster up a fake smile. "I heard. How did that make you feel?"

She shrugs. "Confused at first because I didn't remember her, but then happy she finally came and saw me. Cassie said we had to go though, so I didn't get to play with her. Will I see her tomorrow?"

"Not sure. I will have to call her and see." Fuck, this is exactly what I didn't want to happen. Now I have to arrange something with Tasha... if she even has the time. Who knows why she's here and how long she'll be in town. I will find all of this out once I call her and chew her ass out.

I give Izzy a kiss before putting her down. Austin also comes out of the fort and I pick him up to flip him upside down. Once I put him back on the floor, the kids go back in it to continue playing.

Aly and Cassie are standing up and they both walk over to me. Aly gives me a hug and I thank her for having us over.

"Oh, stop." She pulls back and waves a hand at me. "You know you guys could move in here if you wanted to."

"We are fine at the house. There haven't been any issues. In fact, I don't think people know I'm even living there. Cassie is the one outside the most with Izzy." I look over at Cassie, who gives me a tight smile. "Good thinking about coming here instead of going home."

She nods but doesn't acknowledge my comment. "Can we go somewhere private to talk?"

I'm sure today was quite shocking for Cassie given the fact that I've barely talked about Tasha and her lack of involvement in Izzy's life. I owe her an explanation and since Izzy's preoccupied with her cousin, now would be the most convenient time.

"Sure," I agree and look at Gavin and Aly. "Do you guys mind watching Izzy while we go downstairs to talk?"

"Take your time," Aly suggests and Gavin gets on the floor and crawls underneath the tent to be with the kids in the fort.

"Thanks guys." I extend my arm out to Cassie for her to go first and I follow her downstairs into the kitchen.

Cassie wastes no time on small talk. "Tell me everything about Tasha, Gunnar."

I blow out a breath and rake my hand through my hair. "Let's sit down then." We take a seat at the counter and I tell her everything about Tasha and the events leading up to today. She listens intently and it actually feels good telling her everything.

"So when Tasha moved to California, how frequently was she calling to talk to Izzy?" she asks.

She moved two years ago, so I had to stop and think about it. "At first, it was every day and then as time went on, it started dwindling down to only twice a week. The last six months have been the longest she has ever gone without calling."

"Didn't you find that odd?" Cassie questions with narrowed eyes. "Were you not concerned about her well-being?"

I scoff at that. "Fuck no. She hasn't been concerned about her child's well-being enough to call her consistently so why should I be concerned about hers?"

"I get it, Gunnar. You are angry and bitter, but she's your child's mother."

"Yeah, and she chose partying over her own family. Izzy is better off without her in her life."

Cassie smiles sadly at me. "My mother was an alcoholic as well. My parents divorced when I was in high school and she eventually died from the disease, so I understand your resentment."

My chest tightens and the overwhelming need to comfort her washes over me. I reach over and grab her hand, squeezing it for support. "I'm sorry, Cassie. I had no idea."

"I know you didn't. I haven't offered up that information." She lets go of my hand and I already miss her touch. "But the difference between my mother and Tasha is that my mother never went to rehab for six months. Sure, she attended some Alcoholics Anonymous meetings but never stuck with it. She didn't want to put the time in to get better. Tasha cared enough to put herself through extensive rehab. Will it stick? Who knows. Some people go to rehab once and never touch a drink again. Others go to rehab multiple times and never get sober."

"Maybe her boyfriend forced her to go. I find it hard to believe Tasha would go willingly. She always had a motive."

"Maybe you're right or maybe she hit rock bottom and wanted a change. People can change if they really want to, Gunnar."

Cassie's words sink in and I see the shadows of the past lurking in her gaze. My palms are itching to grab her and hold her tightly. I hate to hear what she went through and this is exactly what I don't want for Izzy.

"What are you suggesting I do?" I ask, because I care about what she thinks. The thought of disappointing her doesn't sit right with me.

She fidgets with her hands before looking at me. "You need to meet with Tasha and hear her out. Let her talk about what she learned in rehab. Ask her if she wants to be in Izzy's life and what she thinks that will look like because she can only be in it if she's sober."

I shake my head. "I don't want to talk to her on the phone, let alone be in the same room as her."

"I get it, but it's not about you, Gunnar. It's about Izzy. Do it for her. You don't want her thinking you kept her mother from her just because of your personal feelings for Tasha."

Cassie's words hit home and I know she's right. I groan, not wanting to do it, but I will for my daughter. "Okay, I'll call her right now and go meet with her."

She places her hands over her heart and the smile she gives me makes my breath hitch. "Thank you, Gunnar."

"I'll meet you and Izzy back at the house?" I ask and she nods. We stand up and she walks me to the door. It takes all my willpower not to pull her in for a hug and instead, I wave goodbye and head to my car. Once I'm inside, I call Tasha.

She picks up right away. "Hi Gunnar. Thanks for calling me back." She doesn't say it sarcastically. In fact, her voice sounds solemn and defeated.

"Against my better judgment, it's probably best we speak in person. Where are you located?"

"I'm staying in a rental by the Green Hills Mall."

"Meet me at the cheesecake restaurant that is inside the mall. I will be there in fifteen minutes," I tell her and I can hear her sigh with relief.

"Thank you, Gunnar."

I hang up without saying another word and start to my car, praying that Tasha has changed for the sake of our daughter.

◌ ⬡ ⧓ ⬡ ◌

By the time I return home, it's past dinner time and Cassie is putting Izzy to sleep. I hear Cassie reading her a book as I near her bedroom door. I stand in the doorway and watch the two of them together, their heads touching as they get lost in the story together. *Cassie's going to make a great mother someday*, but the thought of another man touching her, let alone impregnating her, makes me clench my hand into a fist.

"Daddy!" Izzy's voice clears away my angry thoughts and I smile at her.

"Mind if I take over reading to her?" I ask Cassie, who shakes her head and moves to get out of the bed.

"Good night, Peanut, see you in the morning," Cassie tells Izzy and then glances my way. "I'll be in the playroom finishing Aly's painting if you want to talk when you're done."

I nod at her and watch her walk out of the room before resuming where she left off reading to Izzy. It doesn't take Izzy long to fall asleep. I sneak out of her bed and quietly close her door. I go to the playroom and knock, not wanting to scare Cassie while she paints. She turns around and smiles, motioning for me to come in.

"Wow, that's beautiful," I tell her as I admire her work. The sun rises above the ocean in colors that evoke warmth and joy upon looking at it.

"Thanks. She wants the baby's room to be relaxed and

inviting and to me, that's sitting on the beach, with the sun's rays shining down." I watch her tilt her head as she analyzes her painting and then looks back at me.

"It's perfect. She's going to love it."

"I hope so." She puts her brushes in a cup of water and lifts the straps of her apron over her head. "Let's sit down so you can tell me what happened with Tasha." She places her apron on the table and follows me to the couch. I sit down and Cassie sits at the opposite end from me, making sure there's ample distance between us.

I take a deep breath and begin telling her what transpired. "We met at the cheesecake restaurant inside the mall. When I first walked in, I didn't recognize her. Tasha used to wear revealing, tight clothes with her hair and make-up always done up, even when we would go to the grocery store. The Tasha that showed up tonight was the total opposite. She was still dressed nicely, but in clothes that were modest. She wore no make-up and just looked…natural." I shrug, not really knowing how else to describe her.

"I wasn't there for small talk, so as soon as we were seated, I demanded to know where the hell she's been these last six months, and why she hasn't called Izzy. She told me she has been in rehab, working on her alcohol addiction and confidence issues, and learning how to live a sober life. She got into a bad place while dating Marcus and he eventually dumped her for the woman he was cheating on her with." I give Cassie a small smile. "Talk about karma, right?"

"After Marcus kicked her out, she moved in with some friends and continued partying and spiraling out of control. Her rock bottom was getting arrested for disorderly conduct. Her parents came to California, got her out of jail and took her straight to an inpatient rehab facility in Texas. She was there for ninety days and then spent another three months in a sober living house."

"Wow," Cassie whispers. "That's a lot."

"She said getting arrested was a blessing in disguise, because if she hadn't been arrested, she probably would be dead or would have killed someone when she was drinking and driving. It made me sick when I would come home from a game to see her drunk, knowing she drove with our daughter in the car."

Cassie nods and looks down at her hands. "It's good that she sees it as a blessing. My mother got arrested numerous times and she would only last a couple of months before falling off the wagon again."

I move closer to her, feeling the urge to comfort her. "That's what I'm afraid of though. What if she's not strong enough to stay sober? I don't want Izzy exposed to that."

"Izzy would be protected by supervised visits."

"Yes, but now that Izzy is older and can start recognizing when her mother is sober or drunk, I don't want her to have to deal with that. One of the reasons I stopped picking up the phone when Tasha called was because the last couple of months before she got arrested, she would call Izzy drunk and then not remember the conversation the next morning."

"Your fear is valid, Gunnar. How did she even know where to find us?"

"I forgot that I gave her parents my new address because they wanted to send Izzy some of her favorite things that she left at their house. They gave her my address and she probably followed you guys to the park." I bring the palms of my hands up to my eyes and rub them. "Her being here is my fault. I enjoyed her silence and got stressed when she started calling again. If I had just answered her calls and let her talk to Izzy, we wouldn't be dealing with her presence."

"You don't know that though. If she's truly on a path of sobriety, she will make her way to wherever her daughter is so she can be in her life."

I look up at her and nod. "That's exactly what she said.

She wants to move here so she can be close to Izzy. Her plan is to enroll in school to get her degree in addiction counseling so she can help others."

Cassie gives me a sad smile. "That's really admirable of her."

I snort. "There's nothing admirable about Tasha."

She ignores my comment. "So what happens next?"

"She wants to see Izzy, but I told her no."

Cassie frowns. "Why not? I can be with her when she sees her."

"That's not your job, Cassie. I want a state supervisor at all visits until Tasha can be trusted and even after that, I still won't be comfortable leaving Izzy alone with her."

"Okay, but can she at least FaceTime with her until that gets set up?"

I shake my head. "I told her I needed time to think about things."

"Time to think? You leave for a road trip after tomorrow's game." Cassie stands up in frustration and looks at me. "How are you going to think about things when you are away and need to concentrate on your job?"

I stand up as well and glare at her. "Why are you acting like this is my fault? She's the one who put herself in this situation."

"You can give her my phone number to FaceTime with Izzy."

"Hell no!"

She places her hands on her hips. "Why not?"

"Because it's not your job to have to deal with her. It's mine and I don't want to do it just yet."

She throws her hands up in the air and scoffs at me. "You just aren't listening to what I'm saying," she grinds out in anger. "She's trying to get sober for Izzy, Gunnar. If she's allowed to see or speak to her daughter, that might be the motivation she needs to keep going, knowing she has a future with her kid."

I rear back, not used to seeing Cassie this upset. I can see the trauma of her past battling to the surface within her and she's struggling to keep it at bay.

"Your relationship with Tasha is irrevocably damaged, but Izzy's is not. She barely remembers Tasha and if Tasha can stay sober, this will be the fresh start Izzy gets with her mother." Her eyes start watering and I can see she's barely keeping it together. "God, how I would've given anything for my mother to do what Tasha is doing. She never fought her demons for us…for me."

The dam that was holding Cassie's tears back breaks. She shields her eyes with her hands and starts bawling. Within two strides I take her in my arms and hold her tightly. She wraps her arms around me and buries her face in my chest. Her tears soak through my shirt and the wetness pierces my skin and breaks my heart.

"I'm so sorry, Cassie," I whisper against her ear, not knowing what to say to make her feel better. So I just hold her. I hold her until her shoulders stop shaking and the tears stop leaking. When I feel the time is right, I pull back slightly and take her head in my hands and lift up her chin. Her gorgeous blue eyes look into mine just as two tears splash down her cheeks. I use the pad of my thumbs to wipe them away.

"Please set up a daily call for Tasha to speak with Izzy. It can be through Izzy's iPad that we both can monitor. I promise Gunnar, if she calls intoxicated, I will hang up and block her number."

I hesitate and she grips my wrists and squeezes. "Please do this for Izzy."

I rest my forehead against hers and squeeze my eyes shut. "Okay," I whisper and I open my eyes to see her tears start to fall again. "Cas, please…I can't stand to watch you cry."

Without thinking about what I'm doing, I bring her face closer and start kissing away the tears. I go back and forth from each cheek, trying to catch the tears. I rub my nose against hers and before I can stop myself, my lips find hers in a searing kiss.

God, how I fucking want her. I crush her to me and she whimpers while opening her mouth and giving my tongue full access. I groan, our tongues dueling with each other as she holds my head at the perfect angle before we break apart to gasp for air. My lips find her neck and I roughly suck while my hand roams down to her ass and plasters her pelvis to mine so she can feel how hard she makes me.

"Please, Gunnar," she moans as I suck on her earlobe.

"Please, what?" I want to hear her say what she wants.

"I want you so badly." Her hands reach for my shirt to untuck it and I feel her fingers against my bare skin as she rubs my back.

"Tell me what you want, Cassie, and I'll do it." I cover her mouth with mine hungrily, needing to taste her over and over again.

She claws at my back while I devour her. A small warning is going off in my head, trying to convince me to stop. This is going to change everything and I might not like the outcome, but right now I just don't care. I can't stop myself.

I don't want to stop.

She abruptly pulls back, grabs the hem of her shirt and pulls it up and over her head, revealing those magnificent breasts of hers encased in black bra.

"I want you, Gunnar." Before I can even respond, she grabs my face and recaptures my lips. She alternates between sucking my tongue and nipping at my bottom lip, and the combination drives me wild. I walk her backward until her calves hit the back of the couch, forcing her to sit down. She starts working the button of my jeans while I grab the fabric of my shirt at the back of my neck and pull it over my head. I throw it to the ground just as she unzips my pants. She pulls the top of my jeans and underwear down, making my cock spring to life in front of her face. She immediately grabs it and sticks it in her mouth. I inhale sharply as her mouth suctions against my shaft and she starts bringing me in and out of her mouth.

I throw my head back in ecstasy as I feel her tongue lapping against the tip of my cock. My hands snake through her head, holding her closer and she moans, the vibrations sending shivers up my spine.

"Fuck, you do that so well." I look back down at her and almost come undone watching her mouth attached to me. My need to be inside her grows more urgent and I tighten my hold in her hair and gently pull so she looks at me. "Keep doing that and you're going to make me come. If you want me to fuck you, then lay down on the couch."

She releases me from her mouth and fervently takes her clothes off. I lose the remainder of my own and cover her with my body, but I stop myself from entering her.

"Shit, I don't have any condoms," I groan out in disappointment.

"I'm on birth control," she says, her hand guiding me to her entrance. With one sweeping motion, I'm inside of her and we both moan with how incredible it feels.

"God, I've missed you," I murmur as I start thrusting inside of her. Her body is warm and tight as my cock slides through her wet heat, impaling her in the perfect spot that makes her back arch, her soft moans of pleasure heightening my own. Her mouth latches on to the hardened peak of my nipple, eliciting an animal-like growl from deep within my chest as electricity starts to ping pong throughout my body.

She feels too good and as her walls start pulsating around me, I pound into her harder and faster. She cries out my name and, fuck, if I don't love hearing her say it. Her palms rest against my ass as she gyrates against me in search of her release. It doesn't take long before I feel myself about to combust just in time for her to come.

I'm panting into her neck, trying to stop my hips from continuing to grind into her, but the feeling of her in my arms, wrapped around my body is euphoria itself.

And I never want to give it up.

CHAPTER 22

CASSIE

I thought Gunnar and I would have a conversation about us breaking the rules about sleeping with each other. I was expecting the whole speech of *"This can never happen again,"* and *"We need to be professional,"* but instead he's been quiet and using his job as an excuse to avoid me.

The couch wasn't the only place we had sex on that night. We also christened his shower and his bed. We were insatiable for each other and I had no regrets nor did I care about the consequences of crossing the line with him. But as I was falling asleep, he gently reminded me that I needed to go back to my room in case Izzy woke up and found me in the wrong bed. For some reason, that stung. I know I was in my head, but at that moment, I felt used. My feeling of rejection is silly considering I was a willing participant, and I know we aren't planning on being in a personal relationship together. He's my boss, I'm his employee, and if he wants to occasionally have sex with me, then I'm down for it. I'm tired of denying our attraction to one another. I've convinced myself that I can handle casual sex with him.

But my heart doesn't seem to be on board with it. It's being stupidly irrational and hurt at him dodging me.

He was out of the house the next morning earlier than usual, meaning he barely slept, which showed in his performance at his game later that day. He went 0-4 with three strikeouts, zero runs and zero RBIs. That's unheard of for Gunnar. His mood was gloomy and dark when we saw him afterward to say goodbye before he left with the team for their next road trip. He barely spoke to me or his family and the only person he even smiled for was Izzy.

Before he left, he set up Izzy's iPad so she could have scheduled daily calls with Tasha. Normally when he checks in on Izzy, he calls my cell phone. This time he called her iPad. He was cordial when I would answer it if she wasn't near, but his interaction with me was brief before returning to his usual self with Izzy. He got back late last night and I decided to give him a dose of his own medicine—I left the house before anyone was up to avoid the awkwardness. Today's his day off, which means it's technically mine as well, but I was invited to Gavin's party that he's throwing for both Aly and Gunnar. I was excited to be included in the festivities, but now I don't even want to go. Grace is going with Carter since all of Gunnar's teammates and their partners were invited. I'm torn on what to do because I still want to celebrate Aly's pending birth and give her the painting I made for her.

Maybe it's for the best that he avoids you, Cassie. You need to protect yourself and just do your job. You told him you didn't want a relationship, so he's actually doing you a favor by being a grumpy asshole.

With my mental pep talk, I decide I'm still going to the party. It's a pool party, so I put on the smallest, sexiest bikini I own, which probably covers up more of my body than what the other beautiful women in attendance will be wearing. Then I put on some jean shorts and a high-neck tank top and slip on my sandals. I pack a change of clothes, a towel, and my floppy hat to wear so my face doesn't burn. After that, I carefully wrap Aly's painting. Once I'm done, I grab my backpack, throw it over my shoulder, pick up the painting and head out of the house. My plan is to get there right as the party starts, spend time with Aly, Valerie, and Grace, play in the pool with Izzy for a little bit, and get out of there within a three-hour time span. I don't want to stay too long because I need to get back to my dad' s house and continue working on my painting for New York.

Which I still haven't told Gunnar about.

I sigh, knowing that conversation needs to come up sooner rather than later with me needing a whole week off. I compared the dates I need off to Gunnar's schedule and the majority of the days will be during his All-Star break. His only plans during the break are to relax so his body can recover. Aly and Valerie already offered to help with Izzy during the days he does have games, so my time off shouldn't be a problem.

I arrive at Aly and Gavin's house within twenty minutes and already there are tons of cars lining their street and driveway. I find a parking space a couple of houses down. I gather all my things out of the car and start walking to their driveway. I get closer to their front door and see Gunnar's car right by the garage. I'm sure he came early to help get things set up. I take a deep breath, mentally prepare myself to be ignored by him again, especially in front of all these people. I put the painting down to ring the doorbell, but when no one answers and I can hear the music blaring from outside, I check the door knob and see it's unlocked, so I let myself in.

Their place is packed with people I've never met before. I politely say hello to the guests who are hanging out inside and go to the windows in their living room that show off their backyard. I look out over at the pool and find Izzy, but it's her daddy that draws my attention. He's in the pool, throwing her up in the air and catching her before dunking her under the water. He's wearing his baseball hat backwards, aviator sunglasses shading his eyes and his megawatt smile on full display as he laughs with her. His smile is contagious and I grin just watching them. The pool is crowded, but I notice a couple of women checking out his incredible body. His upper torso glistens in the sun and my mouth goes dry, soaking in the full effects of his essence.

"Cassie, you're here!" I hear my name and turn around to see Aly coming toward me. Her hair is pulled back in a bun and she's wearing a floral sheer cover up over her light blue maternity bathing suit. She's glowing and barely looks almost nine months pregnant. I give her a hug and lift up her present for her to notice.

Her eyes light up as she sees what I'm carrying. "Is this for the baby?" she asks and I nod. "Ooh, I'm so excited. Let's go upstairs to the baby's room and do the big reveal."

"Don't you want to wait for Gavin to open it?"

She waves her hand at me. "Pfft, heck no. He won't be paying attention to any of the gifts. He's just using my pregnancy and his brother's move to throw a party. The man loves being around people and is a better host than I am." I laugh and follow her up the stairs to the baby's room.

The walls of the room are painted white with light tan hardwood floors and matching beams on the ceiling with a big, beautiful light fixture hanging down in the middle of the room. There are multiple accent rugs covering the floors and the furniture is a similar shade of neutral light brown. It is a very boho chic baby nursery instead of whimsical and with the modern style furniture and decor, it's the perfect room for any gender. Once the baby is here, she will add some more color.

Her plan is to hang the painting over the custom-built changing station, so we walk over to it and I lean the painting against the wall. I turn to look at her and smile. "If the painting doesn't match the vision you have for this room, please tell me and I will paint a new one. It doesn't hurt my feelings whatsoever, so be honest."

"Okay," she agrees. I hold up one side so she can remove the wrapping paper. She finds one of the crevices and tears it upon. The room is filled with the sound of ripping paper and she gasps as soon as she gets a good look at the painting.

"Cassie, this is perfect!" I remove the rest of the paper and we both stand back to admire it. "I love it so much! It's exactly what I was hoping for. Thank you!" She turns toward me and gives me a tight hug. "Let me get my checkbook and write you a check."

I stop her from leaving and squeeze her hand. "No, silly. It's my gift to you and the baby. Hopefully they will keep it in their lives forever."

"Oh, I love that and I hope they will too. Again, thank you." She gives me another hug and glances back at the painting. "You're so talented, Cassie. This is such a wonderful and thoughtful gift."

"You're welcome. I'm so happy you love it."

"I can't wait to show Gavin later and make him hang it up." She glances at her smart watch. "Speaking of which, he's looking for me. Let's go back downstairs."

We head back down to the bottom floor and go straight outside to their backyard. Aly stops to talk to some of her guests. I notice Grace standing by Carter, so I weave my way through people to say hello to her.

"There you are. I was starting to get worried about you," Grace says while giving me a hug. I do the same to Carter and stand next to her.

"Sorry, Aly wanted to open her gift in the nursery. Fortunately, she loved the painting."

"Of course she was going to love it." Grace nudges my elbow and I smile sheepishly at her. Besides my father, Grace has always been my biggest supporter when it pertains to my art. She tells everyone and anyone that her best friend is an artist. If she wasn't a nurse, she would be my own personal sales woman. Because of her, some of my paintings are hanging in restaurants she frequents and her dentist's office.

The three of us stand in companionable silence, and I notice Carter's arm around Grace, his hand lazily rubbing up and down the back of her arm. I smirk and make a mental note to ask her later what is going on between them because there's no way this relationship is "fake" anymore.

"You can totally pick out who the baseball players are by their farmer's tan," Grace comments, causing Carter and I to both start laughing because it's true.

"Cassie!" A little voice yells out as Izzy gets out of the pool and runs to me.

"Don't run, Iz," I warn her, not wanting her to slip and fall, but she doesn't listen and barrels into my legs. I stumble back and hit something hard. Hands grab me around my waist and save me from falling.

"Whoa, I got you," a deep voice assures me as I stand upright and turn around. The something hard that I stumbled into was a man's hard, muscular chest. He's very tall and I have to tilt my head up just to look at him. His kind eyes smile and assess me and I have to admit, he's very good-looking. He removes his hands and my gaze snakes down to notice he has the same tan lines as the rest of the players.

"I'm so sorry." I wrap one of my arms around Izzy, who's still holding on to my legs.

"No big deal. I'm just glad I caught you and that you both didn't get hurt."

"Yes, thank you so much for that."

"I'm Lucas Hamilton, by the way." He holds out his hand for me to shake. "I've seen you at the ballpark before. You work for Gunnar, right?"

I place my hand in his and he gently squeezes, his touch warm and firm. "Yes, I'm Cassie, Izzy's nanny." I look down at her and she smiles.

I go to look back up at Lucas, but Gunnar cuts in between

us, causing our hands to disconnect. "Are you okay?" He puts one hand on my shoulder and I feel the zing from his touch all the way down to my spine. *Why can't my body react that way to Lucas?*

"Yes, we're fine thanks to Lucas here." I nod at Lucas over Gunnar's shoulder. Gunnar turns around and shakes Lucas' hand.

"Thanks for saving my girls, Hamilton."

My girls? What the heck? I narrow my eyes at Gunnar, not liking this pissing contest he is starting with his own teammate. He has no reason to act this way and I'm annoyed that the only attention I receive from him in almost a week is jealousy over Lucas innocently touching me to make sure I don't fall.

"C'mon, Izzy. Let's go get some food." I grab Izzy's hand but before we go, I look at Lucas and give him what I hope is a flirtatious smile. "Thanks again, Lucas. We'll chat later." I turn around and even though Gunnar is wearing sunglasses, I can feel his stare boring into my back as we walk away.

"What was that?" Grace whispers as she saddles up to my side to walk into the kitchen with us.

"I have no clue but how dare he!" I hiss, not wanting others to hear our conversation as we walk by. "Everyone was watching us too."

"That's why he did it. He was marking his territory." I look over at Grace, who gives me a mischievous grin.

"Yeah, well I'm not his to mark," I mutter and she raises her eyebrow in skepticism. "You're the one to talk, Miss *I'm-in-a-fake-relationship*." Her cheeks flush pink and I chuckle.

We reach the kitchen and I see Valerie, Rowan, Sosie, Gavin, Damien, and Delilah congregated by the buffet table. I grab two empty plates for me and Izzy and walk over to greet them. While we all chat, I fill up our plates with food and sit Izzy down to eat next to where I stand so I can continue conversing with everyone. A rush of energy suddenly flows through me, my body alerting me to Gunnar's presence before his handsome face appears in my line of vision.

You're a traitor, body.

I watch him and Carter grab food and join our group. I focus my attention between eating and Izzy, not wanting to make eye contact with him, and listen to everyone else talk.

"Don't drink too much, boys," Gavin tells Gunnar, Carter, and Damien. "I don't want Declan chewing my ass out for inviting you over if you suck during tomorrow's game."

"We won't, but there's no guarantee that Baby Bear won't," Damien comments. Baby Bear is rookie pitcher Griffin Barrett, who got that nickname for only being five foot eight, which is small for a pitcher. We all glance outside and see Griffin taking a swig of his beer while chatting up a pretty girl.

"I'll say something to him," Gunnar responds before taking a bite of his hamburger.

"Cassie, how's your painting coming?" Sosie asks and everyone's attention turns to me.

I shift on my feet, not comfortable being the center of attention. "It's going good."

"You're an artist, Cassie?" Delilah asks and I nod. "That is so cool. I would love to see your work."

"She has a website with her whole portfolio you can check out," Grace responds for me and I give her a grateful smile.

"You can actually see one of her paintings right upstairs in our baby's room. It's gorgeous," Aly chimes in, joining the conversation. She has a plate in her hands for Austin and she sits him next to Izzy at the table. She then moves next to Gavin and he pulls her into his side.

"Wait, how come I haven't seen it yet?" Gavin asks his wife.

"Cassie brought it up and I opened it to see how it looks."

"And you didn't wait for me so we can see it together?" he

asks with an incredulous look on his face. I press my lips together to avoid laughing out loud from her getting busted.

She shrugs. "I didn't think you would be interested."

"Of course I'm interested. We have a painting from an almost famous artist in our house now."

I laugh and shake my head. "I'm definitely not famous."

"But you will be after New York," Valerie adds and my smile falters when I see confusion cross Gunnar's features.

"New York?" He questions when he looks at me. "When are you going to New York?"

Oh, crap. This is not the best time to have this conversation, but I guess it's going to happen.

Silence fills the air surrounding our group with uncomfortable glances being exchanged by everyone.

"Valerie's friend owns an art gallery in Brooklyn. She sent him my website and he liked what he saw, so he invited me to submit a painting to a multi-artist exhibition. It happens while you're on break, but I have to be up there a week before. Aly and Valerie offered to watch Izzy during the days you have games, so I didn't think it would be a problem."

"Why haven't you told me?" His voice is demanding, and he stares at me with frustration and disappointment in his eyes.

"Because there hasn't been a good opportunity for me to do so." *Did you forget that you've been avoiding me?* Pretty sure he wouldn't want me to reveal that to the group.

As if he can read my mind, his expression grows remorseful. The inner child in me wants to stomp my foot and say, *"Yeah, you should be sorry you big, sexy, jerk,"* but I keep my mouth shut.

He quickly recovers so no one else notices and smiles softly. "That's amazing, Cassie. Congratulations. Of course it won't be a problem for you to go."

"Thank you," I tell him with a curt nod.

"Oh no!" Izzy yells, distracting us all away from the

conversation. I glance over at her to see she has spilled her fruit punch all over herself.

I swiftly put my plate down and walk over to her to assess the damage. "It's okay, Iz. We will clean it up."

"Here's some towels." Sosie hands one to Gunnar before she bends down and starts cleaning the floor.

"But my bathing suit is ruined," Izzy whines and her bottom lip starts to quiver as tears form in her eyes.

"We have an extra suit upstairs in the closet in the bunk bed room," Aly says and starts to put her plate of food down to go, but I stop her.

"I'll go get it," I offer and before she can object, I leave to head upstairs.

Their bunk bed room is a bedroom that was converted to have two sets of built-in bunk beds with toys and a television hanging on the wall. It's where Izzy and Austin sleep when they have sleepovers. I walk through the room and enter the bathroom. I pull open the closet door and find the bathing suit in one of the drawers. I turn around to walk out when I notice a couple of familiar looking boxes in the corner of the closet.

Why are three of my boxes that I use to ship my art in here?

The top of the boxes are open and I flip the flap up on one of them to see one of my paintings that I sold inside, still in its bubble wrap. I bend down to see the shipping label. The name and address aren't even Aly's. *What the hell? How did they get here?*

"Did you find the bathing suit, Cassie?" I hear Aly's voice, but don't answer. I see her feet in my peripheral vision and look up at her. She sees what I'm looking at and guilt is written all over her face.

"Why do you have paintings that I sold to someone else?" I ask, my words deliberately slow as I try to process what I just discovered.

"I can explain," Gunnar says behind her. She turns to her

side and I see he's in the bathroom, Izzy perched on his hip. He puts her down and glances at Aly. "Can you take Izzy and get her dressed while I talk to Cassie?"

She nods and mutters to him. "Gavin warned us this wasn't a good idea." She grabs Izzy's hand and they walk out of the bathroom, closing the door behind them.

I stand up but stay in the closet by my paintings. "What's going on, Gunnar?"

He holds up his hands in defense. "Before you get upset, please try to keep in mind that I had good intentions."

I cross my arms across my chest. "And those were?"

"I was trying to figure out ways to support your art career."

My anger starts to boil as all the pieces of the puzzle fall into place. "So *you* bought my paintings using fake names? What about the addresses?" I reach down and flip through the packages. "They're all different."

"Those aren't fake people or addresses. Some are family and friends of Aly and Gavin's who agreed to have your paintings sent to their homes."

I storm into the bathroom and he backs up into the vanity. "Why would they agree to that? Because they felt sorry for me just like you do?"

He shakes his head. "No, it wasn't like that."

"Then what was it, Gunnar? Because I don't understand why you would spend all that money on my paintings using other people's names and ask them to *hide* them for you if you didn't feel bad for me."

He sighs. "Cassie, I promise you, I didn't mean anything bad by this. No one feels sorry for you. I just wanted to help boost your self-confidence and help you see how talented you are."

"By giving me false hope that a stranger has discovered me and wanted to buy my paintings?" I yell, my rage coming in burning. I'm angry that I was deceived and it hurts like hell that it comes from him.

His shoulders sag in despair. "I can see how you would come to that conclusion."

"How long were you planning on keeping them here before throwing them away?"

"What?" He looks at me in confusion. "They were never going to be thrown away."

"Then what were your plans with them?"

"I was planning on donating them to the children's hospital."

I don't know what to say to that. It's a wonderful idea, but it still doesn't excuse the fact that he was being sneaky. "If you wanted to donate paintings, I would've done that for *free*," I emphasize, hating that I unknowingly accepted his pity money. Because that's what this feels like. The guy with millions, who's banging his nanny, feels sorry she hasn't made it as an artist so he takes pity on her by buying her art using other people's names. "I've sold a total of five paintings, ten tote bags, some pillows and note cards since I've been employed with you. Were all those sales you?"

"No," he vehemently answers. "I bought four paintings and five tote bags."

That makes me feel a little bit better to know he didn't buy everything. "What did you do with the other painting and tote bags?"

"I handed out the bags to some of the ladies that work at the ballpark as ushers and in the concession stands. The other painting is hanging in The Rooftop Replay."

We stand there in silence while I let his words sink in so I can calm down. "I'm so sorry, Cassie," he apologizes, his voice filled with regret. "I wasn't thinking that my actions might be deceitful. I honestly just wanted to help because I'm proud of you."

"Proud of me? How?" I question in confusion.

"You're busting your ass to make a name for yourself. You work two jobs that you give your everything to. Do you know how admirable that is? I just wanted to somehow, someway, help you." He swallows and takes a step closer to me. "But I see how my actions were wrong and I'm sorry."

In my heart, I know he meant well. It's hard for me to stay mad at him when his intentions were good. Hell, hearing his plans to donate the paintings he bought to the children's hospital is kind of swoon worthy.

This man takes my emotions on a rollercoaster ride, but as we continue to stare at each other, the tension shifts and the anger dissipates from my body. The overwhelming urge to be held by him is so overpowering that my heart rate speeds up and all I want to do is kiss him. "What you did was fucked up," I start while I move closer to him. "But also the nicest thing anyone has ever done for me."

Before he can respond, I stand up on my tip toes and plant a hard kiss on his mouth. I don't know what the hell I'm doing, especially since he's made it clear by his avoidance of me that we can't be together. He's caught off guard by my actions and barely moves. Embarrassed by my brazen behavior, I keep the kiss brief and step back. I look down in embarrassment and turn to leave, but he grabs my wrist and hauls me against his chest. "Fuck no, you're not leaving me after that," he growls before claiming my mouth in a scorching kiss.

I sigh in ecstasy, my heart screaming *yes* because I've missed his touch so much. I wrap my arms around his neck and surrender to him. His lips are demanding, he kisses rough as our tongues battle with one another. He turns me around in his arms and walks me backwards until I bump into the vanity. He hoists me up with our mouths still fused together and sits me down on the countertop. I open my legs and he settles in between them.

My hands roam up and down his back as I try to bring

him closer, but it's not even physically possible since I'm already plastered against him. I knock off the baseball cap and sunglasses that were perched on top of his head and plunge my fingers into his hair.

He breaks our kiss and brings his lips to my neck. "Do you forgive me, baby?" he whispers into my ear while he kisses his way down my neck. I nod, not being able to talk due to the spell his heated kisses have me under.

"I need to hear you say it, Cassie." He briefly comes back to my lips before going to the other side of my neck. I tilt my head back, giving him easier access. The only sound I can make are the little pants of desire as he nips at my earlobe, sending shockwaves to my core.

"I forgive you," I rasp and tighten my legs around his hips. I feel his fingers fish the hem of my shirt out of my shorts. He breaks our kiss and with one sweeping motion, my tank top is over my head and lying on the floor.

He leans me back against the mirror and latches his mouth to my clavicle, licking and sucking his way down to my breast. His fingers gently pull the string of my bikini down my arms to reveal my hard nipple. He sucks the taught bud into his hot, wet mouth and I moan loudly in pleasure.

"Christ, if you don't taste like the forbidden fruit that you are." He continues his assault on my breasts, taking turns on each nipple. Waves of ecstasy are crashing inside of me, my body gyrating against his. Something feral unleashes within me and I pull his head from nipple and kiss him harshly.

"I need you, Gunnar," I beg and I hate how I lose all sense of control when I'm in his arms. I've never wanted someone as much as I want him and it unnerves me. One touch of his fingers and my body is under his command.

"Tell me what you need, baby," he feverishly demands in between kisses. The urgency to have him inside of me is too much to bear. My hands glide frantically down his back until

I feel the top of his bathing suit. I push it down and grab his firm, hard ass and squeeze.

"I want you to fuck me." I inhale sharply at my words because I don't even sound like myself, but I can tell he loves it as he growls into my mouth and starts to unbutton my shorts. Once the zipper is undone, I push him back so I can get off the counter top to stand-up. He helps me slide off the top and when I'm stable on my feet, he yanks my shorts and bikini bottoms down to the ground. When I step out of them, he lifts me up and walks us into the separate room that has the toilet. The lid is already down for him to sit on. I slam the door shut and climb on top of him.

I work my hands up and down his shaft, making him throw his head back and moan. Not being able to wait any longer, I push myself up, guide him to my entrance and slowly slide down, impaling myself on him. My walls clench around his hardness and I start riding him, seeking the orgasm he seems to be the master at getting out of me.

"You're so fucking beautiful," he pants while I dig my nails into his shoulders, grinding my pelvis against his. "I don't have the willpower to stay away from you anymore."

"So don't," I whisper before claiming his lips, plunging my tongue to meet his while I throw all caution out the window to seek that high only he can give me.

The invisible strings start tightening around us and I feel the anxious build-up coming. I break our kiss and lay my forehead against his, our breaths intermingling with each other.

"Look at me, Cassie. I want to watch you come undone." His words open the flood gates and I stare into his eyes while fireworks explode inside of me, my walls clenching him as hard as I can with the most intense orgasm I've ever had. I can't stop the scream that starts to come out of me and he grabs my head and silences it with his mouth. He moans into me and I feel him shudder as he reaches his own climax.

We stare into each other's eyes and it's as if he is reaching into me and grabbing my soul for him to own. A silent understanding crosses between us as we float back down to reality and I shiver in the excitement of knowing there will be more to come with him.

I'm a fool to keep telling myself I'm not in love with this man and that things between us are just physical. I should run as fast as I can, quit this job, but I'm in too deep. Not only have I fallen for him, but I love Izzy as if she's my own. I will let my naive heart accept the torture of unrequited love if it means I get to keep both of them for a little while longer, until the day comes that he won't need me anymore and leaves. The pain will be worse than when my mother left, because I had my father to protect me. No one's protecting me now. It's the story of my life at this point.

I just pray that I will be able to recover once more from losing another love of my life.

CHAPTER 23

CASSIE

As the season grinds on into the middle of summer, I'm in my own little bubble of pure bliss, pretending to play house with a family that's not mine to keep. Gunnar and I try to act normal and professional when we are around our friends and family. We keep our hands to ourselves when we are alone with Izzy, but lately he's been bolder; caressing me when she isn't looking, stealing kisses when she runs out of the room. As soon as Izzy goes to sleep, the night is ours to explore each other's bodies and get to know one another on a deeper level. I have an alarm set for five in the morning so I can fall asleep in his arms and wake up to go back to my own bedroom before Izzy gets up.

When Gunnar's on the road, he calls me after his games and we talk until I can't keep my eyes open. He's introduced me to phone sex and bought me my very first vibrator that he demands I use on myself when we FaceTime so he can watch while he jerks himself off. That came in very handy when he was on his eleven-day road trip. He's taught me to be more vocal in the bedroom and to see and love my body the way he does. This is the happiest I've been in a long time and it seems Gunnar is too.

According to one of the sports reporters on our local news, he's playing the best baseball of his entire career. He was voted Player of the Week and I overheard Gavin asking Gunnar one night if he thinks the team is going to re-sign him. My heart dropped when Gunnar told him he isn't hopeful since they might want to add younger, cheaper players in his place. With the trade deadline coming up at the end of July, anything can happen between now and then. I stop myself from going down the deep, dark, rabbit hole of my abandonment issues. I knew there was a possibility I might be with them for only one season, but now that my heart has gotten involved, my chest tightens, throbbing with pain every time I think this might be it for us. Even if we survive the trade deadline, if the team doesn't re-sign him, then he enters free agency. With the way he's playing, there's no way another team will pass him up if they have a need for his skills and leadership. He's talked about how much he's enjoyed playing for the Terrors and he couldn't ask for a better team besides Texas, but this is the nature of the business and the risk you take when you play professional sports.

Tasha has been calling Izzy on a consistent basis and Gunnar has agreed to supervised visitations when she comes back to Tennessee. She's been true to her word so far and has enrolled in school to become an addiction counselor. She's even started dating again and the man is a life coach who encourages her sober living and doesn't drink either. She's introduced Izzy to him via FaceTime and there's a good chance he will accompany her to Nashville next month.

My exhibition in New York is now only weeks away and I'm starting to get nervous. The painting is done and I gave the varnish plenty of time to dry. I've never shipped a painting this large before and I spent the extra money to secure a wood crate for it. I took my time carefully wrapping it with glassine paper, foam corner protectors, and lots of bubble wrap. Fortunately, it made it safe and sound to the gallery and Michael is configuring where each artist will be placed. I already submitted the dimensions, my statement on the piece, headshot, and bio to Michael, so there's nothing left to do but to show up. My dad and Grace will be going with me and we plan on making a vacation out of it, doing all the touristy things New York has to offer. Things are going so well in my life right now, but I have a feeling it won't last. Sometimes I feel like I'm walking on the edge of a tightrope, bracing for the inevitable fall. When I start getting worried about my future with Gunnar and Izzy, I remind myself to just live in the now and take one day at a time.

⊗ ⚾ 🦋 🧁

"Cassie," I hear the faintness of Izzy's voice in my dreams. I try to look for her, but it's pitch black.

"Cassie," I hear it again, this time louder and I feel little hands slapping my left arm.

My eyes jolt open and I blink a couple of times, trying to grasp where I am and what's going on.

"Cassie." I turn my head and see Izzy standing next to the bed, wearing her butterfly pajamas. Her hair is all roused up and it looks like she just woke up. At first I wonder if she had a nightmare, but she isn't crying like she normally reacts when she has one. Seeing that she's okay, my eyes start to close again.

"You okay, Peanut?" I ask in a groggy voice, sleep trying to pull me back under.

"Why are you naked in my daddy's bed?"

My eyes snap open and I look down at myself. *Oh crap!* I grab my phone from the nightstand to see it's seven in the morning. I don't remember hearing my alarm go off at five.

Either I forgot to turn it on or in my state of sleepiness, I shut it off. Either way, Izzy caught us.

"What's going on?" Gunnar mumbles in half consciousness. He rolls over to face me and slowly opens his eyes and squints. "Izzy?" Within a matter of seconds, he bolts up from the bed, swings his legs over the side and pulls up his shorts that were on the floor next to the bed. He grabs his shirt that was thrown on the bench at the foot of his bed and puts it on. "Let's go make french toast, Iz," he suggests, trying to hustle her out of the room. He rounds the bed and picks her up.

"But why is Cassie sleeping with you, Daddy? Did she have a nightmare?"

"Um, no," Gunnar stammers as he heads for the door to go downstairs to the kitchen. "Cassie had an upset stomach and threw up all over herself, so Daddy helped wash her clothes and while he was doing so, she fell asleep in my bed."

"Ohhhh, poor Cassie," Izzy exclaims in her sweet voice as I hear them descend the stairs.

I'm not sure what I'm more shocked by—Izzy discovering us or Gunnar lying so seamlessly. I slowly get out of bed and make use of his bathroom. I find my clothes from last night and put them back on. I walk quietly down the stairs, not wanting to draw attention to myself and sneak into my room before Izzy notices me. I go through my morning routine of getting ready and by the time I'm done, Gunnar has a whole stack of french toast made and Izzy's in the living room watching television.

"I can take over if you need to get ready," I offer because he has an afternoon home game and then afterward, they leave for the road again.

"No, it's fine, I got it," he says in a cold, harsh voice. Dread starts to seep into my veins. He's acting strange and won't even make eye contact with me. Izzy catching us has spooked him.

"Gunnar, we need to talk before you leave." I watch him

cut up Izzy's french toast, pour syrup all over it and place it where she sits to eat.

"Isabear, come eat breakfast," he tells her. She unglues her eyes from the TV and walks over to sit down. He places two pieces of french toast on a plate and hands it to me without a word. He then proceeds to start cleaning up his mess.

"Please don't ignore me, Gunnar." I put my plate down and move to stand at his side. "I'm sorry about this morning. I don't know what happened to my alarm."

"Let's not discuss this in front of her," he whispers before turning on the water to rinse off the bowls he used before putting them in the dishwasher.

I sit down on one of the bar stools and wait, my anger starting to rise at not only him and how he is reacting, but at myself for falling for him. He sits down next to Izzy and starts to eat his breakfast. I don't even touch the french toast he gave me since I have zero appetite at the moment.

I listen to him tell Izzy about what city the team we are playing against this afternoon is from and then he shows her on his phone where it is located and the other city he is traveling to tonight after the game.

Ten minutes later, Izzy announces she is done eating. Gunnar helps her clean up and then he tells her to go brush her teeth and get dressed. We watch in silence as she runs to the stairs and climbs them up to her room.

He turns to me and says, "What happened this morning can't ever happen again." He finally looks at me and his eyes are distant and emotionless. "I don't want her confused by our relationship. She shouldn't have seen her nanny in the same bed as her daddy."

The realization that I'll only ever be the 'nanny' to him is a slap to my face. *Why are you so surprised, Cassie? He promised you nothing. You're the idiot who fell in love with him.* I cast my eyes down, not wanting him to see the tears that are threatening to fall. I swallow down the bile that has risen in my

throat at the thought of another person I love not wanting me.

I clear my throat and mentally tell myself to keep it
together. "You're right," I tell him in a calm, cold voice, yet
my insides feel like they are burning up in despair. "This
needs to end. From now on, I will only sleep here when you
are on the road. After you come home from your games, I will
return to my father's house." I turn around and head to the
stairs to help Izzy get ready for the day.

"Cassie, you don't have to do that," Gunnar calls out and I
hear his footsteps following close behind me. "Cassie, stop!"
He demands and I halt right before the stairs. "Please look at
me," he pleads and I slowly turn around to face him. I look at
him and I know he can see the anguish in my eyes. "I'm sorry
if I've hurt you or gave you mixed signals. That was never my
intention. I thought we were on the same page of both of us
not wanting a relationship."

"Sometimes you can't prevent feelings from developing."
I stare at him, hoping he will now admit to me that feelings
have developed for him too. Instead, he winces and briefly
closes his eyes before opening them back up and giving me a
small smile. He grabs my hands, but I immediately jerk them
away. "Don't touch me," I hiss, not wanting to feel those
rough hands and remember how good they feel on my body.

"You're young, Cassie. You only feel this way because of
the sex."

His comment makes me angry and I see red. "You don't
get to tell me how I'm feeling."

He holds up his hands in surrender. "I'm the fucked up
one, Cassie. You deserve someone who doesn't have the
emotional baggage I have. Someone around your own age
who hasn't been jaded by a bad relationship."

I scoff and shake my head. "You choose to hold on to your
emotional baggage."

He takes a step back, surprised by my assessment of him.

"Maybe you're right, but you deserve someone who puts you first. Anyone would be lucky to call you theirs."

"I guess that will be anyone but you." I turn on my heel and march up the stairs, needing distance from him. *You're so stupid, Cassie. You knew this was going to happen and yet you took the risk anyway.*

I step into Izzy's room and find her playing with her dolls. "Izzy, let's put those away and get out of the house." I'm about to ask her if she wants to go to the zoo when my cell phone starts to ring. I pull it out of my pocket to see Aly's name flashing across the screen.

"Good morning," I greet in a fake, cheerful voice. I have to act normal in front of Aly. One slip of my emotions and she will be hounding me with questions.

"Having contractions. On my way to the hospital. Do you think you and Izzy can spend the day with Austin? My mom is with him right now, but he was kind of freaked out when he saw I was in pain. I think having a distraction like Izzy would be good for him. Gavin is on the phone with Gunnar right now as well." I can hear Gavin talking in the background as they drive.

"Of course we will and we can even sleepover if need be."

I hear her sigh in relief. "You're amazing! Thank you so much. Gavin will text everyone once the baby has arrived."

"Don't worry about Austin. We'll make sure he has a great time. You just stay calm and do your breathing exercises."

"Screw those breathing exercises. I need an epidural."

I laugh. "Everything is going to go smoothly. Have a safe and speedy delivery. We can't wait to meet the baby."

"Thank you. Hopefully it won't be too speedy or no epidural and I will rage on Gavin if that happens," she laughs and I suddenly feel bad for Gavin. He better pray she's not too far gone to get one.

We hang up and I look down at Izzy. "Congratulations, Iz. You're getting a new baby cousin soon. Let's pack your bathing suit and go play with Austin while we wait to meet the baby."

Izzy jumps up from the floor and screams in excitement. We head together to her closet and start gathering items to take with us. This will be the perfect distraction for me as well and a great excuse to miss Gunnar's game today.

I gave Gunnar the keys to my heart and he used a wrecking ball to shatter it into a million pieces. It's going to take time to put all the pieces back together. After today, I'm done taking risks. No more casual sex. No more falling in love. I will stay on as Izzy's nanny through the end of this season and then I'm done no matter if Gunnar stays in Nashville or not. While the thought of leaving Izzy hurts my stomach, I have to for once put myself and my feelings first.

CHAPTER 24

GUNNAR

The next three days on the road are pure torture.

I think about Cassie and what transpired during every waking hour. Every time I close my eyes to sleep, all I see is the pain I caused her reflecting back at me in those pale eyes of hers. I'm miserable and I only have myself to blame for the emptiness I feel inside. The way I treated her was unacceptable. I'm ashamed and embarrassed at how I handled Izzy finding her in my bed. I've tried to apologize to her numerous times, but she won't take my calls and when I text her, it's one-word answers. Even when I call for Izzy and ask Cassie to stay on the line afterward, she tells me unless it's related to Izzy, there's nothing for us to discuss. Her dismissive behavior puts me in a foul mood and everyone is in my path of irritability.

"It's the nanny, isn't it?" Diesel asks while we're all on the field, stretching. Tonight is our last game on the road before the All-Star break and I'm itching to get out of here so I can try to talk to Cassie in person. She can't avoid me in my own house.

"What about her?" I snap impatiently, not wanting to discuss Cassie with my teammates.

"Something's happened between the two of you, otherwise you wouldn't be such a grumpy asshole."

"Why would you think that? Maybe I've just been tired and off the last couple of games."

"Just look at your stats," Kelton James, our right fielder, chimes in and I give him a confused look. "You were killing it your first couple of weeks here, probably due to wanting to give your old team a big fuck you for getting rid of you. Then your dick came alive from the grave with a gorgeous stranger and you were all satiated and satisfied."

"Jesus Christ," I groan as the rest of the boys laugh. If looks could kill, Kelton would be a dead man right now.

"Then your mysterious lady appears out of nowhere to interview for the nanny position and your stats go down again because fate wanted to fuck with you and you played like ass. Conveniently, your mom gets injured and your lady has to become your nanny because no one else is available. Hats off to karma right there for you."

"Is there a point to this?" I interrupt while we switch stretching positions and start arm circles.

"Sure is. You've been blasting out bombs the last six weeks and were having career-high games. I'm guessing you and the nanny started shacking up again. But something happened and the last four games have been the Gunnar we've seen previously when the nanny has been in your head. So, what did you do?"

"Why do you automatically assume *I* did something?"

"Because Cassie's too nice to dick you over," Evan answers. Cassie and Evan's girlfriend, Christy, have been hanging out and having playdates between Christy's son, Nolan, and Izzy. "I also noticed Carter didn't sit with you on the bus to the airport."

Cassie obviously told Grace, who told Carter, and now he won't talk to me. He looks at me in disgust and refuses to be anywhere near me. He usually plays cards with me, Jake, and Chase when we're on the plane, but didn't this time.

We start doing high knees and once we're done and I catch my breath, I tell them. "Izzy caught us in bed together."

"Wait, like in the act?" Jake's eyes bulge out at the thought and I can't help but chuckle.

"No, we were asleep."

"So what's the big deal about that?" Diesel asks after the athletic trainer tells us to do hip flexor stretches.

"The big deal is that she found her nanny naked in my bed, and we aren't girlfriend and boyfriend. That's confusing to a child."

Diesel scoffs. "Isn't your kid like five-years old? You really think she's going to remember and be scarred for life by this?"

I roll my eyes at him. "Of course not."

"Then that's just an excuse. What's really your problem? Is it because you can't seem to forget that when you were twenty-one, she was ten?" He grins and I would love nothing more than to punch that smile right off his face.

"Fuck off, Diesel," I growl while I move my body into torso twists.

"Still not understanding why she isn't your girlfriend if you both like each other," Evan comments and I grit my teeth. I've had enough of this conversation and them meddling into my personal life.

"It's complicated, guys. Enough of this conversation and let's focus on getting a win tonight."

"You're the complication, McNeer. You're just being a scared little bitch and might let the best thing that ever happened to you, outside of your daughter, fall through your fingertips," Diesel comments and starts doing walking lunges away from the group.

His words resonate with me throughout the game and I

use my anger and aggression when I'm at bat. I strike out twice but manage to get a home run my next time up. I drive the winning run in and we end our road trip with a win we desperately need.

By the time we land back in Nashville, it's past midnight. Cassie heads to New York tomorrow, and I don't want her to leave and not be on speaking terms with her. It's imperative that we talk tonight.

When I arrive home, I knock lightly on Cassie's door and open it, only to find her room empty. I go upstairs and check the playroom, but the lights are all off in there as well. It's when I check in on Izzy that I find Cassie asleep, her arm wrapped around Izzy as she holds her against her body. I lean against the doorframe and sigh with regret. It's evident that these two love each other and Cassie treats her as if she's her own daughter. I've fucked up majorly and I have a sneaking suspicion she's going to leave us when the season ends. Who could blame her? If the roles were reversed, I would be gone. I'm lucky if she stays for the remainder of the season.

If she does, it's because she's a better person than you are, you bastard.

I don't want to wake Cassie up, so I decide our talk can wait until the morning. I close the door gently behind me and retreat to my room.

But when I wake up in the morning, Cassie is already gone.

⚾ 🧤 🦋 🧁

"**M**cNeer!" My name is shouted by Andy Stokes, our third base coach. I look over at him from where I'm doing dumbbell squats in the gym. "Declan wants to see you in his office."

I drop my weights, grab my towel and wipe the sweat off my face. I take a swig of my water and start walking. Murph sits up from his bench presses and raises an eyebrow in a silent question. I shrug, not knowing what this is about but I can speculate. Either he's going to tell me I'm being benched for tonight's home game or they've opted not to sign me to a new contract and I'll be a free agent once the season is done. Or worse, I'm being traded again and will be placed on waivers. All options suck, and I'm praying that it's just me being benched for tonight.

I turn left out of the gym and walk to Declan's offices. When I get to his door, I knock and the door is opened by Walker Martin, our bench coach. "Come on in, Gunnar." He opens the door wider for me to walk through and that's when I see Billy Richards, our general manager, sitting in a chair against the wall. My heart sinks because seeing all three of them in the room together is not a good sign.

"Take a seat, Gunnar," Declan says while seated behind his desk. He points to the remaining empty chair left in the room. I walk over to it, sit down, and fold my hands in my lap. I keep my facial features stoic while I wait for the bad news to be delivered.

"Sorry for interrupting your workout. I'll keep this brief," Declan starts, leaning forward with his forearms braced against the top of his desk. "As you know, the trade deadline is coming up and we're making moves."

Fuck, here it comes, I tell myself and my mind can't help but wonder how Cassie's going to take the news. Is she going to be happy to see me go or sad? Because I know sure as fuck I'm going to miss her. What am I going to do with Izzy? This is when being a single parent is really difficult. My mom's ankle is all healed, so maybe she can come out wherever I land and take care of Izzy for me.

"When we traded for you from Texas, we were looking for a player to fill in the gap that our team had. We needed a consistent offensive performer and someone to take on a leadership role inside the clubhouse. We felt those were the two key ingredients we were missing to take the team to the next level." Declan looks down at his stat sheet, my name and stats highlighted in yellow. The turmoil in my personal life has affected my play and I'm sure that's the reason why they want me gone.

Not only did you screw things up with Cassie, but you've screwed up your job as well.

I don't want to leave Nashville. I like it here, not to mention being back in the same city as my brother has been wonderful.

Maybe you should retire and stay in Nashville where you can be with your brother and be with Cassie?

The thought leaves my mind as soon as it enters it. Cassie hates me right now. I've sent her numerous texts and they all go unanswered. The only way I know she's okay is when I check Izzy's call logs on her iPad to see Cassie has been calling her at least once a day while she's at Aly's house.

"We've talked to your agent and well, we feel these terms would be best for both parties." Declan slides over a sheet of paper and in his scrawny handwriting, it reads: '2 years, 50 Mill.'

My head snaps up and I look between Declan and Billy. "Are you fucking with me? You want to sign me to a two-year contract for fifty million?"

Billy nods. "Hell yeah we do. We've been very happy having you here."

"Holy shit." I rub my face and laugh as the nervous tension leaves my body. "I thought you guys were done with me."

"Do you want us to be done with you?" Declan asks in concern. "I know this was a big transition for you and your daughter, but I thought with your brother being here, that you were actually enjoying Nashville and the organization.

Everyone in the front office likes you and the players seem to respect and value your advice and leadership. If we got the wrong impression, tell us and we will let you become a free agent."

I shake my head. "I can honestly say that coming to Nashville has been a blessing in disguise. It's been an honor and privilege to be here. I don't take that for granted whatsoever."

Walker leans over and squeezes my shoulder. "We're glad to hear that. Our hope is to retire you as a Tennessee Terror. Keep yourself healthy and we might be back in here sooner with a contract extension."

I chuckle and nod. "I'd love that and will do my best to stay healthy."

I stand up and shake Billy's hand while giving bro hugs to Declan and Walker. I walk out of Declan's office on cloud nine and head back into the gym. I open the door and stop in my tracks. All my teammates are looking at me, waiting to hear what happened. I pretend to look upset and put my hands on my hips with my head down.

"Oh shit," I hear someone mutter, but I can't keep up this charade for very long. I lift up my head with a shit-eating grin plastered on my face.

"Buckle up, ladies. You're stuck with me for another two years," I tell them. Cheers go up and soon I'm surrounded by congratulatory hugs and high-fives.

When the excitement dies down, I go to my locker and grab my cell phone. Without thinking, I immediately dial Cassie, but my excitement wanes when she sends me to voicemail. I don't bother leaving a message, because the chances of her listening to it are slim. I prefer she hears it from me rather than the news, so I text her. I call Gavin and my parents on a three-way conference call to tell them the news. My parents will fly in tomorrow to see my new niece, but I didn't want to wait until then. While I'm talking to them, I feel my phone buzz and see Cassie texted me back. I open my messages while Gavin talks about us celebrating and read her message.

Cassie: Congratulations. You deserve it.

But you don't deserve her, my brain tells me and it's right, I don't.

⊘&🦋🧁

Three days later, I'm at Gavin and Aly's house, helping Gavin cook steaks on the grill. Izzy and I have been spending time here during the break, relaxing with my parents and gushing over the newest member of the family, Abigail McNeer. Izzy loves holding Abbi and comments all the time on how cute she is. Austin doesn't seem as excited about his new baby sister as the rest of the family, so we've made sure to pay him lots of attention and even bring him some presents from us and his new baby sister.

Even though the past couple of days have been filled with excitement over my new contract and the baby, I still feel this empty void inside me, reminding me that Cassie isn't here with us. I miss her like crazy and our house doesn't feel as warm and inviting without her. There are reminders of her in every room and it's been so unbearable to be there that we've spent the last couple of nights sleeping at Gavin's. Tomorrow night is her exhibition and I wonder how she's feeling about it. Has everything gone smoothly this week leading up to it? Is she nervous? Does she like New York and want to move there?

You should be there with her, asshole.

But I don't deserve to be, not with the way I've treated her.

"Can you pass me the vegetables?" Gavin's voice interrupts my thoughts and I pass him the plate with the shish kabobs. I watch in silence as he adds them to the grill and closes the lid.

He turns to the side and tilts his head while looking at me. "Are you happy, Gunnar?"

I raise my eyebrows, surprised at the question. "For the most part, yes. Why?"

"Because you don't seem to be. You've been walking around in a trance like you're half here with us and half somewhere else. Would that somewhere else happen to be New York?"

I give him a pointed look. "Don't start with me, Gavin."

"It's pretty amazing the things that come out of a five-year old's mouth." He lifts open the hood of the grill, flips over the kabobs and puts it back down. "Izzy was watching us undress Abbi for her first bath. She helped Aly wash her and commented on how she was naked. Then she said the darnedest thing and told us that she saw Cassie naked in your bed."

I clamp my jaw shut, cross my arms over my chest and stare at him while he continues on. "Not that this news is shocking to us. It has been obvious for weeks that something was going on between the two of you. You looked like a love sick school boy every time she was in the room with you."

"I'm not going to ask what happened, Gunnar, because I can pretty much guess how you fucked it all up since I know you so well. But as someone who loves you, it's time to give you some tough love. You are letting an amazing woman who loves you and your kid walk out of your life. Who the fuck cares about her age when she's more mature than all of your teammates combined?"

The corner of my mouth lifts at that because he's right, she's way more mature than everyone on my team.

"As for your fear of Izzy getting hurt if your relationship doesn't work—you're the one doing more damage to Izzy by not having a mother figure in her life. Here you have one and you're pushing her away with your selfishness. Cassie is not Tasha. She's not going to use you and I would be damned shocked if she ever cheated on you. Cassie is also the type that if your relationship with her didn't work out, she would ask to stay in touch with Izzy."

"You're right, she would," I agree, impressed with his observation of her.

He turns off the burners of the grill, opens the hood, and puts the steaks and the veggies on the platters I have ready for him. "When your career in baseball is done and over with, what's going to make you feel fulfilled in life, Gunnar? What else besides Izzy will make you happy and content?"

His words are like a bucket of cold water slowly being poured over me. "I honestly don't know."

"Well, I know. I've never seen you as happy as you were last month when you and Cassie were together. Imagine how much happier you would be if that was a *real* relationship."

I briefly let myself fantasize about what life would be like if Cassie was my girlfriend, and eventually my wife. It would be heaven.

"Be honest with yourself and with me: do you love her, Gunnar?"

I don't even hesitate with my answer. "Yes, I do."

"Then be with her. We all love her and love the idea of you guys being together."

I shake my head and give him a sad smile. "I've really fucked it up this time. She refuses to talk to me."

"Well, then you need to do something grandiose," he tells me and an idea for winning her back begins to form.

We carry the plates of food back inside the house and put

them in the kitchen. Gavin announces that it's dinner time and Izzy runs into the kitchen with Austin. I pick up my daughter and give her a tight hug and kiss on the cheek.

"Let's eat, Isabear, because we need to get home and pack."

"Pack for what?" she asks with a confused look on her face.

"We're going to New York."

CHAPTER 25

CASSIE

New York has been a whirlwind of activity, which was the distraction I needed to not think about Gunnar. On our first day in Brooklyn, we went straight to the gallery and met with Michael in person. He showed us where my painting was located and walked us through the narrative of the other artwork leading up to mine. Imposter syndrome started to kick in while viewing the other incredible paintings and reading the artists' descriptions behind their masterpieces. If my painting doesn't sell on opening night, it will be displayed for a few more months before being shipped back to me. Regardless of the outcome, I'm forever grateful to Michael for giving me this opportunity.

We ate and drank our way through the city, went to every popular tourist attraction New York City has to offer and saw two Broadway shows. Grace and I went shopping for my big night because she claimed that my wardrobe was lame and I needed to look the part of being a New York City artist. I was skeptical of finding something within my budget, but as luck would have it, we found the perfect floral-print silk handkerchief dress at a second-hand consignment shop with matching emerald green heeled sandals and a clutch to complete the outfit. This week has been magical and tonight is going to be the perfect ending to one of the most memorable occasions of my life.

Despite my excitement for this evening, reality is starting to sink in of what's waiting for me back home. I've been ignoring Gunnar's texts and calls, but I wonder how I'm going to handle seeing him when I get back to Nashville. I thought I was doing well until Carter surprised Grace and showed up last night. She's been sharing a room with me this whole trip, so a night to myself with my sadness and pervasive thoughts broke the dam that was holding my emotions back. While I'm happy for Grace, Carter's sweet gesture was salt being rubbed into my wounds.

"There's no amount of concealer that's going to cover up these bags underneath your eyes," Grace comments while helping me do my makeup. "Did you not sleep due to nerves?" She studies me a little more closely. "You've been crying, haven't you?"

I give her a sad smile and nod. "All of the above. Guess my body needed it. Wish it would've chosen another night to be a running faucet of tears and snot."

"Oh Cass, I'm so sorry." Grace puts down the concealer brush and gives me a hug. "You should've called me. You know I would've come down and stayed with you."

"And interrupt your sexy time with Carter? Not a chance." Grace's cheeks turn pink and she giggles. I grab her hand and squeeze it. "I'm really happy for you, Grace. Carter seems like a great guy." Carter and Grace finally confessed their true feelings for each other and their relationship is no longer fake.

"He is," she says with a smile and continues applying my makeup. "Not at all like his butthole of a teammate." After I had told Grace everything that happened, she refuses to say Gunnar's name out loud. "Carter says he's been pretty miserable to be around, acting like the asshole that he is."

I don't say a word although a small part of me is happy to hear he's suffering as much as I am.

"Let's not even think about him. Tonight is your night to be happy and excited."

"And I'm nervous. Very, very nervous," I chime in with a laugh.

"What's there to be nervous about? It's not the end-all-be-all if it doesn't sell tonight."

"This is true. They will keep it for three months and ship it back if it hasn't sold by then."

"It will sell. It's too beautiful not to," she reassures me.

"I don't know. It's a very poignant piece. Not all people would want that hanging up in their personal space."

"It's going to sell. We're manifesting it right now," she says and I laugh, needing all the positivity and manifestation I can get.

⚾ 🧤 🦋 🧁

We arrive an hour before the doors open like Michael requested and meet the other artists whose work is also being displayed tonight. Michael goes through a rundown of events and lets us know he expects us to schmooze with the guests until it's time for the Q&A session. Each artist will have ten minutes to describe their work and answer questions. Since there are six artists being featured tonight, the session will take us to the end of the show.

Once the doors open, I'm pleasantly surprised to see how quickly the gallery fills up. I get a lot of compliments on my dress, which opens the door for conversation. Michael comes around and introduces me to some other gallery owners and people in the industry. I've been so busy networking, that I lose track of my dad, Grace, and Carter. After I finish conversing with a potential buyer, I go on the hunt to find them. My mouth drops open when I see not only Grace's parents are here, but so are Valerie and Rowan.

"What are you guys doing here?" I ask in surprise when I approach the group and start giving my new guests hugs.

"You're like our second daughter. There's no way we were going to miss this," Katherine tells me after giving me a tight squeeze.

"You look absolutely stunning," Valerie comments once we finish hugging. She takes a look around at the crowd in awe. "This place is packed, Cassie! I'm so excited for you."

"I wouldn't be here if it wasn't for you and your connection to Michael. Thank you so much for making the introduction."

"Oh, please." She flicks her wrist as if it was nothing. "You got in because of how talented you are. You would've gotten yourself here eventually without my help. Aly wishes she could be here, but a newborn baby had to spoil all her fun."

I laugh and give her a fake pout. "We'll just have to come back another time, just us girls."

"Yes!" Valerie pulls out her phone and opens up her camera app. "Let's take a selfie and make her jealous." She positions the phone above us and takes our photo.

Michael comes up and gives Valerie a hug and meets Rowan for the first time. They chat for a couple of minutes and then he glances at his watch to check the time. "Excuse me, Val, but I need to grab Cassie and have her go to the back of the gallery for the Q&A session."

I wave good-bye to my crew and follow him to the back. I get in line with my fellow artists and Michael uses the microphone to ask all patrons to come back for the Q&A session. He waits a couple of minutes for the room to fill up and then greets the audience and tells them each artist will speak briefly about our paintings and then answer a couple of questions.

I listen intently to my fellow artists, enthralled like the rest of the audience about their paintings and what inspired them to paint. My palms start to sweat when the artist next to me starts their turn. I'm not a fan of public speaking, nor do I like to be the center of attention, so my plan is to make this go as quickly as possible and pray that I don't get asked a lot of questions. Pretty sure the person next to me had the same idea, because all too soon, it's my turn and Michael is introducing me. He hands me the mic and I can hear Grace yelling out my name, her voice being recognizable as the loudest and most enthusiastic person in the entire gallery.

"Good evening, everyone. Thank you so much for coming tonight. My name is Cassie Warner and my painting is called The Darkness In Her Light. It is a dualistic portrait showcasing the stark contrast between the woman's radiant, well-groomed, sunshine and roses side versus her opposing dark side of being out of control, disheveled, and somber, that ultimately reflect her struggles with addiction. It's what I imagine the fine line is before the addiction takes full control of your body."

I hand the microphone back to Michael, who continues talking. "Cassie, what drew me to the painting was the details you used in her expression to convey her happiness versus darkness and the symbolism of light versus shadow to represent the dichotomy. I think it's safe to say that all of us felt the magnetism of emotions and the painting sucked us right in. Am I right?" He looks over the crowd, who starts clapping with people shouting, "Yes." I flush with embarrassment over his compliments, but seeing the crowd's reaction gives me a sense of fulfillment and the awareness that I've made one of my dreams a reality.

"Let's open up the floor to a couple of questions for

Cassie." Michael looks around and points to a woman with her hand raised. "Go ahead with your question for Cassie."

Michael hands the mic over to her. "What was your inspiration for this piece?"

I look out in the crowd for my father and see him give me a nod of encouragement. "My mother was my inspiration. She died of alcoholism a couple of years ago."

I hear a couple of murmurs in the crowd and I look down at my feet, not wanting to see the pity on their faces.

"This must have been a difficult piece for you to paint," Michael comments, giving me a sympathetic smile.

"It was actually very therapeutic. Portraits are not something I normally paint and the vision just kept coming to me. I took it as a sign that I needed to paint her, almost as if it was closure for me. If that makes sense?"

I look out at the crowd and people are nodding. "That's beautiful, Cassie." Michael says, "And someone else must've thought the same thing because The Darkness In Her Light by Cassie Warner has officially been sold."

I look at Michael in shock and the crowd cheers and he whispers in my ear, "I'll introduce you to the buyer when we are done with Q&A." I nod in excitement and look for my people. Grace and Valerie are giving me a thumbs up and my dad is wiping away a tear. Tears of happiness are threatening to stream out of my own eyes and I tell myself to keep it together.

Michael starts to introduce the last artist of the evening and I try to focus my attention on them, but I can't stop looking at the faces in the crowd. As I scan each face, I can't help but wonder which one of them is the buyer until I do a double-take at the face of an unexpected visitor.

Gunnar.

Gunnar is here? My eyes widen in shock and he gives me one of those heart stopping, panty-melting smiles of his that I can never resist. My emotions start swirling out of control like a tornado. I'm immensely happy that he's come to support me, but in the next breath, weary about the reason he's here. I briefly lose sight of him when he breaks our eye contact and he bends down. He pops back up and has Izzy in his arms. My hands immediately go to my chest, my heart wanting to burst with joy knowing she's here with him to see me. He says something in her ear and points to me. She follows his finger and when she sees me, her face lights up in the biggest smile. She starts waving and I smile back at her.

My attention is snapped back to Michael when the crowd starts to applaud at his announcement that the artist next to me also sold their painting. *Wait a minute… did Gunnar buy my painting?* The thought sours my mood.

I'm going to punch him.

That man can't just waltz in here and pretend everything is going to be okay if he buys my painting. A painting that I don't even want due to its emotional baggage.

As soon as the Q&A session ends, I make a beeline straight for Gunnar to confront him. I'm tired of his mind games. Gunnar puts Izzy down, takes whatever she is holding from her, and she runs straight to me. I pick her up and hold her tightly, breathing in her scent. Her arms and legs tighten around me and I feel some of the tension leaving my body.

"I've missed you, Peanut," I whisper in her ear before putting her down. "Thank you for coming to see me."

"I made you a sign, but Daddy says I can't show it to you yet." She grabs my hand and we walk over to where Gunnar is standing. My eyes can't stop assessing how handsome he looks in his black suit and it makes me even more mad. In one hand he's holding a large bouquet of red roses and in the other, Izzy's rolled up sign.

"Cassie!" Michael calls out as he briskly walks over to me. "I want you to meet the buyer of your painting."

"If he's the buyer," I nod at Gunnar. "Then I want you to refund him. I don't want his money."

I see a flash of hurt reflect in Gunnar's gaze, but my attention reverts back to Michael when he says, "He's not the buyer. Mrs. Denise Ford is." A woman with long silver hair steps next to Michael and holds out her hand for me to shake.

Embarrassment stains my cheeks red and I take her hand in mine. "Mrs. Ford, I'm honored. Thank you so much for buying my painting."

"I knew I wanted it the moment I laid eyes on it, but it was your story regarding your inspiration for it that leads me to think this was fate. I own an in-patient addiction facility and was planning on hanging it there before I heard you speak."

I gasp, grab her hands, and squeeze. "Sounds like you have the perfect home for it. Thank you again so much."

"We'll be in touch. I would like to commission some more paintings from you."

"That would be wonderful!"

We say goodbye and Michael whisks her away to meet another artist she bought from. When I turn back around, my dad, Grace, Carter, Valerie, Rowan, and Grace's parents are standing by Gunnar.

My father walks up to me and gives me a hug. "I'm so proud of you," he whispers in my ear. "And she would've been too."

I bite the inside of my cheek to keep from crying and squeeze my dad hard. After a couple of moments, we drop our arms from around each other and he steps back. "Is everything okay?" he asks with a nod at Gunnar.

"Not sure," I respond, before Grace moves in to hug me.

"I promise you I had no idea he was coming and neither did Carter," Grace says into my ear.

"I know you didn't," I reassure her as I look over my shoulder to see Carter and Gunnar in a heated discussion.

Grace's parents come over next to hug and congratulate me. Then next is Rowan, with Valerie lining up last.

"I was sworn to secrecy that I couldn't tell you he was coming. If it's any consolation, I only found out this morning from Aly. Please don't hate me," she pleads.

"I don't hate you. Besides, even if you did tell me, what was I going to do? Not show up to my own exhibition?"

She grins. "True, but we could've hired security to keep him out."

I laugh. "That would make things very awkward for me when I show up for work on Saturday."

She giggles for a moment but then gets somber, her smile fading."Seriously, Cass, we can ask him to leave. Rowan and I will escort him out."

I give her a hug, grateful for this new friendship of ours. "No, don't worry about it. I've been ignoring his texts and calls all week, so I might as well get this over with."

I let her go and turn toward Gunnar, who is holding Izzy's hand and is waiting for me. "Isabear, go stand by Valerie and get ready for my signal to unveil your sign. Val, do you mind holding these for Cassie?" Valerie grabs the bouquet of flowers from him, cradles them in her arms like a baby, and places her free hand on Izzy's shoulder so she stays in place.

Gunnar looks around at our group to see no one is leaving to give us some privacy. He smiles in appreciation over their protectiveness and turns his attention back to me.

"Why are you here, Gunnar?" I question with my guard up.

"I'm here because the woman I love is having a monumental night in her life and I need to be here to support her."

"L-Love?" I stutter out in complete shock because that is *not* what I was expecting him to say at all.

"Pretty sure I fell in love with you the night you told me you would protect my daughter with your life and it has been slowly growing every day since."

I give him a sad smile, my eyes watering up with unshed tears. "How can you love someone and treat them the way you treated me?"

He swallows and nods. "There's no excuse for my behavior and I hate myself for hurting you the way I did. I know you probably think I'm the biggest asshole for the way I treated you and I'm so sorry, Cassie. I let my past heartache and resentment control me, causing me to be an idiot. I risked losing the best person besides my daughter to ever come into my life. I let my fear convince me that we shouldn't be together, but I promise you this." He takes a step toward me, grabs my hands and squeezes. "I will never let that happen again."

"How do you know?" I ask, giving him a skeptical look.

"Because once I realized what a fool I've been for keeping you at arm's length, all my fear about us dissipated. My life is miserable without you in it. You bring joy, sunshine, and love not only to me, but to Izzy as well. You've turned our place into a home with love and warmth and it doesn't work without you in it. I don't want to be your boss anymore—I want to be your partner, your best friend, and your lover."

I don't realize I'm crying until he brings his hands up to cup my face, using the pads of his thumbs to wipe away my tears. "I don't deserve you, Cassie, but fuck I'm going to beg you for a second chance. Please forgive me. Please let me show you how much I love you."

He brings his forehead to mine and I grip his wrist as he kisses the tears from each cheek. "I love you, Cassie, and I know you love me too." I swallow and stare in his eyes that are shining with love and admiration. "There's only one more question to ask." He drops his hands, steps back and walks over to Izzy. He slides the rubber band off her sign and whispers something in her ear. She nods and walks forward with him.

He gets down on one knee next to Izzy and helps her get the sign ready to unveil. He asks if she's ready and she nods in excitement. "Cassie Warner," he says loudly. "Will you please be my girlfriend?" As soon as he says the words, Izzy turns her poster around and in his horrible attempt at block lettering, it reads 'Will you be my daddy's girlfriend?' in bright letters. There are pictures of butterflies, cupcakes, baseballs, bats, and hearts all over the poster surrounding the lettering, but what really pulls at my heart is the family of three Izzy drew on the bottom corner that has my name under the woman holding hers and her daddy's hand.

I tilt my head to the side and press my lips together, trying not to cry even harder. I'm in love with both of them and despite his stupidity over shutting me out when Izzy discovered us, Gunnar *is* the man of my dreams. "Yes," I whisper with a nod. Gunnar pops up to both of his feet, hauls me to his chest, and crushes his lips to mine in the most possessive kiss I've ever experienced.

"I fucking love you," he growls after he reluctantly breaks our kiss due to the cheering and clapping from our family and friends.

"I love you too."

He drops his forehead to mine. "Thank you for giving me a second chance. I promise you won't regret it."

I smile, feeling one hundred percent confident that I won't. "Thank you for fighting for me."

He gently presses his lips to mine. "Always."

I feel something hit my legs and I look down to see Izzy's arms wrapped around both of us. We break apart and I lift Izzy up and give her a hug. "I love you, Peanut."

"I love you too, Cassie."

A calmness washes over me, the ever-present fear of abandonment slowly leaving my body. I'm surrounded by family and friends who love and support me through thick and thin and a boyfriend who will fight his own demons to make sure I'm a priority in his life.

I leave the gallery that night with my heart full of love and my biggest dream coming true as I start the next exciting chapter of my life with Gunnar and Izzy.

EPILOGUE
GUNNAR

Two Years Later

I
t's the top of the ninth inning with bases loaded in the
final game of the Championship. I can't help but feel the
sense of déjà vu from last year when we lost to Colorado
in game six. We were riddled with injuries for most of last
season, but managed to scrape by to get into the postseason.
For the most part, everyone had recovered and was healthy
for the playoffs but even with our strong effort, we lost. It left
a bitter taste in all of our mouths. I worked my ass in the off-
season to make sure I was in the best shape of my life, as did
a lot of the other vets who were still on the team and experienced that devastating loss. This season, our team has been
on the road to redemption and we're one out away from
getting it. The noise level in Music City Park is electric with
excitement and anxiety. If a run is scored by the visiting team,
we go into the bottom of the ninth tied and have to rely on
our offense to not only get us another run, but pray the other
team makes some defensive errors.

As the next batter walks to the plate, Tripp and I jog up to
Carter on the mound. He's in his head after the two walks he

just gave up and the bullpen is warming up in case he walks another batter. He's one of the best closers in the league, so I have full confidence that he can get this win for us with a strikeout. Murph started the game great, but a couple of home runs in the 7th inning were given up and he was pulled. It's been a duel and I'm ready for this shit to be over with and the trophy to be ours.

"Listen to me," I tell Carter, demanding that he looks at me and not at the ground. "You've got this, Carter. You hear me? Get out of your head and just focus on throwing down the center of the plate. Don't think about if he hits it or not, we got you if he does. Strike this motherfucker out like the champion you are." He nods and I tap his chest with my glove before walking away.

I go back to my position and briefly look up at my suite. I see my family and friends standing on their feet in anticipation of what's to come. Izzy is holding her signature game day sign with this one reading: "My Daddy Hits Bombs." I touch two of my fingers to my lips and point to them. Cassie does it right back to me and knowing I have her love, support and encouragement fills me with determination.

I focus my attention on the batter and study him intently. I watch how he scans the field and mentally picks where he wants to hit the ball. He ends his assessment by looking straight at me. I know he's visualizing hitting the ball right over my head. It would be the perfect spot to for the ball to drop and allow them to get one run in if we don't try to throw the runner out at home. His coaches are yelling encouraging words at him and both teams are on their feet in their respective dugouts. The runners on the bases are ready to run their asses off. Both teams are on high alert and the tension is thick in the air.

I call after Chase at third base and Eric at second base and signal to them to be ready. I turn around to alert Evan in left field that the batter might hit the ball in our direction. I squat down and get ready, praying that my intuition isn't wrong. Either way, everyone is lined up right where they should be.

The batter steps into the batter's box, holds up his hand for the umpire to know he's not ready yet, and positions his feet to get into his stance. The umpire puts his hand down to let Carter know he can proceed. Carter takes a deep breath and nods at Tripp's signal. He focuses on the strike zone before kicking up his leg and throws a bullet straight down the center. The batter swings and misses.

Strike one.

"You got this, Carter!" I yell out to him, even though I'm pretty sure he can't hear me above the roar of the crowd. The fans are on their feet, chanting Carter's name. I stand to my full height to shake out my legs before squatting back down.

Carter gets into position again and throws a slider. The batter doesn't swing and watches the ball fly straight into Tripp's glove.

Strike two.

He looks at the umpire incredulously, not believing it was a strike. They exchange some words and the batter steps out of the box for some practice swings. Carter steps off the rubber and shakes off his arm. He looks over at me and I nod at him, knowing he's mentally getting himself ready for this next pitch.

We're one strike away from being the champions and the pressure is on him.

He places his foot back on the rubber and waits for the batter's stance. Carter will be throwing either a fastball or curveball. The goal is to confuse the batter and have him swing and miss. Carter gets into position, kicks up his leg and throws. The batter swings and barely misses the ball.

Strike three.

I toss my glove up in the air and rush towards Carter, throwing him off balance when I fling myself at him. "You fucking beast! You did it!" I shout at him over the deafening decibels of the fans cheering in the stadium.

"*We* did it!" he yells back right before Tripp and all the other players converge upon us. We form a circle around Carter, jumping up and down, dancing and screaming for joy that we are the new world champions.

I lose track of time as the whole team goes through the motions of celebratory hugs, back-slaps, and high fives between the players, coaches, and the rest of baseball operations staff. Camera crews have descended upon us, following our every move and getting into our personal spaces. League operations staff starts handing out championship shirts and hats for us to wear. We all start putting them on so we're ready for the trophy ceremony. I see some children running on the field and I'm staying in one spot so my family can find me.

I look through the crowd and find Gavin running toward me. "Fuck yeah, Gunnar!" he screams before crushing me in a bear hug. "You guys did it!"

I don't pay any attention to the camera crews that are circling around us and I squeeze my brother right back. "I love you, Brother. Thank you for being here with me." Tears of joy stream down my face as it hits me that I really just won the championship—and it will be my one and only since I plan on retiring after tonight. It's not public knowledge yet, but I've talked it over with Cassie, my family, Declan, and Billy. I've fulfilled every dream I've had for myself profession-ally in the last fifteen years. It's time to start enjoying life and be more of a present dad and partner, which is what Izzy and Cassie deserve.

"Where's Aly?" I ask Gavin when we're done hugging and I don't see her around us.

"She's up in the suite with everyone else waiting for you to come up to celebrate."

I look over Gavin's shoulder and see my parents with

Cassie and Izzy heading toward us. Izzy's eyes are wide with apprehension, but also excitement as she takes in the confetti that is raining down all over everyone.

I first gather my parents in a group hug, listening to them tell me how proud they are of me and the career I've had. "I wouldn't have had any of this if it wasn't for the sacrifices you two made when you saw I had the potential. Thank you for believing in me," I tell them before kissing their cheeks. I let them go so they can wipe away the tears that are streaming down their faces.

I reach for Izzy and hoist her up on my hip before grabbing Cassie with my free arm and pulling her into my side. The three of us hug each other tightly and I get choked up thinking about what an incredible support system and partner I have in Cassie. I keep my arms around my girls but pull back so I can kiss Cassie on the lips.

"God, Gunnar, I'm so ridiculously proud of you," she gushes, her eyes sparkling with happiness. "What a storybook ending." She side-eyes the cameras that have surrounded us and I know she's trying to choose her words wisely without accidentally announcing anything publicly. The team wants to do a press conference, so we are keeping my retirement under wraps until the official announcement.

"How does it feel to have all of your professional dreams come true?" she asks and I rest my forehead against hers before giving her another kiss.

"Incredible because I have you by my side," I tell her, watching her eyes start to water with emotion. "But there's one more thing I have to do." She gives me a quizzical look as I put Izzy down. "Isabear, go stand by grandma."

Izzy does as she's told and I grab Cassie's hands before getting down on one knee. Her eyes grow as round as saucers and she gives me a look as if to say I'm crazy.

I am crazy…crazy in love with the woman of my dreams.

"Gunnar, what are you doing?" She starts pulling on my

hands to try to get me to stand back up, but I'm stronger than she is and her efforts are moot. "Get up." She looks around and almost hits her head against a camera that is positioned over her shoulder. "Everyone is staring at us."

This was not how I was planning on proposing to her. The ring is back home at the new house we bought last year, tucked in my safe in my office. We have plans to go to Italy and France this off-season with our whole family and I was going to do it at the villa I rented with Lake Como as my backdrop. These past two years together have been better than my wildest dreams. With the high of the win and this being the end of my baseball era, I can't think of a better way to start this new chapter of my life off right than with a proposal.

"Cassie Warner, you painted color back into my life when it had become black and white. You are the most supportive, loving, and caring partner and an incredible mother figure to Izzy. I can't imagine my life without you. I'm done being just your boyfriend—I want to be your husband for eternity." I squeeze her hands while tears cascade down her cheeks. "Will you do me the honor of becoming my wife and putting up with my older, cranky ass who might gain a pudgy dad-bod due to your delicious baking?"

She laughs and nods. "Yes! Of course I will marry you!"

I stand back up, pull her into my arms, and crush my lips to hers. When we come up for air and hug, she whispers to me, "I love you so much, Gunnar McNeer. I'm yours forever."

Cheers of joy erupt from not only everyone around us, but the fans in the stands as well who were able to hear the entire proposal when it was broadcasted on the Jumbotron. We pull apart and bask in the warmth and happiness from our family and friends who take turns hugging and congratulating us.

I look at my new fiancée and smile. I can't believe this incredible woman has agreed to spend the rest of her life with me. I used to not be a big believer in a higher power, but there's no denying that fate brought me my perfect catch.

❀ ⚾ 🦋 🧁

Thank you for reading The Perfect Catch. If you loved this book, I would so appreciate it if you can leave a review and tell your fellow romance reading friends about it.

The next book up to bat is Strike Zone by Mignon Mykel that follows the team's catcher, Cassidy "Tripp" Nash, as he starts a secret relationship with team photographer Cheyenne Meyer. Click HERE or turn the page to start reading.

Curious about Gavin and Aly McNeer's love story? You can read it in Love At The Bluebird by me and Aurora Rose Reynolds. Click HERE or turn the page to start reading.

You can also read Rowan and Valerie Pryor's love story in Until Valerie, available in Kindle Unlimited.

Grace and Carter's love story, Perfect Save, will also be in Kindle Unlimited.

❀ ⚾ 🦋 🧁

LOVE AT THE BLUEBIRD

BY AURORA ROSE REYNOLDS AND JESSICA MARIN

GAVIN

I drum my fingers against the car door panel, impatient energy coursing through my veins while watching the outside scenery pass by. Sosie, my assistant, is driving us to my show tonight, and for some reason, I feel nervous. My pre-show jitters are usually due to the anticipation of the high I get while performing, so this nervousness is a foreign feeling. Maybe it's because I'm tired. Yesterday was a long day with continued interviews and time spent in the studio working on a song for another artist. I didn't get home until close to midnight and crashed as soon as I turned the lights off.

"What's up with you?" Sosie asks, giving me a strange look out of the corner of her eye. She notices everything, so I know I won't be able to weasel my way out of this unwanted conversation.

"Nothing. What's up with you and those bags under your eyes?" I question with concern as I study her more closely. She has her hair up in a messy bun and her thick red glasses on, but those glasses only accentuate the deep purple bags underneath her blue eyes. Something is going on with her that she's not sharing. When I'm in the studio working for other artists, Sosie isn't on the clock, meaning she was done working for me yesterday after lunch. What she does with her free time is her business, but when I see her not looking well, I make it a point to make her personal time my business.

"Always deflecting, but it won't work this time, Gav. I'm not answering your question until you answer mine." She gives me a sweet, fake smile before turning her attention back to the road.

"Fine," I mumble, caring more about hearing what's going on with her than my own nervousness. "Honestly, I don't know what the fuck is wrong with me. For some reason, I'm nervous."

"Yeah, I can tell. You're like the Tasmanian Devil over there." I follow her eyes to my left leg bouncing rapidly up and down. I place my hand on my thigh, mentally forcing it to stop. "But you've performed numerous times at the Blue-bird. Why would this time be any different?"

"Possibly because this is a private event being held by another record label." *Their people will be watching me... judging me*, I think but don't say out loud. I shouldn't be nervous. I practically lived at the Bluebird Cafe when I first landed in Nashville. It's the place to play when you're a song-writer wanting to get noticed. It's an extremely small venue, capacity of only 90 people, making the audience seem like they're right on top of you. Food and beverages are served while the crowd listens to singers belt out their songs. The Bluebird has launched the careers of some of today's most famous singers like Taylor Swift and Garth Brooks. You can feel how special the place is the moment you walk through the doors.

"People are watching and judging you every time you walk on stage though," she reminds me.

"True." I sigh, not really wanting to psychoanalyze my mood right now.

"Maybe subconsciously, you're anxious because you know when your contract is up with the devil, you need to change record labels, and Big Little Music could potentially be your future home." I chuckle at her calling Atticus Langston the devil. From day one, Sosie saw right through his weaselly charm and loves telling me, in her heavily laced sarcastic voice, that she prays for my soul every day.

"I don't think so. For one thing, I like being with a big label, because they have more dollars for marketing and advertising."

"That actually isn't true anymore," she informs me quietly. "I know you've heard how Big Little Music's artists love being with them. Plus, they've landed some pretty big names for not being a more well-known label." She starts rattling off the names of their well-known singers, surprising me with not only their lineup of talent, but her knowledge of who they have signed. When Sosie first started working for me, she didn't know shit about this industry. Not that it mattered to me—I was just trying to get her the fuck out of California and away from my toxic aunt and uncle. Since working for me, she has taken her job as my assistant very seriously, immersing herself in the industry, studying the ins and outs of it and who the big players are.

As I let her words settle in, I realize she might have a point. For a small label, Big Little Music has created quite the reputation for themselves. For one, they still care about their artists and not how much money they can get out of them. They are the total opposite of Charisma Records.

Up-and-coming artists like myself don't usually get signed by labels like Charisma. They already make enough money on their current catalog of talent and don't need or want to take a chance on nobodies. The only reason I got signed is because I wrote a hit song for Tori, who ran home and told her daddy about me. I highly doubt she raved about how truly talented I was—more like she wanted to keep me around and happy so I could write more songs for her. Fortunately, I signed only a single album deal with Charisma. Yes, it sucks big giant, Texas-sized balls that they get to own the rights to my songs for ten years, but that's the price you pay when you sign on the dotted line sometimes.

We pull into the parking lot behind the Bluebird. Since there are no dressing rooms for artists to wait in, most just arrive at their designated time slot or hang out with other performers in the back by their cars. I wave at a couple people I recognize as I get out of the car then retrieve my Martin D28 acoustic guitar from the back and start to warm up while standing there. Sosie always makes sure we arrive ten minutes before call time, which I know is padded with a few extra minutes. Once I'm warmed up, I head over to a group of people gathered near the back door.

"How's the crowd tonight?" I ask, greeting Scotty Wilkins with a pat to his shoulder. I've known Scotty for years and have even wrote a couple songs with him. Despite his overinflated ego, he's a good guy.

"Great crowd tonight. I might stick around to make myself available, if you know what I mean." He winks at Sosie, who responds by rolling her eyes in disgust at him.

"You're barking up the wrong tree, man. My cousin would chew you up and spit you out." I give him a cold smile, hoping he catches my warning when our eyes lock. I know Sosie can handle herself, but I can't help the protectiveness I feel when it comes to my baby cousin. Anyone disrespects her, they'll answer to me.

Scotty chuckles and shakes his head while smiling. "You know, it's pretty awesome how tight you two are. I wish I had that family dynamic." For a moment, something that resembles sadness flashes in his eyes, but Scotty is quick to blink it away and go back to his usual cocky self.

What was that all about? Not that he would tell me anyway. We aren't close, nor will we probably ever be. I purposely keep my circle close and tight. In this industry, I've learned you don't know what people's motives are, so it's best to keep everyone at a distance until they prove themselves to be loyal.

"A couple of us are getting together next week to jam. Look at your schedule, and if you're free, come join us. It would be worth your time." Having worked together before, Scotty knows how I operate. For him to say it would be worth my time piques my interest. I look over at Sosie, who nods at me while typing notes in her phone to check my schedule.

"I'll text you tomorrow with my schedule and you let me know where and when," I tell him, trying to remember what's going on next week. If I recall correctly, it's a slower week, with the end of the month being crazier.

"Good luck in there tonight," Scotty says with a nod at me. He pats me on the shoulder, waves at Sosie, and heads toward his car to leave.

"So much for him staying to make himself available," Sosie snarks sarcastically while watching him drive away.

"You like Scotty Wilkins?" I narrow my eyes at her, trying to gauge her reaction to my question. Sosie has shown zero interest in anyone since moving to Nashville. Her douchebag of an ex-boyfriend did a number on her, so it isn't that surprising to me that she's so standoffish when it comes to the opposite sex.

"Seriously, what *is* wrong with you tonight?" She huffs in annoyance, my smirk only seeming to rile her up even more. "That question doesn't even warrant a response. Get your head out of your ass, because it's time to perform." I laugh at her not-so-motivating pep talk and follow her up to the back door.

We check in with the staff and wait for them to signal me through. I hear the audience clapping and see the performer who was just on stage walk back to us. I smile in acknowledgment at her and then start walking when she's cleared the hallway. Once I appear into the main room, I keep a smile on my face, my eyes trained on the stool for me to sit on. The room is silent, no one applauding in greeting, because the rules of the Bluebird Cafe are that you are here to listen and immerse yourself in the experience and emotion of the songs. No one gets rowdy here. No one gets up to dance. This is a true, musical experience of listening and dissecting every word and meaning of these songs.

"Good evening, everyone. I'm Gavin." Introductions are always informal at the Bluebird, because here, everyone is on equal ground. Doesn't matter how many accolades you have on your resume—we are all songwriters in this room, just trying to make a living doing what we love. My eyes scan the room, noting the heads nodding in recognition at me. I flash a genuine smile in their direction, forcing myself to hold it steady when noticing how many record label executives are here, some of them less than three feet away from me.

Calm the fuck down, Gavin, I tell myself after I talk about the background of the song I'm about to sing. I try to get into a comfortable position, placing my guitar on my thigh, take a deep breath, and close my eyes. I go through my meditation of zoning everyone out before internally repeating my personal motto:

You deserve to be here. Now show them why.

I peek down, watching my fingers strum the introductory notes to the very first song I wrote for someone else called "Needing You Now." My eyes slide closed once more when I start to sing, letting the familiar chords of the song wash away my nerves as I begin my tale. I open them again so I can find that one focal point to concentrate on when I need it.

As I sing the last line of the first verse of the song, my eyes suddenly do a double take when they land on the face of one of the most beautiful women I've ever had the pleasure of looking at. Long, black lashes surround brown eyes the color of whiskey. Her face is lightly tanned with a dusting of natural-looking makeup brushed effortlessly across her face. Her hair seems to be the color of caramel, long and falling in waves down her shoulders. Her eyes are warm, inviting me into their abyss as everyone else starts to slowly fade away.

My mind screams at me not to blink, that she might be a figment of my imagination. As I start into the chorus, the emotions of the words force my eyelids shut, feeling the desperation of wanting that special someone to love you, support you, be there for you. I chose to sing this song tonight because of the power of its meaning and the emotions that it should evoke from the crowd.

My mind still pictures her as I sing out a long chord. My eyelids spring open, seeking out those stunning eyes as I mentally count the three beats of silence before continuing to the end of my narrative. I watch her expression as my voice registers up into my vibrato and an overwhelming need to impress her comes over me. Her eyes widen as I hit my note, her luscious pink lips parting in awe, telling me that I just nailed the ending of the song.

My heart beats rapidly in my chest as I stare at her while the crowd loudly cheers. I slowly start to smile at her, enjoying seeing her cheeks pinkening. She's sitting close enough that I can see the pupils in her eyes dilated from what I hope is pleasure. I reluctantly break our eye contact to acknowledge the crowd, thanking them before continuing to talk about the next song I plan on performing.

As I get ready to move on, I know right then and there she's going to be the one I sing to for the rest of my set, and I don't give a fuck if people start talking about how I'm staring at her like a creeper. I want to watch every single expression that crosses over that angelic face of hers. I start the chords to my next song, not even needing to look down, because the encouragement from her eyes is all I need. All I want.

This woman has captivated me like no one else has ever before.

I need to know the identity of the woman I can't take my eyes off of.

With our gazes locked together once more, I can't help but wonder who she is. Her attendance tonight means she's either in the industry or associated with someone in the industry. *Please, dear Lord, if she's associated with someone, let it not be a husband or a boyfriend.* The only other person at her table is another woman I don't know.

I look to see if I can spot a ring on her left hand when she takes a sip of whatever she's drinking. Her hand is bare, and I can't contain my smile knowing that the chances of her being married are slim without the hardware on. My only obstacle would be if there's a boyfriend, and it would be surprising if there wasn't. Most women who look like her are always taken, but then again, most women who are taken don't look at strangers the way she's looking at me.

She seems to be just as enthralled with me as I am with her. When I sing a seductive verse from my song, she rewards me with a sexy smirk that makes my dick instantly harden with want. I start to feel overheated and know damn well it isn't from the lights. This woman better be single, because my body is now buzzing with adrenaline, and a different kind of anticipation is now coursing through my veins.

I'm going to make that girl mine.

As soon as the song ends, I grab a bottle of water and take a big gulp from it, my eyes never wavering from hers. I need to figure out a way to meet my mystery lady fast. I'm the last performer of the evening, and with this being an industry event, hours of socializing afterward usually occur. I have to talk to her before that happens and rapidly get her number, since we won't have any privacy once I'm done performing.

I'm about to sing my last song for my set and decide to change things up and sing the song I wrote for Tori, "Thief of

My Heart." I see disappointment touch her eyes when I announce this will be my last song for the evening. Lord help me if this woman is as sweet and delectable as she looks, because if so, then I might just have to put myself out there.

◎ ✂ 🦋 🧁

ALY

Stop staring at him, Aly!

He's going to think you are some pathetic psycho if you don't stop.

Wait, is he staring back at me?

Oh my God, he is!

I don't know what the hell is going on, but since the moment I locked eyes with Gavin McNeer, I haven't been able to look away. I've been staring at him for the last twenty minutes, infatuated with his voice, his eyes, his face... all of him. My body feels alive with a connective energy flowing between us, and with the way he's smiling back at me, he's either feeling it too or having pity on my poor, delusional soul.

You're crazy! my mind screams at my heart, and with the way my sister, Valerie, is looking at me when I glance in her direction, she's thinking the same thing.

I can't believe this is the first time I'm noticing him, really noticing him. It's not uncommon for songwriters to become performers, so Gavin hasn't really been on my radar the last two years. I've heard about his reputation as the gorgeous-as-sin songwriter from Austin who's extremely professional and talented. But any interest I had of learning more about the sexy Texan died when I saw the headlines that he was dating Tori Langston. This industry is small, and especially here in

Nashville. We're all on pretty good terms, so everyone knows what a snake Tori can be.

When the gossip mill ran rampant about how and why they broke up, I didn't even bat an eyelash, because honestly, I wasn't surprised. I also couldn't care less. I have no desire to get caught up in the rumors, and sometimes, this industry gets a little incestuous with who dates who, which is another reason why I've stayed away from dating anyone in the business.

I take the opportunity to let my eyes wander while Gavin explains the next song he's about to sing. Pictures really don't do this man justice. They don't capture the sparkle in his green eyes when he looks at you or how his smile can be adorably crooked. You definitely can't appreciate from photos how well his clothes mold to his body. His short-sleeved T-shirt is white with a special low-cut V-neck that shows off his sternum, giving you a peak of a hard, muscled chest underneath. You can tell he's tall by how long his legs are, which are encased in dark denim that clings to his hard thighs and have stylish slits on his knees. His clothes might be plain, but I have no doubt there probably designer labels.

I don't spend too much time assessing his body, because as soon as he starts singing again, my eyes are drawn right back to his handsome face. I become enraptured with his performance and start to daydream he's singing to me and only me.

"Why is he staring at you like that?" Valerie whispers in my ear while she nudges her elbow into my side once he finishes his song. "It's creeping me out!" I look at her and just blink my eyes, not understanding how she thinks he's creepy when all I see is how beautiful he is. She gives me a wide-eyed look and mouths, *What is wrong with you?*

I wish I had an answer for her, but for the life of me, I have no idea what's wrong with me. I've never reacted to someone this way before.

Snap out of it, Aly! He's just a man.

Yeah, a man who rattles my nerves by just looking at me. I turn my attention back toward him when he announces he will be performing his last song for the evening. I suddenly start to feel sad, as if this will be the last time I ever see him again, which is ridiculous, since we don't even know each other. He starts playing the first chords of "Thief of My Heart," and once again, his voice floods my senses and he weaves a dream around me with his lyrics.

You're the one for me.
I'm coming for you.
I'll steal your heart.
Run away with me.
Forever.

I keep my eyes locked on his as the song becomes a tale of broken promises and hearts. Then, all too sudden, the song is over. I look around the room in a daze, seeing everyone on their feet, applauding. Then it dawns on me that every other woman is staring at him the same way I am. It's as if we've all been possessed by the devil himself. A devil we're all ready to sin with. Seeing their reactions snaps me out of my trance, and I start to wonder if I imagined how he was looking at me.

Don't be a fool, I tell myself, annoyed I let my mind wander for a man I've never even met before. I have zero clue as to what kind of person he even is. I give my head a shake and stand up to leave, telling myself that none of this matters anyway. He's a musician, and therefore, these silly fantasies of him will stay just that. *Fantasies.*

"Ready to go?" I ask Valerie, who's still looking at me with concern. She nods and we grab our purses off the back of our chairs to leave.

"Excuse me," I hear a husky voice say, making my head snap up to confirm who I hope it is. Gavin is standing in front of me, his height causing me to look up into his mesmerizing eyes. "Call me," he tells me in a commanding voice, handing me his card. My eyes widen in shock, causing his serious expression to change into a devastating smile. "Please?" There's a plea to his tone that turns my insides into complete mush. He's robbed me of my voice, so all I can do is smile back at him and nod. His gaze flashes briefly to my lips before looking back at me with apologetic eyes as people begin to approach us.

Soon, he's lost in the sea of bodies surrounding him, and I know our moment is gone. I clutch his card in my hand and turn to leave, shaking my head at my sister when she narrows her eyes at me and starts to open her mouth to ask questions.

"Not here," I interject with a stern voice before I turn away and search for the exit through the crowd. Just when we're about to clear the front door, I hear my name being called. I turn around to see Shane, my boss, coming up behind me, motioning for me to meet him outside. With an unfamiliar pit in my stomach, I walk toward the end of the building to wait for Shane.

"Did I just witness Gavin McNeer giving you his card?" he inquires, staring me down with inquisitive eyes. Crap, if Shane saw that, then that means other people might've too.

"He sure did," Valerie answers for me, her gaze mirroring Shane's. Both of them cross their arms over their chests, and I know there's no way I'm getting out of this conversation right now.

"Do you know him? Because the way you two were eye-fucking each other all night long made even *me* feel uncomfortable."

I can't contain the blush that flushes up my cheeks from Shane's words. The evening air is cool, but just the mere thought of being in any kind of sexual position with Gavin is causing me to sweat.

"You're being dramatic." I wave my hand out in front of me, trying to downplay this situation, and the two of them just roll their eyes at me. "And no, I don't know him. Tonight was the first time I've ever seen him."

"And it looks like it won't be the last!" Shane breaks into an evil smile, rubbing his hands together as if he's coming up with a secret plan.

"He's a musician!" I sigh. "I'm sure he gives his card out to every single lady he thinks is pretty." I dismiss the two of them as I start to dig into my bag for my keys, not wanting them to make such a big deal out of something that probably doesn't mean anything.

"Actually, he doesn't," a voice comes up from behind us, startling me. I turn around to see a pretty blonde with a messy bun on top of her head and chic red glasses that match her lipstick standing next to us. She has startling baby-blue eyes that have a hint of annoyance to them. "Giving out his card to anyone," she says as she looks me over, "is something he doesn't do. In fact, I've never seen him give out his number to some random girl before. Regardless, I didn't mean to eavesdrop, but Gavin wanted me to remind you to call him later." She looks me up and down one more time before leaving without even introducing herself. Can we say *rude*?

"Wow, she's rude." Valerie huffs as we watch Gavin's messenger walk back inside the cafe. "Shane, do you know who she is?"

"I think that was his assistant, who's also his cousin. I always see her with him when it's work related. Who cares about her?" He groans. "Can we talk about how he sent her out here to remind you to call him not less than ten minutes after he gave you his number? That's hot!" Shane grips my forearm and squeezes, excitement radiating from his eyes. "You better do as he says and call him tonight."

"You know the policy, Shane," I remind him with a knowing smile. "No dating anyone in the industry."

"Rules are meant to be broken. Besides, that policy is for

dating within our own company, not within the entire music industry!" He places his hands on his hips when I shake my head at him. "You listen to me, Alyson Marie Dawson…"

"Her middle name isn't Marie," Valerie tells him, and my lips twitch at seeing a what the hell expression on her face.

"I'm sure it isn't, but since I don't know what her middle name is and I'm trying to be all parental on her right now, Marie sounded good," he explains in exasperation, causing me to chuckle at how ridiculous he's being. "Listen to me, Alyson whatever-your-middle-name-is Dawson! You have got to stop letting these opportunities pass you by! First Brodie and now Gavin? Child, are you *insane*?" he screams the last word out.

"Can you lower your voice? You're causing a scene!" I hiss at him, not wanting the attention his shouting is bringing our way, judging by the looks we're starting to receive.

"All I'm saying is that you need to live a little and see where this goes. You may have just met your soul mate."

"Soul mate?" I scoff. Now it's my turn to roll my eyes at him.

He throws his arms up in irritation. "Valerie, can you please talk some sense into your sister?"

"Nope, I actually agree with her. I don't think she should call him. He's a musician, meaning girls throw themselves at him and he will also have to tour eventually. I don't approve of a long-distance relationship for my baby sister," Valerie states firmly, looking him in the eye to show how serious she is.

"Thanks for being supportive there, Val," Shane says with heavy sarcasm. "Side note—I'm really digging this hot-for-teacher look you've got going on with the sexy glasses and high ponytail. Too bad you're going to look this way when you're ninety and single with that kind of attitude!"

Even Valerie can't contain her laughter at that comment. I do have to agree with Shane though on the subject of how my sister looks. She has a certain sex appeal in her work attire. She's gorgeous with her light-blonde hair and ice-blue eyes— the complete opposite of what I look like. Nobody guesses we're sisters when they first meet us, but our bond is as tight as if we were twins.

Shane looks between the two of us, shaking his head in silence. "I'm done with this conversation, as it's giving me heartburn and now I need a drink." He gives Valerie and me a kiss on our cheeks and looks one more time at us both. "It's a shame, really. Two of the most beautiful girls I've ever seen, single as the day they were born. Aly, I do hope you change your mind about calling Gavin. I'll see you tomorrow." And with that, he leaves us and goes back inside.

Valerie and I walk to our cars in silence, both of us deep in thought. Shane's words repeat over and over in my brain. What do I have to lose by calling Gavin? Sure, it goes against my policy of not dating musicians, but every cell in my body is screaming that he seems different and to give him a chance. The memory of his handsome face with those intense eyes demanding I call him causes me to shiver, a smile creeping up on my lips, because I actually liked that he demanded I call him.

Give him a chance, Aly! You've got nothing to lose.

Oh sure, just my heart if he breaks it into a million pieces.

A phone call is harmless and doesn't mean anything.

"You aren't seriously going to call him, are you?" Valerie's question interrupts my internal debate with myself. I look over at her to see she's waiting outside of her open car door, and I realize we didn't even say goodbye to each other, since I was lost in my own thoughts. I take a deep breath and flash her a bashful smile, knowing she isn't going to like my decision.

"Of course I am," I confirm, giving her a playful wink. Feeling high with adrenaline and confidence, I pull out my phone and type in his number. While his phone rings, I blow her a kiss goodbye and get into my car to start the engine. My Bluetooth picks up the call and I start to think I'll be leaving a voicemail when he suddenly picks up on the fourth ring.

"Hello?"

"Gavin? Um, hi, this is Alyson, the girl from the Bluebird Cafe," I say, trying to sound somewhat cute and not like a complete dork. "The one you gave your card to," I remind him, hoping he hasn't been handing his card out like candy on Halloween night.

"Alyson," he repeats my name in his deep voice, and a chill slides down my spine. "Do you go by Aly?"

"Yes," I rasp out, my voice shaking a little at my nervousness. "Most people call me Aly."

"Well, all right then… Aly." Why does my name sound so exotic coming from him? "I'm sorry if you can't hear me very well. I'm still at the Bluebird. Can I call you when I get home?"

"Oh right! I'm so sorry. Your assistant demanded I call you, and she's a little scary," I joke while I smack my hand against my head for being the dumbass I am. Of course he's still at the Bluebird, since it hasn't even been five minutes since I left. Why didn't I think to wait to call him?

Fortunately, he's chuckling at me and I marvel at the sound. "I hope she wasn't rude to you. Sosie's always pretty serious."

"No, she wasn't rude at all." I grimace at the lie. "Call me whenever you get a free moment. I should be up for a while. I mean, call me another day or whenever," I stammer, rolling my eyes at myself for how stupid I sound.

"I'll call you in a little bit, darlin'. Get home safe and I'll talk to you soon," he tells me before saying goodbye and hanging up.

"What an idiot you are, Aly," I groan out loud, mad at myself for calling him so soon and seeming desperate.

Knowing there is nothing I can do about it now, I turn on the radio, hoping it will distract me from my thoughts of Gavin.

I pull into my driveway fifteen minutes later and I go inside. I feed my cat before putting on my pajamas. After I wash my face and brush my teeth, I look at my clock and see it's only 10:00 p.m., so I decide to get into bed and continue reading the current book I'm obsessed with. Apollo joins me and curls into my side. I check to make sure my phone is on full volume and not on vibrate so that I won't miss Gavin's call. With my phone settled next to me on the nightstand, I lie against my pillows and start to read.

Two hours later, the words are starting to blur together and I'm afraid that if I don't go to bed soon, I will be jolted awake by my Kindle smacking me in the face. I put it aside and reach for my phone. Disappointment rears its ugly head as I see how late it is and he hasn't called me back like he said he would.

"Chin up, Aly. Don't waste any pretty breaths on him," I tell myself, repeating the old motto my mother used to say to me when a boy I liked didn't like me back. I turn my light off and settle into the covers, praying that a certain green-eyed devil doesn't occupy my dreams.

◎ ❈ ✿ ☕

Ready to read some more? Click here to get your copy of Love At The Bluebird by Aurora Rose Reynolds and Jessica Marin.

STRIKE ZONE BY MIGNON MYKEL

TRIPP

November — Off Season

Well, I'll be damned.

Seeing the woman who's had the starring role in my dirty fantasies for the better part of a year, 1600 miles away from the city I know her in, wasn't on my bingo card—but there she is.

Chey—

"Cheyenne! Your chai tea latte with two shots of espresso is ready for pickup!" is called from the end of the coffee kiosk, at the same time the barista in front of me asks if I need more time to decide.

Oh. Right. I was ordering a drink.

"Um. No, I'm good," I answer, tearing my gaze away from the bubbly blonde who shouldn't be in Arizona. "I'll just have a large caramel macchiato, please. Iced."

Holding my phone over the card reader to pay, I hope this exchange goes quickly because I can't lose her...

But then the scent of summer sidles beside me. "Well, I'll be damned," Cheyenne whispers the very words that were on my mind moments before. "As I live and breathe. It's...you."

"Your receipt?" The barista sounds exasperated with my lack of attention but I give her my classic, crooked grin and shake my head.

"No, but thank you, Rina." For good measure, I pull a bill from my pocket and stuff it in the tip jar, not really caring if it's a one, five, or twenty.

"First name basis with the baristas?" Cheyenne teases, taking a step to the side. Her coffee cup is raised to her lips but she doesn't sip from the lid.

"She wore a name tag," I point out, glancing down at the photographer assigned to the team I've spent the majority of my professional baseball career with. Her tiny stature brings the top of her head just below my chin, but what she lacks in height, she makes up with curves—curves on nice display today, thanks to the fitted shirt and jeans that look like they were made specifically for her hips and thighs.

And fuck, that blinding smile that is so notably her. I don't know if I've ever seen her without it.

"What brings you to Arizona? Our warm winters?"

Is that a blush on her cheeks?

"I live here," she answers with a shrug. "Well, for a few months out of the year, anyway. I'm a desert girl, didn't you know? A 'native,' as so many Arizonans like to say." She finally takes a cautious sip from her cup, wincing almost immediately. "Frick, that's hot." She sucks her top lip into her mouth, pressing her finger there as well, and a frown mars her brows.

"They should fix those machines."

"Fix them?" It takes her a moment to catch on to the dad joke my own father has been spouting in some form or fashion since I can remember. "Ha. That's funny." The words are flat and monotonous, but it isn't long before she shakes her head and that gorgeous smile is back on her face.

"I've been known to tell a joke or two." I cross my arms and scan the coffee kiosk. It's not terribly busy. It's why I chose to stop here at the one inside the grocery store, instead of the standalone drive-thru cafe on the other side of the parking lot. "Have we talked about you being from Arizona?" I would have remembered that detail.

I remember the day I met her, on a road game to Miami. At the time, that's where the league assigned her. One of her primary tasks on game day is to shoot images of the players entering the clubhouse. We usually travel in groups on away game days so a lot of the work credited to her is of the home team, but this particular day, I was solo.

"All by yourself today, Tripp Nash?"

The voice came from behind a large camera lens and I grinned for the photo. When the camera was lowered, I got my first look at the face that went with the voice, and if I waxed poetic, I'd say the world stopped spinning and angels sang.

The first thing I noticed was her blinding smile. Then, the way her eyes danced with the same joy that radiated from her entire being.

"Just early today," I answered, instead of giving in to the desire to stop and have a conversation with the woman. She wore black from shoulders to ankles, only breaking up the dark color with white crew socks and tennis shoes.

"Well, welcome back from your injury. Have fun out there!"

It was the only time I saw her that season...but then there was last season's home opener.

"Hey, I know you."

I looked toward the familiar voice and saw the face that'd been popping up in my dreams off and on over the last eight months. My smile had nothing to do with her bringing her camera to her face and everything to do with, well...

Her.

"I never caught your name," I told her, slowing my stride down the hallway as I neared. Unlike in Florida, today she sat on the floor—still in all black with white feet—and after she placed the camera gently on the concrete beside her hip, she wrapped her hands around a raised knee.

"Cheyenne." She said it with a small nod of her chin but a wide smile on her face. Did the woman ever not smile?

I wanted nothing more than to stop right there and ask her questions—how long had she been doing photography; was sports photography always her goal or did she have other pictures she liked to take; what did she do in her freetime… maybe I could "accidentally" cross her path—but I had a meeting with the coaching staff before hitting the weight room to focus on hip mobility. Ever since my injury the previous season, I'd been feeling my age. Keeping every joint warm and ready was a high priority.

Instead of stopping, I smiled down at her as I neared, then passed, her. "Nice to meet you, Cheyenne. Officially. You ours this season?" I added over my shoulder, and a quick thrill hit my chest to see her twisted, watching as I headed down the cold, gray hall, and toward the bright hallways that made up the clubhouse.

"I am."

I remember when she and another photographer taste-tested Hi-Chew candies during arrivals, and that she prefers the strawberry ones.

That she sometimes dances in the hallway when she doesn't think any players or staff are around.

And I remember the way she celebrated with the guys when we clinched a division spot last season.

The other photographers were in the locker room with us, of course, but Cheyenne's joy, her smile that night, is definitely one of those core memories everyone talks about.

"No," Cheyenne says now, bringing me back to the present. "We haven't. But I know you're from Arizona, kinda sorta. Went to high school in Deer Valley, and then college out in Tempe." Her face pinches. "Probably shouldn't have admitted that. But in my defense, it's on your stats page. Well, college anyhow. And you're one of the hottest catchers of our generation." That blush from before deepens. "Hot, as in, top of your game. Everyone knows you. Wants you. On the field!" Her eyes widen as her speech quickens. I should stop her, give her an out, but I'm enjoying this too damn much. "They want you on the field. On their team. Behind their..." she winces and her voice finally comes down to a near whisper, "plate. Gosh, that was—"

"Order for Cassidy!"

I wink at Cheyenne. "Saved by the barista." My face is recognizable enough that using my given name isn't doing me any favors in the incognito department, but I try to keep the fanfare to a minimum.

After picking up my iced drink and accepting the straw the barista holds out, I turn and find Cheyenne isn't nearby anymore. A moment of panic courses through me—I can't do anything about my attraction to her during the season, but here? In the off-season and not even in Tennessee? This is my opportunity, and it can't just be...gone—but then I spot her around the corner at the condiment bar.

It's my turn to step beside her. She doesn't glance at me, but I'm pretty sure the hand holding the cinnamon shaker trembles slightly. Nerves? This bubbly woman who talks a mile a minute damn near 100-percent of the time?

"I have one of my fundraisers this weekend," I answer her earlier question. "That's why I'm here."

"Ah." She nods and places the shaker back in the space labeled for it. "I'm hanging out with my parents' tortoise before I head out on a trip."

"Tortoise?" I absently swirl my plastic cup, holding it from the top with the straw sticking out from between my index and middle fingers.

"Bowser the Sulcata." Cheyenne finally glances up at me and for the first time since knowing her, I catalog her eyes. I always thought they were light brown, but in reality, the browns and greens mesh with yellow, making a nearly golden hazel. "He's fifty-three, and my mom got him from a fair when she was four. She didn't want the goldfish, and my grandparents didn't think the teeny tiny turtle was going to end up as an eighty-pound monster, so they said okay."

"Damn," I chuckle lightly. "That's a commitment. Don't they live for a hundred years or something close to that?"

Cheyenne's attention goes back to her chai as she replaces the lid. "I'm pretty sure Bowser's sections on their estate and will are higher than mine." She reaches for a napkin to clean nearly unnoticeable latte droplets from the counter. "But it's important to have a plan in place when you have pets that live that long. I always wanted an African grey parrot, but their lifespan is something like twenty, twenty-five years, and that's a long time to keep something else alive."

"Especially when they act like they pay their vet bills," I add, recalling the many ... spirited ... horses I grew up with, with similar lifespans.

"For sure."

This time when she looks at me, I can feel the goodbye between us and I'm not ready for it yet. "I was going to grab a few things. Walk with me? Or do you have places to be?"

Her eyes stay locked on mine for a solid three heartbeats before she nods. "Okay. I need to grab some airplane snacks while here. Don't let me forget."

⚾ 🧤 🦋 🧁

Turned out, she didn't just need airplane snacks, but some hiking sustenance pointers, as well.

"I can't believe you thought peanuts and peanut butter

M&Ms would be 'good enough' when backpacking New Zealand," I tease lightly, pushing a half-full shopping cart out of the store and toward my rental. She also said she was picking things up in-country and stopping to enjoy local spots, but there was no way her meager choices were going to be enough.

"Then it's a good thing I ran into you this afternoon." Cheyenne swings two plastic bags from her right hand as she walks beside me. Our coffees, forgotten about, are both in cup holders attached to the cart, and when the wheels bump over the concrete curb, some of her chai bubbles from the sipping hole. "Who'd have guessed there were better protein options for traveling." I sense a hint of sarcasm in her words, but there's zero annoyance.

The rented Yukon I'm driving this week is at the far end of the lot, but Cheyenne walks beside me the entire way. She even helps place my groceries into the back.

"Where are you parked?" I ask, handing her the still-warm latte. It had to have been steamed extra hot before.

No wonder she burned her lip.

"Oh, I walked. My parents only live a few blocks away."

"Can I give you a ride there?"

"It's okay, you don't have to."

"Please?"

With a playful sigh, Cheyenne shakes her head. "If you must."

"I must." I hit the unlock button on the key fob. "Hop in. I'm just going to return the cart."

When I pull myself into the cab a few moments later, I set my iced macchiato in the available cup holder but notice Cheyenne still holds hers. "You can put it in here, if you want."

"I'm okay, thank you."

After hooking my arm around the headrest behind her, I check my surroundings, as well as the mirrors and camera, to reverse from the parking spot, then head toward the main road. "Which way?"

She gives basic directions and I nod, committing them to memory. This isn't the exact area I spent my teenage years, but the major crossroads that travel east and west are the same regardless of which side of the Phoenix valley you're in.

Yuma is always south of the 10, with McDowell above it—at least, until you run into the 51—and Camelback is Camelback, regardless if you're nearing Verrado to the west, or running straight into the mountain the road is named for, over on the east side.

"The fundraiser this weekend," Cheyenne breaks the small silence between us, "is this the one you do for youth baseball programs?"

I nod, and explain the weekend in depth. There's a hit-a-thon for local high school baseball players, and then a mini-tournament with different teams who pay a small $50 fee to be part of the brackets. There are a few high school teams signed up, but also, two of the local fire stations, a police department, and even the Maricopa sheriff's department, that are expected to play. It's meant to be a fun tournament, and funds are raised from tickets to the games, but also from raffles people purchase tickets for.

"Last year, this event raised about ten-grand and was split between three programs. This year, I'm focusing more on at-risk youth and I found two programs that specialize in the population."

"Is there a reason for at-risk youth?"

"Personally? No," I shake my head as I reach for my macchiato, sipping from the straw before returning the cup. "I'm just very aware I grew up in a privileged environment, even when we were on my family's ranch in Montana. Not every family can just up and leave their home state so their kid can get a better chance for a future in the sport he loves." I shrug my shoulder as I hit my turn signal. "Just trying to leave good behind."

After turning right into her parents' neighborhood, Cheyenne gives more detailed instructions to get to their house.

"The two-story at the end of the cul-de-sac."

"Got it." As I drive closer and closer to the Spanish-style home, the thought this impromptu afternoon went way too fast hits hard.

I should ask if she wants to come by my place. Grill out. Watch a movie.

Tell me more about this backpacking trip she's going on, her plans for the holidays, when she's heading back to Tennessee...

Instead, I pull the large SUV to a stop in front of the house. "It was fun seeing you without a camera attached to your face," I joke, trying to keep things light.

This time, her smile isn't as bright and bubbly as it typically is. "Of all places to run into you..."

"See you this spring?" It hadn't dawned on me that she might not be ours next season. It should have. Maybe she gets a new assignment every season.

But she nods, cutting off the sudden worry that this might be it, for real. "Yeah. I'll be there. Bells and whistles."

Thank fuck. I may not be able to do a damn thing about my attraction to her during the season, but seeing her face is a bright spot in my otherwise monotonous daily schedule.

"Will you be assigned to spring training, too?"

"I won't find that out for a few more months. If I recall correctly, the league invited me around January this past year. Pre-season assignments aren't usually the same as regular season, but I'm for sure assigned to the Terrors for regular season. So, if I don't see you in February, then definitely March."

I badly want to come up with something else to talk about,

more reasons for her to stay sitting beside me, but I'm coming up blank.

Well, hell.

"Have a good night, Cheyenne, and enjoy your trip. Stay safe."

At 'trip,' I swear she dips her eyes briefly toward my mouth. I almost wonder if I imagined the brief moment, but then her lips tighten slightly as she swallows hard.

It's not just me who's attracted to the other.

I'd kiss her in a heartbeat if I was sure it was what she actually wanted.

Attraction is one thing.

But I'm not sure what kind of gray area there is in her contract with the league.

Sure, it's the off-season right now…but I have a feeling I'm not going to want to pump the brakes, stop whatever good thing we have going, come February when all those rules are in place once more.

"Have so much fun with your fundraiser," her voice is soft, as if she's also digging deep for words when she isn't ready to leave. I know I'm not imagining it. "I know it's going to be a hit."

She puts her hand on the door to push out, but before she slips out of the vehicle and away from me, she turns her head, a contemplative look on her features. "Do you maybe want to do dinner or something tonight?"

TENNESSEE TERRORS BASEBALL CLUB SERIES

Bases are loaded … but love is on the line.

Welcome to Music City Park, where the lights shine bright, the stakes are high, and the players of the Tennessee Terrors don't just risk it all on the baseball field — they gamble with their hearts too.

From second-chance romance to forbidden love, grumpy meets sunshine to enemies to lovers, single moms and single dads, fake dating and opposites attract, these baseball stars are about to learn the game doesn't end when the ninth inning does.

Batter up …

Let the season of love begin!

All books are interconnected stand alone novels, but you can read the series lineup as follows :

Diving Catch by Lauren Runow following Evan Parker, the team's left fielder.

Faking it … At First by MJ Fields following Damien "Diesel' Donovan, the team's first baseman.

The Perfect Catch by Jessica Marin following Gunnar McNeer, the team's shortstop.

Strike Zone by Mignon Mykel following Tripp Nash, the team's catcher.

Legal Catch by ML Preston following Jake Reynolds, the team's center fielder.

Grand Slam by CA Harms following Kelton James, the team's right fielder.

Stealing Bases by Tarrah Anders following Chase Thorne, the team's third baseman.

Double Play by L.B. Dunbar following Declan Wylde, the team manager.

Curveball by Ruthie Henrick following Max Murphy, a pitcher on the team.

Perfect Save by Brittany Holland following Carter Callahan, a pitcher on the team.

ALSO BY JESSICA MARIN

LET ME IN SERIES

Heartbreak Warfare

Perfectly Lonely

Edge of Desire

Half of My Heart

BEAR CREEK RODEO

The Irish Cowboy

The Celtic Cowboy

STANDALONE NOVELS

Until Valerie (Part of Aurora Rose Reynolds' Happily Ever Alpha World)

Love At The Bluebird (co-written with Aurora Rose Reynolds and connected to Until Valerie and The Perfect Catch)

Shopping For Love

The Perfect Catch

ACKNOWLEDGMENTS

Thank you to all of the readers and bloggers who take the time out of your day to read my work and support me. Your positive feedback and love mean the world to me.

Thank you to my family, especially my husband and children. Without their support, I wouldn't be able to continue living my dream.

It truly takes a village to make a book come to fruition and I couldn't have done it without the following people: All the wonderful ladies on my ARC Team, Tracey Vuolo, Dorothy Bircher, Kati Dickerson, Barbara Hoover, Emina Ros, Brittany Holland, Anastasia Ant, Kate Farlow, and the other wonderful authors of the Tennessee Terrors, especially Lauren Runow.

Thank you to my Misfits for your continued love, support and promotion of all things Jessica Marin.

Please make sure you follow me on all of my social media pages and visit my website at https://jessicamarinbooks.com for new books and exclusive merchandise. I look forward to our next adventure together!

Peace and love,

Jessica

ABOUT THE AUTHOR

Jessica Marin began her love affair with books at a young age from the encouragement of her Grandma Shirley. She has always dreamed of being an author and finally made her dreams of writing happily ever after stories a reality. She currently resides in Tennessee with her husband, children and fur babies.

Jessica would love for you to join her on all of her available social media outlets. Do you love being a part of exclusive reading groups? Then join Jessica Marin's Misfits on Facebook!

Jessica Marin's Misfits

Don't do social media? Join Jessica's newsletter to stay up to date with everything in Jessica Marin's world, including new releases, exclusive teasers and FREE BOOKS!

Newsletter

Love signed paperbacks? Check out my store to get yours personalized (US Markets only)

Jessica Marin's Website

amazon.com / shop / authorjessicamarin
facebook.com / authorjessicamarin
instagram.com / authorjessicamarin
tiktok.com / @authorjessicamarin